THE VIPER

A BROKEN RIDGE NOVEL

AMANDA MCKINNEY

HH TISEVICH

Paperback ISBN 978-1-7358681-6-5
eBook ISBN 978-1-7358681-5-8

Editor(s):
Pam Berehulke, Bulletproof Editing
Nancy Brown, Redline Proofreading
Cover Design:
Damonza

https://www.amandamckinneyauthor.com

DEDICATION

For Mama :)

ALSO BY AMANDA

THRILLER NOVELS:

The Sketch Artist

The Perfect Murder

The Stranger in My Bed

A Marriage of Lies

When I Disappear

The Wife's Silence

The Widow of Weeping Pines: A Thriller Novella

The Raven's Wife: A Thriller Novella

The Lie Between Us: A Thriller Novella

ROMANTIC THRILLER NOVELS:

THE ANTI-HERO:

Mine

BESTSELLING STEELE SHADOWS SERIES:

Cabin 1 (Steele Shadows Security)

Cabin 2 (Steele Shadows Security)

Cabin 3 (Steele Shadows Security)

Phoenix (Steele Shadows Rising)

Jagger (Steele Shadows Investigations)

Ryder (Steele Shadows Investigations)

Her Mercenary (Steele Shadows Mercenaries)

Her Renegade (Steele Shadows Mercenaries)

ON THE EDGE SERIES:

Buried Deception

Trail of Deception

THE BERRY SPRINGS SERIES:

The Woods (A Berry Springs Novel)

The Lake (A Berry Springs Novel)

The Storm (A Berry Springs Novel)

The Fog (A Berry Springs Novel)

The Creek (A Berry Springs Novel)

The Shadow (A Berry Springs Novel)

The Cave (A Berry Springs Novel)

THE ROAD SERIES:

Rattlesnake Road

Redemption Road

The Viper

Devil's Gold (A Black Rose Mystery, Book 1)

Hatchet Hollow (A Black Rose Mystery, Book 2)

Tomb's Tale (A Black Rose Mystery Book 3)

Evil Eye (A Black Rose Mystery Book 4)

Sinister Secrets (A Black Rose Mystery Book 5)

And many more to come...

LET'S CONNECT!

Get early access, exclusive deals, and a behind-the-scenes look at Amanda's world.

Join Amanda's newsletter for new releases, limited-time promos, personal notes, and the stories behind the stories—sent straight to your inbox.

https://www.amandamckinneyauthor.com/contact

THE VIPER

A renegade DEA agent and a ruthless private detective collide in this seductive small-town tale of revenge, murder, and the unbreakable bond between sisters.

They say revenge is a dish best served cold. Apparently, they haven't met the Archer sisters.

Owner of Archer and Archer, Inc., a prestigious New York private investigative firm, Colette Archer embodies effortless perfection in her couture suits and trademark chignon. But this private investigator has a secret. When night falls, Colette slips on her wig and into the persona of a tequila-guzzling hustler who occasionally fancies two men instead of one. This double life comes as an unwelcome side effect of a horrific past that she and her sister, Jade, a bohemian martial-arts-instructing renegade, decide to settle once and for all—regardless of who they must destroy in the process.

Obstinate DEA agent James Black is one mistake away from spending his career crunching numbers in the confinement of his six-by-six cubicle. In a last-ditch effort to save his floundering career, James seeks the assistance of ice queen Colette Archer. Despite the spark of heat between them, she seems to despise him almost as much as poly-blend fabrics.

After following Colette and her sister to a sleepy small town in Montana, James learns of a devious and dangerous pact the sisters have made to avenge their past. Using Colette's weakness to his advantage, James tricks her into helping him uncover the whereabouts of a ruthless drug lord. But when Colette is brutally attacked, James realizes he has inadvertently set wheels in motion that might not only cost him his job, but also the woman who's stolen his heart.

1

The Watcher

I watched the smoke curl from my nose, ghostly tendrils catching in a breeze I didn't feel, eventually spiraling into nothing.

Nothing. The exact place I intended to go at that moment.

Closing my eyes, I welcomed the burn in the back of my throat as I angled my head upward, rolling it from side to side a moment before finally relaxing against the backrest.

Though my nose had been desensitized long ago, I inhaled deeply, the experience of the smoke just as important as the effect. I loved the smoke, became obsessed with it long ago as one might a significant other, boy or girl. It was a loyal friend that was always there for me. A friend in my deepest, darkest hours.

One that I'd die for.

I closed my eyes, picturing the smoke around me. As it always seemed to do, the gray cloud morphed into *her* face before thinning, spreading, contorting her mouth into a scream that eventually ripped apart before fading into nothing.

Hand trembling, I took another hit, allowing the buzz to spread from my lips, across my face, down my body, and finally circling back to settle in my brain, a thick haze that pushed everything away—thoughts, fears, and memories. My dear friend removing me from consciousness and leaving me with . . . nothing. The only place I felt peace.

As if separated from my body, my hand slid from the armrest, falling onto my lap like dead weight. The tingle on my skin moved to my legs as the floating sensation enveloped me like a warm hug.

It was a cold autumn night, the leaves just past their peak, slowly shriveling up before falling from the trees to litter the ground in browns and blacks.

Another season coming and going. Autumn, the harvest time of year, a time to acknowledge growth and maturity. The moments before death.

Outside, a branch ticked against the window like the fingers of a skeleton, slowly pulling my attention to the frame of blackness. Staring into my distorted reflection in the window, I lost myself in the past, a time when there were no windows. Only gray concrete, steel bars, coiled barbed wire, and stun guns. I remember how badly I wanted to be a part of the night again—outside, free, with the breeze on my skin. Experiencing the change of the seasons at my leisure.

Turns out, being free again wasn't really what I thought it was going to be.

I closed my eyes and rolled my head back to forward position.

"Take me away," I whispered in a singsong voice to the nothingness around me. "Awaaay . . ."

I don't know how long passed as I sank into the high

before taking another hit. I knew I'd need one more before passing out.

Staring blankly into the fireplace in front of me, I listened to the pitiful pops and hisses as the fire slowly died, taking the light with it. I'd forgotten to turn on a lamp before I settled in.

Too late now.

I'd forgotten to do a lot of things since the drugs began to take control years ago. I didn't give a shit, though.

Funny how that works, the vicious cycle of addiction. You use to forget, so you can be happy, yet soon the drugs become the only thing that makes you happy. The more you use, the more your body breaks down, making you miserable—therefore, the more you use to counteract this physical and mental pain. You try to quit, then memories come back, so you use to forget, so you can be happy again. And on and on we go.

A howl of wind rattled the windows. Otherwise, the house was eerily quiet that night. I didn't own a television or a radio.

Hours passed as I sat there, staring into the fire as I did every night. Alone in the middle of the woods with only the ghosts of my past and my pipe to keep me company.

They visit me sometimes. The ghosts. Not just in my nightmares but in my waking hours too. Materializing from nothing and just staring at me. That's all they do. From across the room, they observe me closely, blurry apparitions with black holes for eyes fixed directly on me. For hours, they watch.

At first, I'd run. Out of the house, into the woods, to the bar, anywhere but my house. Not anymore, though. Now, I stay. I stare back, ready.

God, I'm ready.

The twitch of my fingers pulled my attention, and I realized I could feel my legs again. As I reached for the lighter, the faint click of a door opening froze me in place.

They're here.

I knew they'd come. And in that moment, I realized I'd been waiting for it.

Like a switch flipping, my brain suddenly jolted to life, hyperawareness overcoming me. Survival instinct, I suppose. But while my brain was screaming at me to react, my body retained the reflexes of a wet washcloth, a side effect of the drugs.

Instead of reacting, I slowly gripped the armrests as if steeling myself for what was about to happen.

My focus funneled behind me as I strained to listen for any sounds or movement. Although there were none, I could feel a presence in the room as if the devil himself had risen from the ground beneath my feet.

My heart pounded and a wave of nausea washed over me, the adrenaline and the drugs warring in my system.

Every hair on my body stood on end as I heard the break in the stillness around me, a second before a black cloth sack was pulled over my head. I surged forward but was instantly knocked back into the chair, momentarily blinded by pain as something hard smashed into my skull.

Disoriented, I tried again to scramble off the chair—for what, I don't know—but was struck again.

And again.

And again.

My attacker was unnaturally quiet as they moved, the only noise in the room the splitting of my skin with each blow, the breaking of my bones.

Sometime later—minutes or hours, I didn't know—I woke up on the floor with warm liquid running from my nose and mouth, my brain feeling too large for my skull. Aside from the black bag still wrapped around my head, I was naked. My clothes had been removed, my hands bound at the wrists, my feet at the ankles.

Swimming in and out of consciousness, I focused on the sound of the faucet in the distance, something clanking against the side of the sink.

Not a single word had been spoken during the attack. I didn't know what was happening anymore. Drifting, I was somewhere between this life and the next.

Footsteps approached. Two hands pinned my head in place against the rug, seconds before a tidal wave pummeled into my face.

Choking, wheezing, gasping for air, I screamed, my gurgled pleas and cries interrupted by sputtering coughs. My bindings sliced into my skin as I thrashed like a wild animal, though it was useless. I was blind, paralyzed, and now drowning.

Eventually, the flow of water stopped.

My chest heaved as I desperately tried to suck in air through the saturated bag. It felt like trying to breathe through a straw. My chest burned like fire.

I'm going to die.

A panic I'd never experienced before overcame me, replacing all rational thought and common sense, the idea of dying spinning me into an uncontrollable whirl of energy as I bucked and screamed on the floor.

That's when a searing-hot pain burned into my throat. A knife, I assumed. A flesh wound, an inch from my jugular.

The voice that broke the silence stilled me, sending a ripple of goose bumps crawling over my skin.

And then I knew. I knew exactly why this was happening to me.

While in prison, I'd once heard someone say *repent and you shall be saved.*

So I did.

I confessed my sins and named the other watchers, a moment before the fire engulfed me.

2

Colette

New York City

Glancing over my shoulder, I tugged at the sleeve of my charmeuse silk blouse, careful to conceal the bruises that mottled my wrists. Not even my sister's largest, most obnoxious beaded cuff could cover the scabbed-over purple spots. I flexed my fingers, wincing at the sharp pain in the joint of the middle one.

Ironic.

The scent of autumn was thick on the cool night air, a mixture of spice and damp earth. Musty, dirty, cloying. The parking lot was dimly lit, the only working streetlight blurred by a thin fog, its dingy orange glow flickering with every shift in the wind. My focus turned to a dead twig tumbling across the cracked cement, a few brittle brown leaves desperately hanging on for the ride, soon to be at the mercy of the wind.

A black car with a neon racing stripe sat idle at the end

of the lot, the heavy bass from its sound system muted by the traffic on the interstate a few yards away. Though almost midnight, the atmosphere stirred with energy and desperation, that insatiable craving to feed addiction, whether it be through a needle in the arm or the dark fetishes of the immoral.

This part of the city never slept—or talked.

It was a place I never imagined myself to be. Funny the turns life takes us down.

Goose bumps prickled my arms as I checked the time. Fall was advancing on the East Coast like a freight train, with winter weather predicted for later that week, the earliest snowfall in over sixty years. Once a self-proclaimed heliophile, I used to despise the winter, mourning the loss of the heat and humidity like a snake retreating into its hole deep in the ground, where it lay in wait until the warmth of the sunlight shone once again.

But there is no light anymore. Not in fourteen years.

Now, I revel in the cold. The bleak backdrop of lifeless vegetation, the short days, long nights. The darkness.

It suits me . . . now. It suits me *now.*

A car door slammed behind me but my stride didn't falter. I knew the slamming door belonged to the 1998 Lincoln Continental parked in the third spot west of the dumpster next to the motel office.

Lifting my chin, I sniffed, like an animal sensing its prey, and began to count the heavy footfalls of the man who had sat behind his steering wheel, Marlboro in one hand, cell phone in the other, for exactly eight minutes after sliding into the spot at six miles an hour.

Caucasian, five foot ten, two hundred twenty pounds, the beginning of a receding hairline concealed by a NO BOUNDARIES red, white, and blue baseball cap likely purchased from the discount bin at the local Walmart. Drunk, based on the slight stagger in his step, and fighting ragweed allergies, based on the loogie he hocked onto the windshield of a nearby car.

The man's steps faded into the alley behind the motel, and I wondered what poison he was seeking that night.

Addiction fascinated me, a disorder of the brain characterized by compulsive engagement in a substance or behavior despite adverse consequences. It is a power so strong that the need to sate these desires overcomes all else—our health, our safety, our relationships, replacing the innate drive of human self-preservation. That basic instinct to survive.

Most people sum up addiction by the number of deaths it causes, but that is only half the picture. The number of marriages, relationships, jobs, bank accounts, and livelihoods it destroys is far greater. Addiction changes us to the very core, slowly consuming our values, beliefs, and priorities like a virus. In almost all cases, addiction arises from the attempt to numb a pain—past or present.

It is a power that I'm drawn to, both as an observer and as an active participant.

Perhaps one caused the other—I'm not sure. And I didn't care. All I knew on that night was that I needed my escape. My hit.

My punishment.

A used tissue caught in the wind, spiraling around my Louboutin heels. Red soles to match my lips; black patent leather to match my mood. Not even the shiftiest pickpocket in the deepest depths of hell could drive me into second-hand rags. Been there, done that, and that's where I drew the line. If I was going to die, dammit, I was going to go out in a blaze of diamonds and couture. The definition of self-made success . . . right?

I considered doubling back to grab my jacket from the back of my car, but decided against it. Past experience had taught me the more layers I wore, the longer the delay and greater chance for second-guessing.

Men in that part of the city weren't used to the well-made fasteners of a Von Furstenberg suit jacket. I'd changed in my office after working late as usual, opting for a flowy blouse unbuttoned just enough to show my ample cleavage, untucked over a pair of skinny jeans from the stash I kept locked in my safe, next to the wigs.

Headlights cut through the night as a sixth car turned into the lot. Pivoting, I stepped deeper into the shadows because I didn't have time to record the plates or take a mental picture of the junkie behind the wheel. My pace quickened over the cracked asphalt, echoing in the darkness like the moan of a cat in heat. From somewhere deep in the shadows, voices went silent, heads turning in my direction.

Two men, I'd noticed immediately upon my arrival, undoubtedly waiting for their deal to go down. One that involved more than a dime bag, based on the weapons hidden in their waistbands.

I didn't make eye contact, though I wanted to. I was in a mood that night, one that had become increasingly harder to ignore. The devil on my shoulder, I know now.

Instead, I kept my gaze on my target, surprised that a small part of me wished for one of the men to advance. That night, I'd welcome the challenge.

An airplane roared overhead, blinking red lights against a sky as black as coal. Below it, the airport shone like a beacon, the harsh blinking lights, muted buzz, and energy that comes with fighting the clock. The hurry to wait. The excitement beyond all that glittering glass, the hope, the fear, the anxiety, the change. The busyness of life.

I wondered who had found their way to the parking lot that night. Wary travelers seeking a cheap room and even cheaper drink after flights canceled or missed? Some by accident, others by meticulously planned distractions? Or perhaps hopeless wanderers with simply nowhere else to go?

Those were my favorite.

The whispered voices returned once I stepped out of view, and the sound of my heels was drowned out by drunken laughter coming from the brick building on the corner, otherwise known as my target.

My pulse rate picked up, that familiar tingle of excitement increasing with each step. Salivating, for a moment, I contemplated two at a time.

Depends on the crowd, I decided as I maneuvered between the beat-up trucks and sedans. Two with car seats in the back.

Kids. Little beings of dreams and wonder. Naivety and ignorance. A husband, a family. A thought so foreign to me.

I chanced a peek into one of the cars and found myself staring for a moment at the half-eaten granola bar sitting next to a pink sippy-cup in the car seat, a momentary pang of protectiveness stealing my focus.

Was she safe? Warm? Well-fed?

But why did I care? It was all merely an illusion. One misstep, one single bad decision that would shatter the child's entire family surely awaited her.

A fire sparked against that excitement I'd felt moments earlier.

Yeah, I was in a mood that night.

I had to refrain from running to the flickering neon sign that read BAR, as if the windowless brick walls, puke-stained sidewalks, and duo of whores out front weren't clear enough.

The women turned to look at me as I stepped out of the shadows. A cigarette dangled from the tall one's lips, which were swollen and bruised. Her brow cocked as she gave me the once-over, turning fully toward me. The other stepped closer, almost protectively, one eye blackened, her lips pale and cracked.

Keeping my eye on the tall one, I turned my attention to the footsteps of the two junkies coming up the sidewalk behind me.

Just then, the thick metal door of the bar swung open and two chortling truck drivers stumbled out.

My attention lingered on the whore, my sudden hesitation surprising me—and pissing me off. Turning away, I caught the door and slipped inside, reminding myself of the purpose of the evening, which was not to save those who didn't want to be saved.

Like the smell of fresh coffee in the morning, the scent of stale beer and cedar made every nerve sensor in my body tingle, anticipating what was about to come. A Pavlovian response conditioned after many, many years of repeated stimulation.

The barroom was dimmer than usual. One of the only three working lights had burned out since my last visit. A thick haze of cigarette smoke snaked around the scattered tables, where lonely souls slumped over pints of beer and shots of cheap whiskey.

Taking a steadying inhale to calm my pulse, I slid seamlessly into the huntress that I spent all week pining to become once again. Casually scanning the crowd, I crossed the warped hardwood floor, my heels sticking and peeling off with a loud squelch.

That night, eight men and one woman had found their way to the seediest bar just outside the airport.

Five locals, judging by the mindless daze of their boredom, and three travelers. One, a middle-aged man in a Tommy Bahama with black Chaco sandals and a white tan line around his bare ring finger. An overnight bag was parked at his feet.

Another man, this one older, wearing the business attire he'd carefully chosen to arrive in for his big meeting with the partners, and another, glued to his cell phone with a panicked expression on his face as he awaited confirmation from his travel agent of the rescheduling of his missed flight.

Only one local piqued my interest. New to the bar. New to drinking away pain.

So, I had four options that night.

After sliding into my usual bar stool, two down from the end, I settled in, careful to avoid the mysterious glob oozing down the side of the wooden bar top.

As usual, I carried no purse to keep an eye on. Only my key fob, credit card, driver's license, and a switchblade tucked safely in a back pocket of my jeans. Purses revealed too much, I learned long ago.

The same cloudy, cheap liquor bottles crowded the mirrored back wall as they had days earlier, although a bit lighter now. The same news channel looped on repeat on the box television mounted to the ceiling above the kegs. Same ripped black leather booths lined the far wall.

"What can I get ya?"

A tall, skeletal man with sallow skin, yellowing eyes, and an abnormally large head walked up. He wiped his hands on a towel tucked alarmingly deep into his trousers.

I didn't recognize him, though "new" was definitely not a word I would use to describe his appearance as he carried the same despondent disinterest and perpetual boredom of the prior barkeep. A lifelong bartender, I decided, before placing my order of tequila on the rocks, otherwise known as my go-juice.

It wasn't lost on me that the barman didn't ask for my ID. My appearance had become a source of insecurity over the years. Long days, long nights, and constant stress had slowly sucked the youthful glow from my skin and made me appear older than my thirty-three years.

The Eagles' "Lyin' Eyes" kicked on from the jukebox in the corner.

After delivering my drink, the man lumbered away, leaving me to my thoughts.

Wrapping my fingers around the cold, sweating glass, I took a moment to watch the ice swirl in the deep amber. I found myself thinking about the hookers out front, worrying about them. Pushing the emotion away, I inhaled deeply, then sipped, welcoming the burn down my throat.

With the tequila warming my insides, I closed my eyes and mentally sang along with the song, the only place I could consistently remain in tune.

You can't hide those lying eyes . . .

I took another sip, deeper this time, and leaned back.

Your smile is a thin disguise . . .

"Is this seat taken?"

My pulse kickstarted to life. *And we begin.*

It was the local, I guessed, based on the quiet, unsure tone of his voice.

Waiting a moment, I swirled the glass in my hand, then slowly turned.

A game. It was all a game. One that I'd become very good at.

A portly fellow, the man had round ruddy cheeks and thinning hair a few years from falling out. His thin blue button-up and faded khakis told me he'd just left the same blue-collar job he'd had for the last decade. Deep-set frown lines suggested it was a job he hated but must keep in order to pay for his three-bedroom, two-bathroom, cookie-cutter house in a cookie-cutter neighborhood, and his wife's obsession with scrapbooking.

But the faded sparkle in those chestnut-brown eyes also suggested that there was a time, long ago, that this man had big plans. The hardworking grit of someone with the intent to be successful and work their way to the top of the company they'd so proudly signed on with, fresh out of the college they'd willingly put themselves into debt to attend.

But year after year, this man's lack of assertiveness cursed him into being overlooked by the younger, hungrier, smarter versions of himself. As hope faded, along with his checking account, he'd let himself go, evidenced by the thick waist and what was surely an unfortunate case of man boobs under the poly-blend fabric. Probably developed soon after falling into a depression he'd yet to acknowledge, losing that zest for life along with his wife, who he decided he no longer loved.

Because why else was he so unhappy?

I gestured to the seat next to me and smiled.

The corners of his dry, chapped lips curled up as he dropped his weight onto the stool next to me, a waft of cheap cologne following seconds later. As he selected the perfect spot for his Bud Light on the bar, I took another sip of my tequila, internally wagering on which pickup line this stranger would go with first.

From experience, I knew there were four main openers.

The first, and far most common, was leading with a comment about the weather. Whether it be rainy, sunny, wet, or dry, men have learned that there was always a guaranteed response when prompted about the conditions beyond the bar top. It was a safe, comfortable conversation starter, used most often by the newly divorced.

The second most common was "You from around here?" This pickup line was riskier than the first because it was more personal. The more confident, forward strangers used this line, and were more often than not more aggressive.

The third most common pickup line was "What are you drinking?" This usually came from the less advanced pickup artist who tended to leave much to be desired in the way of conversation skills. You see, once I informed the interested stranger what I was drinking, he'd respond, and boom, we were back to square one. These men had a lot to learn.

And finally, "What's your name?" This was always used by the most aggressive man in the room by far. No preamble, no bullshit. The man never cared what my name was—he simply wanted in my pants. He was a man I'd dated several times in my past.

My past . . .

I set my drink down, keeping my eyes low.

The man cleared his throat, then began with, "I thought winter wasn't for another month."

And just like that, we began the dance.

Based on his choice of pickup line, I presumed he was either newly divorced or perhaps still separated, because he couldn't fully cut ties with his family until he found what he was looking for. Little did he know, it was within himself.

I smiled as I took another sip.

His curiosity fixed on me, assessing me assessing him. "You don't look like you belong here, if you don't mind me saying."

I didn't mind him saying that because I put a lot of effort into not appearing like the whores outside. Men always wanted the woman in the bar who didn't look like she belonged there. It was all about the fantasy. They wanted everything their wives—their lives—weren't.

"That's correct," I lied. "I'm just here for a little bit, for work."

"What kind of work?"

"Culinary school." A smile lit my face, my back straightening in excitement at this plot twist. A chef. Wouldn't that be a cool job? There was a time, long ago, that I'd considered going to culinary school.

That dream never came to fruition.

I paused, wondering why the past had crept up on me in that moment. And then I remembered the time of year.

He smiled, a big toothy grin with a gap in the middle that you couldn't help but smile back at. "No kidding? A professional cook?"

"That's the goal."

He surveyed my trim one hundred twenty pounds, sculpted meticulously with five-mile daily jogs and hour-long hot-yoga sessions.

His smile morphed into a flirt. "A professional cook—I wouldn't have guessed that."

"Am I to take that as a compliment?"

"Yes . . . *yes*."

"Thank you then."

"How did you get into cooking?"

"My sister. She—" I froze, the single word catching in my

throat like a ball of wax. "She loved to cook," I said, quickly recovering. "Taught the whole family. I'm the only one who decided to turn it into a career."

"Very nice. Definitely plenty of culinary jobs here in New York. Where are you coming from?"

"Louisiana."

His brows popped. He seemed pleased by this. "You drive or fly?"

"Fly, and was delayed for five hours at the connection. I just got in." I glanced at my watch. "About two hours ago."

"And pulled into the first motel you saw?"

"Bingo."

His gaze swept over my face with a nod that suggested he was calling this coincidental meeting kismet.

It was.

The bartender walked up, wiping his long, skinny fingers on his towel as he bitched about the score of the football game now playing on the television. Mr. Bud Light bitched back. Apparently, my suitor and his shadow had bonded over pigskin before my arrival. What else had they discussed?

Not liking this, I decided it was time to go.

The man next to me had other plans, however, and ordered another beer for himself and "another one for the lady."

When the barkeep walked away, the conversation continued, my new drinking buddy quick to inform me that he was a linebacker in high school. Thirty years ago, I guessed.

Surprising myself with my patience, I settled back, pretending to listen, a cat eyeing the mouse. He was oblivious to this, of course.

"What's your name?" I asked finally, as Chatty Cathy took a break to wet his throat.

"Berry."

"I'm sorry." I grinned.

He laughed boisterously. "I know. Berry with an *e*, not an *a*. Destined to be overweight from the start, right?"

I hated his insecurity. I hated it for him.

"What's yours?" he asked.

"Sarah." Otherwise known as the most perfectly inconspicuous, forgettable name.

"Ah." He chuckled. "I know two other Sarahs."

They always did.

I glanced at the clock. "Well, Berry-with-an-e . . ." I drained my drink and waved for the bartender. "I've got a large pepperoni pizza and a game of solitaire waiting in my motel room for me."

"You play cards?"

"Since I was a little girl."

"Poker?"

I snorted. "Which kind?"

His brown eyes sparkled. He glanced at my drink, at his, then back to me, and I smiled. He hesitated, while I had officially stepped on pins and needles.

"One game of poker," he whispered, as if anyone cared he was about to make a bad decision with a woman at a bar. "Winner pays the other's bar bill."

"You're on."

Like a puppet on a string, Berry stood when I did and obediently followed me across the room.

I felt the eyes on us as we stepped into the cool evening air. The hookers were gone, and I welcomed the privacy once the door slapped shut behind us, leaving the remaining clientele to focus on their empty pint glasses and their screwed-up problems while I attempted to sate my own craving.

For the next seven months, I could do whatever I wanted to do, be whoever the hell I wanted to be. Because seven months was all I had left.

Seven months to right the wrongs.

3

Colette

With Berry-with-an-e hot on my heels, I walked briskly down the sidewalk, my gaze locked on the flickering neon sign that read MAHALO MOTEL hanging crookedly over a thick metal door.

Apparently not as drunk as I'd like, Berry hesitated, his heavy footsteps pausing behind me. "Wait. Didn't you say you already had a room?"

Ignoring him, I pushed open the office door and stepped under the blinding fluorescent light, a stark contrast to the inky blackness outside. The familiar scent of burned coffee and stale cigarette smoke greeted me as I watched Berry in the reflection of the window as he cautiously stepped in after me, glancing over his shoulder, uncomfortable now.

This amused me, knowing that despite that red flag going off in his head, he would press on, the need to satisfy his cravings far too powerful.

That addiction.

The sad motel office was badly in need of a renovation,

as was every room in the motel itself. To the left, two mismatched plastic chairs leaned against the wall, awkwardly facing each other, an artificial tree canted in its woven base, filled with Styrofoam riddled with holes, likely from a family of mice. A small computer sat in the middle of the front desk, and behind that, a narrow doorway led to a smaller office for personal use.

Obnoxious bells jangled from above the door as Berry gingerly guided it closed behind us.

My attention was pulled to movement from the back office as the motel manager pulled herself away from *Nick at Nite,* blaring from a tiny television teetering on the edge of a desk cluttered with yarn and knitting needles. The leather chair groaned as she pushed herself up, taking a moment to find her knees. The woman would be a sitting duck in a motel frequented by gangbangers, if not for the Colt 45 I knew she kept under that desk.

Taking her time to cross the postage-stamp-size office, MaryAnne finally stepped into the light, wearing a sweatshirt adorned with a crocheted kitten and a ball of yarn. Around her neck was the gold cross she wore every day.

I was pleased to see that MaryAnne had put on weight, and assumed she'd finished her last round of chemo. I made a mental note to check with my connection at the oncology clinic and rearrange the payment schedule as needed.

A spark flickered in her tired, milky eyes as our gazes met. But just as quickly, she regrouped, glancing at the man standing timidly behind me.

"How may I help you, ma'am?" Despite the extra pounds she carried, MaryAnne's voice was weak, and something deep in my heart broke. But just as quickly, I forced away the emotion.

Because death comes for us all. She was lucky to have lasted that long.

"One room please, ma'am." I handed her my credit card, though just for show.

MaryAnne took it from my fingers, quickly turning the plastic upside down so Berry wouldn't be able to read my real name across the front. Avoiding eye contact, she focused on the computer, her fingers clicking at a dizzying speed across the keys, although the rest of her moved in slow motion. I always wondered what she was typing at that moment.

"You're in luck," she said, still avoiding eye contact. "I've got one room left tonight. Five C—on the corner."

After swiping the card, she handed it back, along with a receipt with pink streaks running down the center. I scribbled my signature and handed it back, knowing that MaryAnne didn't care that it was illegible. She was paid not to.

Our eyes met for a second, and she blinked. *Thank you.*

I dipped my chin. *Thank you.*

Turning, I breezed past Berry, who was surely wondering at this point if the innocent chef he'd just "picked up" from the bar was a prostitute.

Not a word was spoken between us as we fell into step together down the sidewalk, Berry now at a loss for words.

The door to the room on the end opened as smoothly and quietly as if it were on greased hinges, and I was glad MaryAnne took my advice to replace it.

I stepped inside as Berry fought an internal battle whether to follow. It was a deciding moment, a turning point in the middle-aged man's life. Because once you entered the motel room, there was no going back.

Crossing the room, I clicked on the table lamp, its dim

light revealing my reflection in the smudged mirror above the dresser.

That night, I'd chosen a long, pin-straight black wig. It was a stark difference from my pale skin and the honey-blond hair I had tucked carefully underneath. Thick black bangs brushed my brows, the blue hue of my eyes contrasting with the black. That, with the red lips, gave me a vampire vibe. I liked it, I decided.

"I'm . . . not sure about this," Berry said quietly from the doorway, caught in that very sticky spot between the angel and the devil.

"Then leave," I said, keeping my back to him while rearranging the pillows on the bed.

"I've never done this before . . ."

"What?" I glanced over my shoulder with a smirk. "Play poker?"

I refocused on the bed, my smirk widening into a smile as I listened to one loafer, then two, enter the room, and finally, the click of the door shutting behind him. The devil won that battle.

"So. How do we do this?"

After yanking the curtains closed over the window, I turned to him. "The first thing you do, Berry, is quit thinking."

His throat worked with a deep swallow.

Keeping my eyes on his, I backed up to the bed as I stepped out of my heels, watching his face flush and that little vein pulsate next to his eye.

The energy in the room shifted. The once still, musty, vacant air was now charged with raw lust. Rational thought had been cast aside by the human's purest, most powerful desire. Sex. An orgasm. That euphoric explosion like nothing else in the world. I could practically feel the blood pumping between his legs, the throb matching my own.

My eyes locked on his, I took my time unbuttoning my silk blouse. Because a handful of minutes is all I ever had, so I reveled in each one.

The shirt dropped to the floor. His gaze remained on my chest, flickering between the nipples peeking out of my white lace bra. Next, my jeans.

Sweat beaded on his forehead.

Shifting my weight slightly, I pulled the blade from my back pocket and slid it onto the nightstand, next to my phone. Berry didn't notice this. They never do.

This was when my arousal started to peak. Everything was in place at that point.

My heart pounded as I reached back, unclasped my bra, and felt it sweep past my nipples as it tumbled to the floor.

Wiping the sweat now saturating his forehead, Berry swallowed deeply.

I loved this moment, when the man became putty in my hands. Weak, ignorant creatures so easily manipulated.

Leaving my panties in place, I demanded he undress.

Berry obeyed, removing his clothes with the smoothness of a teenage boy fumbling his way through his first masturbation. His swollen hands trembled. His balance was off, his entire world at that moment centered on the hole between my legs. A woman's most powerful possession.

"Boxers," I said when he hesitated, not knowing what to do next.

He nodded, then pushed them down, a thick, short veiny penis springing up with the movement.

"Now lay down."

"Where?" he asked, innocent like a child.

"On the bed, on your back."

The bed squeaked and groaned under his weight as he crawled onto the obnoxious paisley-print bedspread that MaryAnne washed every day, regardless of my schedule.

He glanced at the lamp. When I shook my head, he nodded. "Aren't you going to—"

I slid out of my panties and tossed them into the corner.

His eyes flared with heat.

My heart began to thrum as I crawled onto the bed and straddled his body on my knees. I could smell him—hot, ripe, the pungent scent of pheromones rolling off his hairy, splotchy chest.

Pinning him down, I placed my hands on his chest, the coarse springy hair worming its way through my fingers. Spit pooled in my mouth.

As I lowered myself to just above the head of his penis, my cell phone vibrated.

He blinked.

"Stay." Keeping one hand on his chest, I plucked the phone from the nightstand, clicked it on, and read the text from my sister. Then I tapped into my tracking app and pinned her location. Once I was sure she was safe, I replaced the phone next to the switchblade he still had yet to notice.

I refocused on him. "Rules. Do not touch my face, my neck, or my lips, Berry. If you do, the only way you will leave this room is in a wheelchair. Do you understand?"

He nodded, his eyes widening with that intoxicating mixture of fear and excitement. A dangerous, dangerous addictive combination.

Berry was mine now. The man would do anything and everything I wanted.

Fool.

I pulled a condom from the top drawer—always fully stocked—ripped the foil, and slowly rolled it over his erection. Jerking at my touch, he breathed hard, his chest heaving as adrenaline coursed through him. It had been a long time since I'd seen a man that excited.

My fingers slid between the hairs on his chest as I spread my knees wider and positioned myself over Berry's throbbing penis.

"Keep your hands at your sides."

"Okay," he whispered.

I lowered slowly, until the tip penetrated my lips. "Are you ready, Berry?"

"Yes," he choked out, and his voice cracked.

"What are the rules, Berry?"

"No lips, face, or neck. Hands at my sides."

Smiling, I exhaled and slipped into the darkness.

For the next twenty minutes, I rode Berry like a wild animal as tears streamed down my face. Grabbing, slapping, scratching, cursing. Uninhibited. Uncontrolled. Unrelenting.

Unhinged.

I came with a dizzying explosion, that vile mixture of ecstasy and revulsion releasing from me with a guttural scream. As I clawed at his chest, Berry emptied himself into the latex. He fell limp below me, but I wasn't done. Pinning him in place, I ripped at his chest hair as I kept going until dryness shredded my insides and the pain was no longer bearable.

For twenty minutes, I punished myself for the decision I made fourteen years ago.

The one decision I could never take back.

4

James

"Eagle One, in position."

My focus shifted to the rooftop across from mine where a red aviation warning light blinked against the pitch-black night sky, every two seconds.

Two seconds.

A shadow slipped past the vapor funneling from the pipes, the silhouette briefly backlit by the red light—revealing my partner's location to anyone who might be lurking in the shadows.

From my spot behind a turbine vent, I spat out a curse.

Two fucking seconds, yet somehow the man responsible for my overwatch missed his window of darkness. This didn't sit well with me. We were trained for moments like this. Entire careers were built on moments like this. And lives were lost because of moments like *that.* Two seconds was enough to make or break an entire mission. Unfortunately, I knew this all too well.

I wasn't used to having to worry about the men around

me. In the Marines, my team and I were one, trained to think as one, speak as one, act as one. A single impenetrable unit. There was no I. No missed windows. There were no mistakes.

Was . . .

That familiar rush of anger pulsed through my veins.

Since accepting a job with the Drug Enforcement Agency, I'd been told that I came off as too edgy to my coworkers. "Arrogant and hotheaded" were the exact words used, if I recall correctly. My boss, George Clancy, had added "unreasonably obstinate" to the list.

Lifelong federal agent George Clancy had been married and divorced three times, had no kids, and had recently lost his mother to cancer. People literally hid when he walked into the room. I considered *unreasonably obstinate* a compliment coming from him.

I'd been called many things in my life, but stubborn wasn't one of them, and I couldn't help but wonder where this restless energy was coming from.

I'd expected my new job to include much more seizures and arrests than gathering evidence and composing reports behind a computer. As the new guy, I'd been assigned every desk job imaginable to, as they said, "learn to crawl before blowing shit up."

At this rate, I was going to be crawling until I could no longer hold my own shit.

I needed action, movement, the ability to use my skills beyond a Word document or an Excel spreadsheet.

This was my first official high-stakes raid with the DEA since accepting a position with the department a year earlier, and was the only thing standing between me and securing a seat in my current division's Special Response Team. Not only was I the "greenest" man on the team that night, I'd fought tooth and nail to be included on that particular op, using every bullet in my belt until the team supervisor caved and allowed me to participate.

I was out to prove myself that night—and nothing felt right about it.

Above me, stars blanketed a crystal-clear autumn night sky. The moon shone like a massive spotlight hellbent on exposing our team. I examined the tilt, calculating the time. I wore a watch but never needed to check it.

I wasn't a fan of full moons. The inky blackness that came with a moonless night had always been my friend. Someone I could count on.

Not that night. The slums of Harlem were bathed in an eerie silver light. Long, dark shadows stretched between one dilapidated, abandoned warehouse to the next. Shards of glass from the busted windows covered the narrow alleyways, reflecting the moonbeams that exposed concrete walls stained with graffiti and years of human piss. The stench of that night rivaled the shitholes I'd stormed in the caves of Tora Bora.

Movement from the corner of my eye drew my attention. Sliding my finger over the trigger of my Barrett MRAD, I focused my scope and peered downward to the black cat creeping between dumpsters. It was a good sign. Feral cats didn't wander in alleys already filled with predators.

Careful to remain in the shadow of the turbine vent slowly spinning next to me, I shifted back into position.

A brittle dead leaf fluttered slowly down from a tree I didn't see. The air was cold that night, coldest of the season, if I remember correctly. It reminded me of my tours overseas. Blazing-hot days and ice-cold nights. Again, I felt that anger, that longing for my old life.

Regret wasn't an emotion I readily accepted. Until that

point in my life, I'd lived my twenty-eight years with only one regret, one heavy enough to last a lifetime. After that, I'd promised no more. Regret—guilt—would eat you alive.

So, why the fuck are all these feelings coming back now?

For a moment, I imagined myself back there, in the Marines. Pretending to sleep under the cover of camouflage netting, my brothers asleep next to me.

They could always sleep. Exhaustion, I assumed.

Me? I never could. Not during an op. As the team leader, I'd replay the mission over and over in my head, as we'd practiced. I'd plan for every scenario under the sun with one end goal in mind—the target. If you lost focus for even a second, if you allowed emotions or fear to creep inside, the op fell apart like a bad game of Jenga.

Work the plan. Move as one. Always keep your eye on the target, and only the target. Successful completion of the op was all that mattered.

It took a brother dying in my arms to learn how wrong I was.

I kept my eye on the rooftop, my faith quickly waning in my new partner, Adam Dabrowski. I tried to convince myself that it was okay. That it wouldn't be the first time someone had failed me and I had to pick up the slack. But the truth was, it *wasn't* okay.

Mistakes aren't okay. They are not acceptable.

My partner's location being exposed by his inexperience was *not* acceptable.

Thinking back, that should have been my first sign that things were about to go very, very wrong.

My earpiece crackled. "Bear Bait, in position," was followed by another crackle. "Black Cat, in position."

My pulse rate picked up as adrenaline built in my veins,

heightening my senses, sharpening my focus. I welcomed the feeling, thrived on it.

This was life. *This* was what I was made for.

My fingertips began to tingle.

I took another look at the rooftop next to me, but this time, I didn't allow myself to question my partner. There was no time for that anymore.

Phase three of the raid had commenced.

Scanning the perimeter, I envisioned the team attaching the explosives to the breach point, a reinforced steel door installed days after one of the largest drug cartels in the area secured two hundred pounds of fentanyl inside. The DEA had been tracking the shipment since it crossed the US/Mexico border a week earlier.

It would be the second largest fentanyl seizure in US history, valued at three million dollars. But the drugs weren't the only focus of this operation. The goal was to capture and interrogate the main players of a rapidly growing international drug cartel known as the Salazar Organization.

I had my eye on one man, Enrique Salazar, the rumored second-in-command of the organization's North American trade. Known as El Hoguera, or Bonfire, Salazar was known for his vicious retaliation against snitches in his inner circle, most notably burning men and women alive while their friends and family watched, then each of them meeting their own demise execution-style.

A rumored playboy, his treatment of women was only marginally less savage, marking those who belonged to him—known as his harem—by shaving off their clitorises so that he was the last man to ever pleasure them. The physical abuse his harem endured was second only to the mental abuse as he forced fentanyl into the women, slowly getting them addicted and turning them into his slaves. Salazar truly was a demon walking this earth, bred of generations of drug smugglers.

I didn't have to be told that Enrique Salazar's seizure could help bring down the entire cartel.

I wanted him. I wanted him to avenge the death of my mother.

My earpiece crackled. "Charge secured."

I shifted into a squat and lowered my night-vision goggles.

"Three . . ."

I closed my eyes, said my Hail Marys.

"Two . . ."

I inhaled.

"One."

My eyes shot open with the sound of the blast. The building shook as I lunged from my position, my life now in my overwatcher's hands. The building shook beneath my feet as screams and shouts rang out below.

Women. They always had fucking women.

Flinging my sniper rifle onto my back, I threw myself over the side of the roof, shimmied down the ladder, and hurled myself feet-first into one of the many busted windows of the sixth floor.

In one seamless movement, I landed silently onto the concrete, lifted my rifle, and scanned the room. It was pitch-black, aside from the moonlight streaming in through the windows, which only illuminated a three-foot square. Large support beams ran the length of the massive empty space, littered with trash, beer cans, and dead leaves.

The pop of gunshots rang through the air. I sprinted across the floor just as Adam flew through the window from the opposite side. We didn't speak as he fell into step behind me, our heads low and rifles pointed upward as we jogged to the stairwell.

According to the intel, the shipment was being held in a renovated basement at the bottom of the six-story warehouse, secured 24/7 by at least a dozen armed guards. A group of leaders from the cartel had begun arrangements for distribution.

An alarm sounded. Loud, screeching wails followed us as we jogged down the stairs, smoke beginning to engulf the stairwell.

The chaos grew with each floor we passed. The moment we rounded to the third, we were met with startled, dirty faces.

Three bullets, between three sets of eyes. None Salazar.

We stepped around the bodies and continued down the stairs, meeting two of our own on the way.

The smoke was thick and cloying, the scent of gunpowder strong as we reached the first floor, the red strobe light grotesquely illuminating multiple dead bodies bleeding out on the concrete. It was at least twenty degrees hotter down there.

Adam slipped in a pool of blood and grasped my shoulder for support. I steadied him as the others blew past us. Our eyes met for a beat as I nonverbally told him to get his shit together.

He nodded, and we split off from the team to breach the left entry of the basement while the other two planned to breach the right.

Dead bodies littered the floor, the smell of blood and urine stronger than the smoke.

Three men emerged from the basement. I took them out one by one, then turned to see Adam engaged in hand-to-hand with an unidentified. Just then, a body fell from the ceiling. I aimed my rifle upward, where at least five masked men had climbed to the rafters, seeking refuge from the breach.

Shit.

Pacing my shots around the goddamn red strobe light of the alarm, I put a bullet between the eyes of the man descending a rope, then grabbed my radio.

"Need backup, first floor. Ambush."

Gunfire exploded around us as I fired back, picking them off one by one, but not fast enough. Adam was down on the floor, struggling with his attacker.

Under a hail of bullets, I aimed upward, pulled the trigger, and sprinted to my partner. A bullet grazed my arm, searing heat ripping through flesh. My magazine was out of ammo by that point, so I swung my rifle at Adam's attacker, slamming the butt of it into the side of his face.

That's when everything turned to a buzz.

I didn't hear the shouts, the gunshots, the groans and dropping of dead bodies around me as I fell to my knees by my partner. The side of his face was gone. His eye, cheek, and jaw was a mushy mess of blood.

And he was *still alive*.

His one good eye locked on mine, his chest heaving as he tried to say something in raspy wheezes, the final pleas of a man who knew he was dying.

A hand wrapped around my bicep as I began to gather Adam in my arms.

Someone was screaming at me, but I couldn't make out the words. Adam's foot was caught in a hole in the floor, probably what tripped him up, causing him to lose a fight he should have won.

Determined, I fought off whoever the hell was pulling at me.

Adam is alive, that's all I could think. *He's still fucking alive.*

Panic gripped me. I couldn't leave him. I'd left someone else in their time of need once, and I vowed to never do it again.

At this point, two of my teammates were trying to pull me back. Their words finally began to register.

"The place is rigged to blow!"

"It's going to blow, Black! We've got to get out!"

But Adam is alive.

With a guttural scream, I shoved the men back and refocused on trying to dislodge my partner's foot from the damn floor.

Adam is alive.

The screams faded as heavy footfalls disappeared out the doorways, shadows slipped out the windows, and I found myself alone.

Me, Adam, and dozens of dead bodies.

I will never, ever forget that moment. The moment the world around me suddenly stilled.

An eerie quiet, seconds before the blast.

5

Colette

Wiping vomit from my mouth, I crawled out of my bathroom on hands and knees. My head lolled like a rag doll's, my blond hair falling into my eyes as I slowly crawled across the carpet to my bed. Despite the frigid chill in my veins, sweat dripped from the tip of my nose.

I stank like sour milk, but I didn't care.

Squinting, I lifted the bowling ball that was my head and found the red light of the bedside clock glowing through the darkness, declaring the time as 1:47 a.m. At least it was past midnight.

I reached up, fumbling through the bottles of pills that cluttered my nightstand. After examining each label under the light of the alarm clock, I opened three bottles, tapped out two pills from each, and popped them in my mouth. The bitterness of the taste made my eyes water as I ground the pills between my teeth, then chugged an old half-full bottle of water peeking out from under my bed.

Eating the pills increased the speed of the results, I'd learned.

Sighing, I collapsed onto the carpet, too weak to climb into bed. I knew that within ten minutes, the nausea would subside, and within thirty minutes, the pain would be gone. I would wake feeling almost normal, shockingly so. Then the pills would wear off, the queasiness and aches would return, and I'd pop some more.

And on and on we'd go.

Seven to ten months. That's the prognosis the doctor had given me when he'd diagnosed me with stage four melanoma.

6

Colette

The monogrammed turban twisted around my wet hair wobbled as I tiptoe-jogged across the bedroom and clicked off the harmonious melodies of "Gradual Wake Number 4," otherwise known as my alarm clock.

Ignoring the droplets of water sliding down my naked body, I paused to check my email—for the fourth time since I'd awakened. Like most people mindlessly scrolled through their social media feeds, completely unaware that they'd even picked up their phone, I checked my email accounts. It was a nasty little habit that reminded me that I needed to expand my team at Archer and Archer, Inc.

Adding another private investigator would allow me to be more selective about the cases I represented, and give each the time they deserved. Maybe I would even be able to take that Bora Bora vacation I'd been hoping to plan for the last five years. Or was it seven?

Regardless, it was too late now.

Dawn had arrived sometime during my shower, the sun greeting me with a brilliant orange glow as it peeked over the buildings that surrounded my high-rise apartment in Tribeca.

The snow-white carpets reflected an unnatural shade of tangerine under the floor-to-ceiling windows that lined my bedroom. A strategically placed mirror caught the sunrise, reflecting onto the clean lines of my modern chrome furniture and its glass tops, the snow-white comforter already tucked back into place, leaving no trace of sleep.

Black, white, and gray. Every single object in my apartment was either black, white, or gray. Clean, I thought, but according to my eccentric boho sister who owned eleven pairs of rose-colored sunglasses, it was boring.

Momentarily forgetting about the unread emails in my hand, I took a moment to appreciate my favorite part of the day.

There's something about this time of morning, when the sun breaches the tops of the buildings, chasing away the shadows and washing away the sins and secrets of the night before. In an instant, the world is illuminated with a fresh, clean light. It's the purest part of the day, a clean slate to begin once again. A free do-over. A baptism of light.

For me, it's the only time of day that energy is abundant and the concept of hope is something that seems attainable.

This optimism only lasts a short time, though, I've noticed. The following hours quickly become weighed down by time, the inevitable disruption to our carefully crafted schedules, the fast-paced chaos of the city. And perhaps the most destructive force, our own false interpretations of reality as we succumb to the drain of a society that revolves around money and power. The early morning hope is so quickly forgotten, or perhaps *allowed* to be forgotten.

Whose fault is that? The thought flitted through my mind, a constant internal battle.

I sensed the buzz of life below me, fellow early birds out for their morning jogs or coffee runs. I wondered if they rose every morning without an alarm clock as I did. I don't know why I set it, other than that it's simply part of my evening ritual. A "just in case" backup plan that I'd never needed.

Fourteen years, and I'd never once needed my alarm clock as a reminder to wake up. For fourteen years, I'd awakened exactly one hour before sunrise, like clockwork.

I wondered who else, on the streets below me, was battling cancer at that very moment. Who else had been given a deadline for their life?

A shimmering tangerine light danced off the high-rise building across from mine, and I wondered how long it had been since I'd watched the sun rise above the natural horizon rather than this manmade one.

Too long.

Tossing my phone onto the bed, I padded across the room. Exactly three feet from the edge of the window, I rose to my tiptoes and peered down, as far as I could see, anyway.

My stomach dipped, but I forced myself to remain in place until the palpitations calmed.

One more step. It's a good day for one more step.

Inhaling, I lifted my foot and shifted my weight to my tiptoes, my pulse beginning to pound.

One more step . . .

A familiar dizziness washed over me, and I was saved by the ding of my cell phone, alerting me to another email that surely demanded my immediate attention.

Exhaling, I pivoted away from the window and hurried across the room.

Maybe tomorrow.

After checking my phone, I hurried back to the bathroom and unwrapped the turban, then hung it on its designated hook next to my robe. Scowling at the blond highlights in my hair that had dimmed, I automatically checked for grays, then reminded myself that it didn't matter anymore.

Keeping one eye on the clock, I combed the strands into a conservative, tight chignon at the base of my neck, smoothing the sides. After exactly four squirts of hair spray, I applied my makeup, taking time to conceal the bruise on my left cheekbone, now several shades of purple.

Once pleased with my reflection, I slipped into a freshly ironed navy Donna Karan skirt-suit, inspected for hair, fuzz, or any imperfection, then stepped into a pair of Valentino pumps and decided on matching pearl earrings and necklace to complete the look.

Effortless perfection took a solid ninety minutes every morning.

After taking a final pass through my apartment to ensure everything was in its proper place and all appliances were off, I popped in my earbuds, tuned to my favorite morning news show, grabbed my things, and made my way to ground level.

The cool air hit me with surprise as I slipped into the sea of pedestrians with the ease of a true New Yorker. As usual, Lower Manhattan was a bustle of activity—horns, shouts, the buzz of a million very important cell phone conversations being carried on at once. The air was thick with exhaust, cars running their heaters for the first time of the season.

Chin up, shoulders back, my right arm free, I took a mental inventory of my surroundings.

The colors and makes of the cars parked along the congested street. The homeless man, new to the neighborhood, and the three bags of aluminum cans next to him. The man leaning against a tree painted red with autumn, smoking a cigarette, watching the crowd as it passed. A group of tourists huddled around a map under an awning. And finally, Alfred, the owner of the newspaper stand, in a moth-eaten vintage cardigan almost as old as he was, arguing with a woman about the cost of a cup of coffee. I catalogued the single dead brown leaf that fluttered down in front of my face. The angle of the shadows, the light reflecting off glass buildings, the steam rising from the vents.

I took a slow inhale to calm my heart rate, and focused on the familiar baritone of the journalist discussing the morning stocks in my ear as I walked the eleven steps to the Starbucks next door.

"Morning, Miss Archer!" Channing, the six-to-one, Monday-through-Thursday barista called out from behind the bar. As he did every morning, the twenty-something hipster had the energy of a goldendoodle. This, combined with his infatuation with "older" blondes, worked to my advantage.

Greeting him with a dip of my chin, I weaved my way through the unusually thick and impatient crowd. Must be the cold morning. A man shifted his weight as I passed, our bodies brushing against each other as Channing thrust forward my morning coffee—large with two honeys and one creamer.

"On your tab, ma'am."

"Thank you, sir." I winked, and with my left hand, took the cup from his long, tanned, tattooed fingers.

He winked back. "See you tomorrow."

Ignoring the snide remarks from the line of customers, I slipped back through the crowd, my eye on the exit.

Something about the crowds. Always something about the crowds . . .

Sipping at my cup, I pushed out the door and almost stumbled at the flavor that filled my mouth—a gallon of liquid sugar with a splash of gut-punching strong black coffee. The mixture of bitter and sweet made my eyes water.

Christ. Channing gave me the wrong drink.

This was unlike him, and I made a mental note to chide him the next morning about it.

Unacceptable. I'd spent months cultivating our relationship so I wouldn't have to waste time in an angry line every morning. My life was built on structure and routine. Every second of every day had a meaning and a purpose, and when any part of that schedule didn't go as planned, the meaning and purpose were interrupted.

Scowling, I examined the cup. The name BLACK was scribbled on the side.

No shit. Black with fourteen tablespoons of sugar. I imagined what had to be a four-hundred-pound man on oxygen waiting impatiently for the drink. Maybe the mix-up was for the best.

I considered tossing the syrup in the trash but decided the headache from the caffeine withdrawal would be worse than the diabetes this drink was surely about to give me.

Irritated now, I hurried my way up the two blocks to the high-rise that housed my business—my baby—Archer and Archer, Inc. The business that, in seven to ten months, would go to my sister, Jade. A fact I'd yet to share with her.

Along with many, many other things.

7

James

"You're off the team."

"The *fuck*?" I spat out.

Lifting my new eight-dollar coffee to avoid the elbows jabbing around me, I pressed the phone to my ear as I weaved through the crowd, observing the uptight blonde who'd strode into Starbucks like she owned the place and stole the cup of joe I'd just ordered.

The beatnik behind the counter apologized, but I got the feeling he was more concerned about Blondie's reaction to the mix-up than mine. Couldn't blame the kid—the woman was striking, in an icy, stick-up-your-ass kind of way. But I *could* blame the leathery-skinned businessman in gold cuff links, old enough to be the woman's father, who leaned into her as she'd passed in a thinly veiled attempt to brush against her chest.

Lifting my elbow, I barreled into the pervert as I passed, sending him stumbling onto the manicured toes of three twenty-somethings who screamed and scowled at the "old man's" clumsiness.

Not even seven in the morning, and I was already wound up.

The four pain tablets I'd found buried in the cabinet under my sink had done nothing to curb the machete piercing my temples, or the soreness lingering in my ribs from being tossed against the brick wall like a rag doll a few nights earlier.

The lack of sleep didn't help either.

Every time I closed my eyes, I saw Adam's bloodied face as he bled out on the warehouse floor, trying desperately to scream. Except sometimes, I saw Jack's face instead, throwing me back into the slums of Afghanistan when my men and I had been given bad intel that walked us directly into a trap.

The debriefing with the DEA hadn't been much different from what I'd gone through with the military and as a cop. A formal debriefing followed by multiple smaller meetings, and then a quick trip to the combat stress counselor so the higher-ups could check that box. Then a funeral to cap it all off.

More of the same, yet so different at the same time.

Needless to say, the mission had failed. Miserably.

Enrique Salazar was never captured that night in Harlem. The single guard who survived the gunfight confessed Salazar had escaped with two of his main associates via an underground tunnel seconds after the breach.

The asshole was gone in the wind, and we'd done nothing but ensure that it would be a very, very long time before he poked his head up from the sand once again.

It had been a total clusterfuck that apparently wasn't over.

"What did you say?" I asked, because surely I didn't hear my assistant correctly.

"You're off the Salazar team. I thought you'd appreciate a heads-up before the boss calls you in this morning."

"What the hell are you talking about . . ." My voice trailed off as I slipped out the door behind the blonde, unnoticed.

Falling into step behind the tall, willowy woman, I studied her confident stride by which she maneuvered through the crowd. The woman walked with her chin up and her spine as straight as an iron rod, punctuated by two pointy shoulders under an uptight skirt-suit outfit that probably cost more than my truck.

The woman's demeanor was so stiff that not even the honey-blond bun at the nape of her neck swayed as she strode up the sidewalk—again, like she owned it. Through the haze of exhaust and the bleak colors of the men and women around her, a single beam of sunlight sparkled off the string of pearls she wore around her neck.

"Sir?"

"What?" I snapped back to the moment, surprised at the stranger's ability to hold my attention, considering what I was hearing on the other end of the phone. "What the fuck do you mean, I'm off the team?"

"You've been removed from the case."

"What? Why?" My stride quickened as I followed the woman with no idea why. And now my brain was also spinning, and I didn't know the reason for that either.

"They're downsizing."

I stopped cold. A man stumbled behind me, but I didn't

move. When he stepped around me, our eyes met. He opened his mouth to spout something off, then closed it and shuffled away.

"Downsizing?" I repeated. "This isn't a fucking family of four. I'm going to need more details here, kid."

My language, that was another thing my boss had suggested that I remedy. I sidestepped a goldendoodle walking her Botox-Barbie owner, oblivious to anything that doesn't involve six zeroes.

"Hang on," Blaze said. "Just a minute."

I muttered a curse as my assistant placed me on hold.

Blaze Nightwalker—yep, that's his real name—was the third assistant assigned to me since I was transferred to the New York office after completing my special agent training in Virginia. I had no choice in the location of the transfer, because if I had, I wouldn't have chosen to live in the armpit of the United States.

Little did I know at that time that being a special agent meant shuffling more paperwork than when I was a cop. It also involved sitting behind a desk for ten hours a day, reading reports, building reports, and reporting on reports.

The remaining time was spent researching on the internet, interviewing anyone and everyone—and their parents—who may or may not know something about drug dealing. And watching video after video of the scum of society who may or may not be involved in drug trafficking.

For weeks, I'd lived in a city where the only grass within walking distance of my studio apartment withered under human urine and dog shit. The only time I got to see the sun rise was during my morning coffee run to the vending machine across the street that sat under a yellow ball that read "Sun's Coffee." Out-of-*Oder* that day, according to the handwritten sign duct-taped to the window.

The son of some big shot over in public affairs, Blaze was twenty years old, and was either a virgin or gay. Because getting ass is impossible when it's glued to the bottom of your custom-made Swedish anti-stress office chair fourteen hours a day. The dude never left the office. A literal genius, I'd been told by the assistant before him, who also believed that the evil eye she had tattooed above her ass crack would help ward off negativity. Little did she know the repelling power of a tramp-stamp went well beyond those who were just evil.

Blaze was one of those super-book-smart kids who was always listening, watching, and waiting for the other shoe to drop so he could swoop in, steal it from you, slide it on, and then judge its poor craftsmanship.

He was one of those Gen Xers who researched too much, knew too much about nothing, and every morning drank a cup of wheat grass with his organic guacamole gluten-free toast. The kid was always on point, always dressed up, and had yet to let a single curse word slip from his lips. He ate lunch at his desk every day—always packed, each calorie counted.

After work, Blaze went to the gym, where he glistened under the harsh spotlight of the scrutiny he didn't care about. For reasons unbeknownst to me, he cared about me, though, particularly my language and my aversion to suits.

Finally, Blaze graced me with his presence again. "You'll have to ask Clancy for details. Sir."

Sir. He also called me sir.

Horns blared to my left, and my attention was pulled to the snarl of rush-hour traffic driving over the litter on the streets.

I shifted back to the blonde and watched her eye a burly

fellow in an oversized jacket. "How do you know this, Blaze? What did he say?"

"I was copied on an email, sent this morning. I assume you haven't opened it."

"No, I haven't opened it. If I had, I wouldn't be having this fucking conversation."

I assumed Pretty-Boy Blaze blamed my backlogged email on an evening wasted sitting at a bar top or under a busty blonde. In reality, my evening was spent slogging through level three of an Excel training class that I spent half my paycheck on—my version of absolute hell.

I dipped under a random umbrella and made my way to the edge of the sidewalk. "You mean to tell me there's a group email that says James Black has been cut from the Salazar case?"

"No, the email says they're reorganizing."

"Then how do you know they're reorganizing *me*?"

A brief pause followed, and it was then that I realized Blaze had probably received the confidential information directly from his big-dick father. And why was he helping me out?

The kid continued. "There are other subsequent emails that have followed, including one that indicates you have been assigned to support the intel officer on the Walton case."

"The *Walton* case? Intel *support*?"

"Yes. Sir."

My grip tightened and the lid to my Starbucks popped off. A volcano of piping-hot coffee exploded into the air and onto the ground, coating my loafers in sticky brown liquid. Cursing under my breath, I loosened my grip, shook off the liquid, and grabbed a napkin from a nearby hot dog stand. I considered tossing the rest, but in all honesty, creamer in my coffee wasn't half bad. It also had a weird flowery flavor that I couldn't put my tongue on. Ironically.

"You have a meeting scheduled with the Walton team lead at nine o'clock this morning."

"Just like that? I'm off?" My jaw clenched as I began to pace.

"Yes, sir. Something about disobeying a superior—"

"Adam was still alive." I sneered into the phone, but it didn't matter.

My partner that night had died minutes after I carried him out of the building. Minutes after ignoring my superiors as they tried to drag me out. Minutes after putting their lives in danger because my ass wouldn't leave my dying partner.

Blaze cleared his throat. "He has requested you pull together—"

"Let me guess. A report for the nine o'clock meeting. Anything else?"

"Not that requires immediate—"

I clicked off the call and shoved my phone into the pocket of my suit pants that were two sizes too big, because I wasn't used to buying suits. In fact, I hated suits. But I'd bought it because I finally got the job I'd worked all my life for. The job that I was already one mistake away from losing.

The thing was, I didn't lose. And Clancy and his team of suits was about to learn that.

I maneuvered through the crowd, finding a less-traveled pathway that hugged the line of buildings and several homeless people begging for change. Well-to-doers don't like to come eye to eye with the homeless. Makes them uncomfortable, so they avoid them.

If they only knew what I'd seen. What I'd done.

From my pocket, I pulled the report Blaze had sent me, at my request, sometime in the early morning hours. Apparently, before the reorganization email. The top, in fancy bold and italic, read COLETTE ARCHER.

I skimmed the overly detailed notes for the second time that morning, studying my target for the day.

Colette Archer, a thirty-three-year-old New York native turned computer super-genius. Received a full ride to Stanford University, where she graduated with honors with a computer science degree. Shortly after, the overachiever opened her own private investigation firm, Archer and Archer, Inc., now one of the most prestigious PI firms in Lower Manhattan. Archer's client list included senators, federal agents, and a former president.

I quickly reviewed the rest of the notes, most revolving around her accolades and articles in which she was featured —successful, smart, smart, smart, got it.

The report gave me everything I needed, except a weakness. Something to exploit.

I retrieved my phone. Super-Blaze answered on the first ring.

"The report you pulled together on Colette Archer, her company's name is Archer *and* Archer, right?"

"That's correct."

"Who's the other Archer?"

Keys clicked rapidly on the other end of the line as I dodged a trio of joggers in spandex tighter than the loafers I thought would stretch.

"Colette Archer and Jade Archer."

"Who's Jade Archer?"

"Her sister, co-owner of the firm."

"Why doesn't your report include anything on her, then?"

"Jade Archer co-owns the business but doesn't work there."

"What does she do?"

"She appears to be a drifter, mostly. A few jobs here and there. Tattoo artist, mechanic, martial arts instructor."

"A computer genius and a martial arts instructor?"

"Correct. Do you need anything else?"

"Yeah. The firm's client list is impressive. What makes this Colette chick in such high demand?"

"She's the best around. Built a reputation from the ground up. Personally handles each case. Rumor on the street is that she's quite the hacker—"

"Computer hacker?"

"Right. And she uses this skill to aid in her investigations, pulling information that no one else can get. Therefore, no one can compete with her. As I understand it, she's extremely picky who she works with and rarely takes new clients."

"And how did her current clients get through the front door?"

"Money. Rumor is Miss Archer charges ridiculous fees."

A woman who likes money. Shocker. And that, I decided, was her weakness.

"Thanks, B." I killed the call and scanned the surrounding buildings as a fight over a cab broke out behind me.

My gaze shifted to the mirrored windows of the high-rise, and above it, a sliver of a sapphire-blue sky. A weird feeling came over me, the one I always got right before something big happened.

More honks and shouts vibrated around me, and for the hundredth time in the last thirteen months, I wondered if I was where I was supposed to be.

I glanced at my watch. Less than two hours until my meeting to secure my reassignment to the Walton case.

Contemplating, I looked over my shoulder.

Technically, I was no longer on the Salazar case.

Technically, I should be sitting in my gray cubicle, catching up on emails.

Technically, I didn't give a damn.

8

Colette

"Morning, Miss Archer." The doorman greeted me with a smile as he opened the shiny reflective door.

"Thank you, Cliff. Any news from the wife?" I asked, maintaining my pace as my heels clicked on the marble floor.

"Yep." The old man smiled proudly. "She got the job, Miss Archer."

"That's fantastic; great news. Get her flowers, Cliffy."

"Yes, ma'am." He laughed as I breezed past him. "Go get 'em, Miss Archer."

Forcing another sip of my coffee-flavored sugar block, I weaved efficiently through the sea of suits and pencil skirts, past the fountain and to the second set of elevators. I looked from one security camera to the next as a crowd gathered around me. Finally, the bell dinged and the door slid open.

I hurriedly stepped into the cab before the crowd to ensure my spot in the back corner.

My lead was followed by a man, mid-fifties, in a knock-off Zac Posen and scuffed wingtips, checking his phone. Behind him, another man, about my age, bathed in cologne and arrogance. He eyed me coolly, unabashedly giving me the once-over.

I met his gaze, held it, then returned my focus to the door.

Next in, two women in long skirts and Velcro sneakers, chatting about the weather. And finally, a young boy, no more than ten, with headphones on his ears and a skateboard in his hands. Visiting Daddy, I guessed.

Though my body remained still, my gaze darted from one person to the next, in order, over and over until the cab jerked to a stop.

Holding my breath, I squeezed through the crowd and stepped onto the thirty-first floor. My shoulders relaxed as I strode down the familiar carpeted breezeway that was rarely crowded. Back in my comfort zone, I was already scanning my phone when I reached the last door on the left.

I paused—but nothing happened. Frowning, I looked up from my phone.

Still, nothing happened.

My focus turned to the keypad glowing next to the handle. The electricity was working.

Just then, the door flew open with the force of a hurricane. While most people would have stumbled backward at the burst of noise, I planted my feet and steeled my spine.

"Oh. So—so sorry." A napkin fluttered to the carpet around the whirl of disheveled energy that was my office manager, Kareena Bashar. "Sorry, Colette."

I watched this sorry excuse for competency stumble backward in an awkward attempt at holding the door open for me while stepping out of the way. Her short brown bob was frizzy, her bangs hanging limply against her forehead, thanks to an unfortunate cowlick that her hairdresser failed to warn her about before cutting the bangs. A bit of coffee splashed over the rim of her mug as she moved with the grace of a wild buffalo. The piping-hot liquid slid down her arm, staining the dingy white dress shirt she'd chosen for the day. She winced in pain.

I glanced at the freshly shampooed carpet—now soaked in coffee—back to the mug in her hand, and finally, back to her.

Kareena cleared her throat. Forcing an innocent smile that gave her a cartoon-like appearance, she lifted her mug. "Sorry I didn't buzz you in. I was in the break room getting coffee."

And not where she was supposed to be. The lobby of Archer and Archer, Inc. was to be manned at all times. *All* times. She knew this.

"Your cheek looks better," Kareena said, though I hadn't asked. "I still can't believe you fell down a flight of stairs."

"Messages?"

I stepped past her, taking note of the new perfume she was wearing. A sharp, tangy scent. Tangerine with a hint of bergamot, a citrusy scent most commonly chosen by those with a high level of confidence. It must have been a gift. From a friend, or a boyfriend perhaps?

"Yes. You have several messages."

Kareena muttered something under her breath as she slid her mug onto the front desk and plucked out a handful of tissues, knocking the box onto the floor in the process.

Christ.

If not for my sister, I would have fired Kareena Bashar years ago. Five years my junior, Kareena was born and raised in the same neighborhood as my family in the Bronx. An inner circle, if you will. Important when hiring, according to my sister.

Competence is more important, I'd argued.

It sounded like a herd of buffalo stumbled into my office after me. Despite her small size, Kareena walked with heel strikes heavy enough to trigger seismographic networks. I often wondered if she lived in an apartment, and if so, who lived below her. A revolving door of tenants, I imagined.

The blinds that covered the sweeping windows of my office had already been opened, just a crack as per my instructions, and the speakers in my bookcase turned on to earth sounds.

She'd succeeded at two out of three tasks for the morning. I wasn't good with two out of three.

After hanging my purse in its designated spot, I opened my briefcase while Kareena thumbed through her notes.

In addition to the new perfume, Kareena had chosen a different color of blush and lipstick that morning. Bright pink instead of nude, adding a splash of color to her pale cheeks. It looked good on her. And I also decided that I liked the perfume.

Definitely a new man. I made a mental note to check into this between meetings.

I watched her closely as she read off my messages and noted my comments to each before moving on to the next.

"Also," she said, "your three o'clock called. Wants to reschedule."

"No."

She glanced up, then froze with the pen in her hand. "No?"

"No. This is the second time Mr. Cornwall has requested to reschedule." I slipped out of my suit jacket. "Tell him to take his business elsewhere."

I felt the shock of her stare as I hung the jacket in the closet.

Heir to a steel manufacturing conglomerate, Charles E. Cornwall was a senator from New York who sought the expertise of Archer and Archer, Inc. (me) to investigate the history, client list, and financial performance of a rival company he was planning to acquire—pending my investigation. Although there were many fringe benefits to working for a United States senator, I didn't tolerate those who were unable to manage their own schedules.

I closed the closet and turned. "What else?"

"A Sergeant Rick Maxwell called from the first precinct, asking for updates in the Butler/Barnes case."

"Please call Sergeant Maxwell back and remind him of the meeting we have scheduled next Monday, and of its itinerary that includes discussing my updates on his case."

"He sounded desperate."

"Everyone is desperate."

"Yes, ma'am. And, um, there was something . . ."

I slid my laptop onto my desk and pressed the power button, watching my office assistant from under my lashes as she madly flipped through the loose papers in her hands.

"And . . . Mrs. Winthrop called again. This makes her eighth call in two days. She says you're the only private investigator she'll hire for the job."

"No."

"She offered double your fee."

"Triple. Triple my fee and work her in. For Tuesday. Work her in for next Tuesday."

Kareena scribbled the number three on her notes because "triple" took too much time to write.

"Lastly, Barb Davenport"—the bell at the front door rang—"wants to come in early today."

"Mrs. Davenport can wait until her appointment." I glanced at the clock on the wall. "In exactly fifty-four minutes."

When the bell rang again, my jaw clenched and I began counting backward from five.

From seven a.m. to eight a.m., Monday through Friday, I sat quietly behind my desk, drank my coffee, prioritized my day, and caught up on emails or reports that had come in the night before.

Kareena knew this. I paid her to know this.

The bell rang again, followed by a tap of ceramic nails against glass.

Three . . . two . . .

Kareena bit her lip.

One.

I sighed. "Fine. Let her in. Tell her I will be twenty minutes. Please close my door on the way out."

"Yes, ma'am."

Kareena spun on her heel and all but lunged out of the office.

"And, Kareena?"

She peeked around the mahogany door she'd been in the middle of closing.

"The carpet cleaner is in the closet."

"Yes, ma'am."

9

James

The air was cool and perfumed with something floral as I stepped onto the thirty-first floor.

I immediately noticed how much quieter this floor was than the others, a contrast to the chaos below, and I appreciated the break from the buzz of the streets below. The end of the hall was framed by a window overlooking the city, still shaded with shadows although the sun had risen hours earlier.

Suite number 3114, home of Archer and Archer, Inc., was at the end of the hall, and the door was locked, of course. I stepped back, noticing the keypad and black security box a second before it squawked at me.

"May I help you?" a young woman barked from the other end.

I didn't like not knowing who I was speaking to, so I peered through slits in the blinds that covered the office window. It annoyed me that I couldn't simply walk in. I'd never been to a private investigative firm that vetted everyone who stepped through the door.

Who the hell was this woman?

"I'm here to see Colette Archer," I said with sarcastic gusto, my voice echoing down the hall.

A moment passed while the woman on the other end recalibrated her hearing.

"Do you have an appointment, Mr. . . ."

"No."

"Miss Archer is currently in a meeting. However, I can check her availability for next week."

"I need to speak with her this morning." The grip around my coffee cup tightened, but this time without a volcanic explosion. *Baby steps.*

"I'm sorry, Mr. . . ."

"Black." I shifted my weight impatiently. Why the hell was I still talking to a speaker box?

"I'm sorry, Mr. Black, Miss Archer is—"

"My name is Special Agent James Black with the DEA. I have an urgent matter to discuss with Miss Archer immediately."

"Oh. P-please hold."

Hold what?

I began pacing. I shouldn't be there. I should have been putting the final touches on the report I had to present in less than two hours.

Grinding my teeth, I pressed all the buttons on the intercom—every single damn one of them.

"Yes, Mr. Black?" The woman behind the box responded calmly, unfazed by my childlike tantrum.

"Miss Archer. *Now.* Please."

"Miss Archer hasn't responded to my request yet."

"For her attention?"

No response.

I took a deep breath, recalling Clancy's words from the week before. *"Being a DEA agent isn't all about going undercover and shooting. You need to work on your people skills, Black. Your patience and ability to read a room is highly lacking."*

A minute passed. Then another.

I was two seconds from hurling myself out the thirty-first-floor window when the door finally buzzed.

Barreling inside the office, I locked eyes with the voice behind the box, a five-foot-tall fairy of a woman with short brown hair and a challenge in her eyes that suggested her morning had gone similar to mine.

"May I see your badge, sir?" the receptionist said in a low, emotionless tone meant to let me know she didn't care much for my presence.

I flipped open my wallet—never gets old—then quickly slid it back into my pocket like they do in TV shows. It was always my favorite part of the day.

She nodded, approving of the plastic card that could have easily been forged. "Miss Archer is with a client right now. Please have a seat."

I didn't sit.

Minutes passed as I paced the small seating area of the office, chugging the remainder of the creamy coffee blend I'd received by mistake from the Starbucks barista.

The small office was pristine. A vase of fragrant white flowers centered a glass table filled with magazines—*Vogue*, *InStyle*, *Elle*, and *National Geographic*—the stack fanned to perfection, each magazine spaced identically apart. I flicked open a few, disrupting the stack's precision, and checked for a name and address. None. A black-and-white painting of nothing, just swirls of colors, was hung above two black leather chairs.

The room was glass, black, and white—and cold.

Ten more minutes ticked by with me pacing a hole in the carpet while sliding the receptionist the side-eye with each pivot. She kept herself busy, avoiding my gaze like the plague.

I sighed heavily and checked my watch.

Waiting, waiting, waiting. Hurry up and wait. The synopsis of my new life.

Suddenly, a muffled sound of raised voices from behind the closed office door stole my attention. Cocking a brow, I looked at the receptionist, who seemed unfazed by this outburst in her boss's office.

I strained to listen.

"I have to know if he's cheating on me. Our entire fortune is at stake!"

"I understand, Mrs. Davenport—"

"No, you don't! This is the fourth time my husband has cheated on me. I'm done. I need proof."

"I understand. But I do not do infidelity cases, Mrs. Davenport."

"Oh yes you do, Miss Archer. You do now. You understand who I am, right? I am—"

The woman's words were cut off by a loud bang of something. There was a slight shuffle, followed by a voice so deep that I wondered if a man was in the room with them. I glanced at the assistant again, finding her still unruffled.

The office door swung open and a well-dressed middle-aged woman stormed out, her eyes wild and cheeks flushed, gripping her purse like a weapon.

I glanced into the dimly lit office, but the barely open

door prevented me from seeing the monster inside. The woman's high heels pounded the carpet with the aggression of someone who demands attention when they enter, or leave, a room.

The receptionist never once looked up from her computer.

The office door slammed shut.

Blinking, I looked at the door, the assistant, back to the closed door, then back to the assistant.

"It'll be just a minute."

What. The. Fuck?

Fourteen minutes later, the door cracked open. That's it —just a crack.

I surveyed the receptionist, who looked up at me with a subtle warning in her eyes. Not an expression meant to remind me to be careful, but more to inform me that *she'd* be watching *me*. Despite the hostile environment of the office, the woman was loyal to her boss.

Interesting.

"You may enter now," she said coolly.

"Thanks." I strolled into the office bracing myself for who—or what—I was about to lay eyes on.

Blinking with surprise, I recognized the woman behind the desk immediately. She was the stick-up-the-ass blonde who stole my coffee.

I was greeted by a pair of squinted blue eyes as cold as ice. The massive black wingback leather chair engulfed the woman, but instead of making her appear small, it had the opposite effect. Like a queen among servants.

She sat with her shoulders pulled back, a pair of perfectly manicured hands folded on a spotless mahogany desk, so smooth and clean it reflected the light from her computer's screen. Immaculately organized too, with only a laptop, notebook, pen, and small stack of papers to the side.

Her chair was framed by a sweeping window covered by black blinds opened just enough to allow thin slivers of light to streak across the room. Everything was black. The dimly lit dungeon-like office was a stark contrast to the bright, natural light of the reception area.

A beam of light sparkled off that blond bun she had pulled so tightly at the base of her neck, and I realized how much blond hair didn't fit this woman. Her hair should be black. Coal black like a raven's wing.

She didn't speak, just stared at me with an expression as hard as the lines of her desk. The only movement she made was her eyes as they scanned me from head to toe.

I shifted my weight, very aware that this woman had somehow thrown me off my game without a single word leaving her plump pink lips.

A piercing squawk from somewhere in the corner pulled me from my daze, and I swung my head around. "What was that?"

"How can I help you, Mr. Black?" she said, my question not worthy of the time it would take her to respond. Her tone was sultry, as smooth as her pale skin—and condescending as hell.

The squawk repeated, followed by a chorus of chirps. I couldn't concentrate.

"What the *hell* is that?"

"It's ambient music." This came from the receptionist sitting just outside the office, clearly eavesdropping. "Nature meditation."

"Door, please," the ruler of the castle barked.

The door was quickly shut.

I was caught in a paralyzing bewilderment of the woman in front of me and the weird-ass music surrounding her.

Where *was* I?

With a perfectly sculpted brow cocked, the queen waited for her servant to speak. "Again, how may I help you, Mr. Black?"

I set the stained, soggy, now-warped coffee cup on her desk. Her nose twitched in disgust. Keeping her hands perfectly folded on the desk, she leaned forward, ever so slightly, and glanced inside the cup.

"Thanks." She leaned back, resuming the uncomfortable posture of perfection. "But I prefer my coffee not half-drunk."

"I get the vibe you don't prefer anything half-drunk."

Her eyes narrowed.

"Where's mine?"

"Your what?"

"My coffee, Miss Archer. The one that you took."

"You can pick it up from the wastebasket on your way out. I'm still regaining taste on the tip of my tongue."

"Too strong for you, Miss Archer?"

Her gaze sliced mine. "Too abrasive."

"That's no way to talk about an eight-dollar cup of coffee, assuming we are still discussing coffee, of course."

"You're here to give me a lesson on manners?"

"I don't have that long." I glanced at the clock on the wall, black with glittering gold numbers. "My name—"

The deep belch of a bullfrog croaked over my words, followed by the pitter-patter of rain, which I knew wasn't coming from outside. A melody of bells chimed over a chorus of ribbits.

Colette didn't so much as blink.

"How can you work with this racket?"

"Quite efficiently, actually. Soundscapes redirect our brain to focus outwardly, on the task at hand. Artificial sounds, such as music, trigger an inward-focused attention, similar to states observed in anxiety, depression, and PTSD."

For a second, I was pulled back to my youth when I spent full days hiking alone in the mountains, listening to the sounds of nature around me. Those are still some of my best, happiest memories to date. But sharing that information, or anything personal with this woman, felt anything but safe.

I refocused—outwardly. "Miss Archer, my name is James Black. I'm an agent with the DEA. I have a few questions about a woman you assisted six months ago. Her name is Avery Bell."

I paused for verification, but I got none. I didn't like that this stranger and I had already engaged in some sort of pissing match about who owned the conversation. And I didn't have time for this bullshit.

"Does the name ring a bell, Miss Archer?"

"I have a confidentiality agreement with all my clients."

"I just have a few simple questions about her."

"I'm sorry. I won't be able to answer them for you, Mr. Black."

"Miss Archer, Avery Bell is rumored to be connected to a very dangerous drug cartel known as the Salazar Organization. I understand she came to you six months ago, requesting your services. I'd like to know why, and what services you provided."

"Ms. Bell came to me regarding her safety—"

"Why? Was she threatened?"

"Ms. Bell believed she was being followed, and wanted a private investigator to verify this."

"Did you?"

"I provided an assessment of her threat and the estimated costs associated with working with me. She declined."

"That's incorrect." I stepped closer to the desk Colette Archer used as a shield. As I did so, I noticed a slight twitch in her hands, still folded neatly on her desk. "You set Ms. Bell up with a brand-new identity and helped her leave the country."

"I can neither confirm nor deny that."

Gripping the edge of the desk, I leaned forward, invading her personal space. Her sanctuary. Something about this woman reminded me of a snake, a Viper, sneaky, conniving, carefully choosing its victims and waiting patiently until going in for the kill. One lethal bite.

Little did I know at the time how accurate that comparison was.

Although Colette tried to hide her immediate discomfort, her neck worked with a deep swallow. She remained remarkably cool, though, aside from the fire shooting from her eyes. And this was when I noticed the purple hue underneath the thick makeup she'd painted onto her face.

I'd been in more than my fair share of physical altercations, both giving and receiving bruises exactly like the one on her cheekbone.

Our eyes met, and her jaw twitched.

A little warning bell rang in my head.

"As I said . . ." Colette tore her gaze away and ever so slightly pulled back her chin in a subtle attempt to distance herself from me.

I made her nervous, and it had something to do with that bruise. I straightened and scanned her desk as she continued.

"I take client confidentiality very seriously, and therefore am unable to confirm or deny my assistance in Avery Bell's disappearance."

"You will confirm it when I return this afternoon with a warrant, Miss Archer."

"Not this afternoon, Mr. Black. I understand new DEA agents require approval from multiple levels before a warrant can be sent to a judge for their approval, which even then, can take days."

So that was what Miss Archer had been doing for fourteen minutes while I waited outside her office door like an idiot. Researching her unannounced visitor.

"What else did you find out about me, while using your computer science degree from Stanford to hack into my private life, Miss Archer?"

"Other than the fact that you were born and raised in Montana, became a cop at eighteen, served four years there before joining the Marines, where you stayed five years, before accepting a job with the DEA? I know that you were just assigned to your first big case, and based on the wrinkles in your shirt and stains on your pants, you aren't acclimating to office life very well. In the course of a few years, you've gone from being top dog in the military to bottom of the totem pole at the DEA. This makes a stubborn alpha male like yourself bitter and morose, and ironically less likely to fit in."

"You forgot abrasive."

"The coffee, Mr. Black." She gestured to the trash can.

"Yes, you were referring to the coffee earlier. *Right*."

"I'm good at reading people," she said, almost defensively, and I found it interesting that she felt the need to tell me this.

"I'm not leaving here until you give me what I need, Colette."

Her lips pressed to a thin line, as if the thought of me invading her precious space more than I already had was more than she could stomach. "I'll make contact."

"Define 'make contact.'"

"I'll reach out to Ms. Bell and we'll have a chat."

"I want that chat to be about Enrique Salazar's current location."

"I'll see what I can do. Now please leave."

"I'd also like a copy of everything you have on Ms. Bell, right now."

"Then I guess I need that warrant, James, *right now.*"

I leaned forward again, this time bending over her desk until my face was inches from hers. Colette forced herself to remain in place, but pulled her hands onto her lap where there was a weapon hidden, I was certain. Her jaw locked as she forced herself to hold eye contact.

But she failed. For one second she glanced at my lips, then looked back to my eyes.

Electricity crackled between us.

"Do you understand, Miss Archer, that by refusing to answer a few simple questions about a client I can easily prove came to you, you are potentially hampering a federal investigation and enabling a vicious drug cartel to continue to berate, abuse, rape, and in some cases, kill women just like Avery Bell?"

I stumbled backward as she shot out of her chair like a ball of flame. Blinking, stunned, I stared into a pair of blazing, wild eyes, brimming with a hostility so fierce that I didn't know what was going to happen next.

Both her body and her voice trembled. "It's time for you to leave, Mr. Black."

I didn't move, continuing to assess what just happened as a million thoughts raced through my head. One of which was wondering exactly how mentally unstable this woman was—and what the hell she was hiding under that prickly facade.

Just then, a cell phone vibrated from the desk.

Colette didn't move, those ice-blue eyes cutting into mine like a pair of twin blades.

Two rings, three . . .

It stopped, then rang again, this call-back breaking her trance-like fix on me.

"Excuse me," she spat out, picking up the phone and turning her back to me.

I understood this was my cue to leave, but I didn't. Like Clancy said, I never was good at reading a room.

"What?" Colette lowered her voice, moving into the corner of the room. "Are you sure it's him? . . . When?"

I could barely make out the voice on the other end of the line, but could tell it was a woman, speaking very quickly, offering much information.

Peeling my gaze from the private investigator's ass, I took the opportunity to scan the small stack of papers on her desk again.

"What time?" She turned to look at the clock.

I quickly stepped back.

Her gaze landed on the stack of papers. "I'll have to catch the later one. You'll have to pick me up . . . Yes. Okay. See you soon."

Colette clicked off the phone, a flush coloring her cheeks now. Our eyes met, and for a second it was as if she were seeing me for the first time and had forgotten that she'd almost just tackled me like a rabid spider monkey.

"I have to go." She began gathering her things, a

completely different woman now. “Please see yourself out, Mr. Black.”

After taking another glance at the papers, I dipped my chin. “Ma’am.”

I strode out of the office. As I stepped onto the elevator, I pulled my phone from my pocket.

I had an airline ticket to book.

10

Colette

Peeking through the blinds of the office window, I watched my unannounced visitor, the annoyingly abrasive DEA agent, step onto the sidewalk below.

I didn't need binoculars to verify that it was him. James Black was the only man in the crowd striding the sidewalk with the cockiness of a king entering his courtyard, and he was also the only person within a five-block radius who soared well over six feet.

I'm tall, yet James towered over me in my office. Eclipsing me—in *my office.*

It wasn't just his size that threw me, but the way he commanded the room the moment he entered it. His aggressive, no-bullshit attitude that, in my experience, was the telltale sign of a loose cannon, and I didn't like loose cannons.

I also didn't like my body's immediate reaction when I laid eyes on the man, the flush of heat in my chest, between my legs, and the rush of butterflies in my stomach.

The definition of an Adonis, James Black looked like

he'd been carved from stone with a sharp nose and jawline that could crack walnuts. His hair was that perfect shade of sandy blond, with natural highlights that I paid hundreds of dollars for. And his skin was a golden tan, sun kissed just enough to give him a rugged appearance, unlike every other pale businessman in the city.

A Greek god came to mind when I saw him. And then he opened his mouth.

Despite his youth, the DEA agent exuded authority, the kind that made you sit up and listen when he spoke. And he did, loudly. Without using a single word, from the moment James set foot into my office, he made sure that I knew that he was displeased with me.

The man intrigued me instantly. Most people, men and women, treated me with the respect and wariness as one might a recently tamed tiger. And that was without knowing about the cancer.

I knew his type. Dominant, alpha, controlling, unwilling to bend or compromise. Basically, my kryptonite.

James checked his watch, and even the way he lifted his wrist was aggressive.

Twenty-eight years old. Five years younger than me. *Why does this fascinate me?*

Probably because James Black didn't act like a twenty-eight-year-old. Quite the contrary, in fact. He carried the kind of confidence usually only seen in men twice his age. Men in high positions, men of power.

Did this confidence come from his time in the Marines? Based on his size and arrogant nature, it wasn't a stretch to imagine that he'd been special ops of sorts. If so, James had likely experienced more than men double his age. Had seen things that many would go three lifetimes without seeing.

What, exactly?

And what was it that made him emit waves of subtle hostility, as much a part of him as breathing. A scar from long ago that never quite healed? From what?

I watched him bulldoze his way through a crowd of businessmen. He was one of them, yet so *not* one of them.

James Black wore the lines of a suit as comfortably as a prostitute wears a cross around her neck. It didn't fit. With the hard lines of his face, the set of his jaw, the wide shoulders and massive chest, the man was built for boots and tactical gear, not a cheap poly-blend suit and synthetic leather slip-on loafers he'd obviously picked out on his own.

He had to be single. No woman would allow her man to set foot in public in a pair of front-pleated slacks. Not since the eighties, anyway.

James Black somehow had the ability to both amuse me and knock me off-kilter. Dare I say, intimidate me. *No, I won't.* I couldn't, because only the weak allowed themselves to be intimidated.

My brain switched from attraction to caution.

How did he know I helped Avery Bell leave the country? What else did he know?

And why did he show up on this day? The day my plan began to spin into motion?

A tingle of warning snaked up my spine. It wasn't a good time to be on the Feds' radar—even one as sexy as James Black.

No, it wasn't a good time for James Black to barge into my life.

With that thought, I closed the blinds, turned, and lifted the papers from my desk. The screen saver on my monitor flipped to the image of white-capped mountains against a crystal-clear sky.

Nerves tickled my stomach.

I refocused on the papers in my hand—airline tickets, itinerary, maps, topographic layouts of the small town known as Broken Ridge, Montana.

I'd never been to Montana, or to any place with a population less than quadruple digits. I didn't like going into the unknown, yet it had to be done.

Inhaling deeply, I studied the landscape on my monitor. I'd heard the mountains were beautiful in the fall. I guessed I was about to find out.

Closing my eyes, I took another deep breath.

It will all be over soon.

11

Leo

Broken Ridge, Montana

Flipping up my shirt collar, I sank deeper into the seat as dead leaves tumbled across the hood of my vintage Mustang. It was a cold, cloudy, overcast day, the usually bright colors of autumn muted by a thin gray mist.

The cold weather seemed to be sneaking in earlier each year, the winters harsher, more brutal than I remembered when I moved here years ago. Then again, Montana was never known for easy winters—or dense population. Ranking just above Alaska and Wyoming, Montana is home to only seven residents per square mile. Compared to New York at four hundred ten people per square mile, these places were like night and day.

I once drove two hours through the mountains and only passed three trucks. It was then that I finally understood why my brother had picked this location when he up and left us at eighteen.

My gaze lingered on the snarl of round barbed wire that secured the top of the fencing that surrounded a gray windowless brick building.

What remained of a dead cedar tree sagged lifelessly at the entrance of Broken County Jail, a few dead leaves caught in its bare, brittle branches. I wondered why they hadn't cut the damn thing down. Probably to serve as a symbol of sort. *This is where people go to die,* it says as you pass by on your way to hell.

I'd been waiting nearly three hours at that point. The coffee in the cupholder was cold, the Coke next to it, flat.

My wrist fell limp against the steering wheel as I stared at the steel doors, wondering what he was going to think when he saw me.

Hell, I wondered why I was there.

What the hell had gotten into me?

How long had it been since my brother and I had seen each other?

The song on the radio switched from Steely Dan to that damn new-age pop-rock bullshit. I turned it down.

Tapping my thumb against the steering wheel, I counted each passing second.

Forty-eight, forty-nine, fifty . . .

Finally, the metal door opened and a guard stepped out. He paused to look around, then nodded at the person beyond the doors.

And then I saw him, my brother, as his massive body dwarfed the barely five-foot-five security guard. Dylan strode past the guard with a confident gait, his shoulders back, as if he hadn't just spent the last six months in jail for aggravated assault.

Bastard.

Straightening in my seat, I took note of the whisper of nerves as I started the engine.

As if sensing something—*me*—Dylan turned his attention in my direction.

For a moment, I questioned everything, but then realized there was no going back at that point. I shoved the car into drive and pulled out of my parking spot under the trees.

Though I knew he saw me, Dylan kept walking. Bastard knew I was there. He was always good at looking over his shoulder.

I watched him for a beat as he crossed the parking lot, wondering where the hell he was going with those long, purposeful strides as if he had a meeting he was late for.

I almost laughed at that thought.

Pulling up beside him, I rolled down the window, noticing the tattoos that covered his arms. More than he had the last time I saw him.

Dammit, when was that?

Deep red splatters stained the front of his T-shirt—the same clothes he'd been wearing when he was arrested, I guessed. The jailhouse hadn't even washed it for him. It bothered me, seeing him like that. I don't know why. It wasn't like anything had changed.

Maybe I have changed.

"Get in," I said.

Dylan didn't respond or even grace me with a glance. The son of a bitch just kept walking as if he was running late for all the plans in the world.

"Dude." I leaned closer to the window. "Get in."

"What the fuck are you doing here, Leo?"

"Get in."

"Fuck you."

I blew out a breath, tapping my fist against the steering wheel. I should have known it was going to go like that. My brother had always been a stubborn, unforgiving asshole.

"I drove all this way to give you a lift. Get in."

Finally, he peered over his shoulder, and I startled at the face staring back at me. My brother had aged. A lot. And he looked rough, not unlike his fellow inmates. A bloodied lip and a black eye suggested he'd spent some time in the hole recently. It didn't surprise me.

"How the hell did you know I was here?"

"Tammy told me."

Bartenders heard a lot and shared a lot. It was one of the reasons I loved them.

Dylan scoffed, then refocused on the road ahead.

I pressed the gas as his pace increased. "I also thought I should tell you . . . Dad died."

I watched closely for a reaction, but got none.

"Two months ago," I said. "Liver failure."

Still, nothing.

Heartless asshole.

A moment passed, and I grew impatient. "Where the hell are you walking?"

"Go to hell, Leo."

I snorted, my gaze shifting to the mountains in the distance. "It won't be long."

For a moment, I lost myself in the red, orange, and yellow splashed against the treacherous terrain. Used to be so bright. Now it just looked dirty.

"I'm going to give you three more seconds, Dylan. Get in, or find your own ride to wherever the hell you're going."

Three . . .

Two . . .

One.

I slammed my foot on the gas, leaving my older brother in a trail of exhaust.

I should have known.

Some wounds never heal.

12

Colette

I pulled my suitcases over the sidewalk warning pad that separated the airport from the cracked two-lane road in front of it. Although it was just past five, the thick cloud cover and flickering streetlights made it look closer to dusk.

A gust of wind blew past me, slicing through the trench coat I'd thrown on over a long-sleeved T-shirt before I left for the airport. A thick mist hung in the air, weaving between the few people who were milling outside the tiniest airport I'd ever seen. The wet fog clung to my long hair, frizzing the ends and sending a chill up my spine. Montana was colder than I'd expected, and I was glad I'd tossed a few sweaters into my luggage at the last minute.

From the moment the wheels hit the tarmac, it had taken exactly fourteen minutes to deplane and retrieve my luggage from one of the only two conveyers. The airport was the size of a tobacco can, and had brass-buckled cowboys to boot.

No one was in a hurry. It was as if I'd entered another world where there was no such thing as time. No plans, no appointments, just a herd of cattle slowly moving from one patch of grass to the next. The crowd took their time, meandering, chatting while going through the gate as if they didn't have a care in the world.

It was maddening to someone who goes from zero to sixty the moment their sleep machine begins to illuminate.

A truck zoomed past, splashing mud onto my sandals.

"Hey!" The menacing glare I intended for the passing vehicle faded to a gasp as my gaze lifted to the snow-capped mountains in the distance.

The vision took my breath away.

I blinked, completely mesmerized by the massive rock structures spearing up from the colorful landscape around them, seemingly out of nowhere, as if they didn't belong among the flat, wooded land where I was standing. Blazing oranges, yellows, and reds colored the base of the mountain range like a painting, quickly fading against harsh, craggy gray rock, lined with divots that I could only imagine could house an airplane. The peaks, tall enough to breach the clouds, were dipped in the purest white.

An astonishing—and for some reason extremely intimidating—view.

I felt small in that moment. Insignificant. And shockingly, it felt good, a little reminder that I didn't run the world. I was merely a tiny speck beneath all its glory.

Growing up in the city, I'd been awestruck by some of the newly erected buildings, but those were manmade. Carefully designed, engineered, planned, funded. Not like this. This was the kind of landscape you only saw in calendars. The wonder of Mother Nature, right there in front of me. So desolate, yet so inviting at the same time.

I didn't realize I'd stepped onto the road until a car slammed the brakes behind me.

Just then, quick blasts of a horn mimicking the riff of *shave and a haircut, two bits* pulled my attention to the left. I frowned, squinting at a massive four-door pickup truck flashing its lights.

Idiot. Some drunk cowboy late for the rodeo.

The truck honked again, this time louder and longer, causing people to stop in their tracks and glance my way.

Just then, a long, skinny, tattooed arm waved manically from the window.

Jade.

Cursing under my breath, I dipped my chin, hiding my face from the watching crowd as I hurried across the road. After shoving my suitcases in the back seat, I jerked open the front passenger door, struggling to climb into the monstrosity my sister had chosen to drive for this blessed event.

"What the hell is this?" I slammed the door.

"A truck." Grinning, Jade shoved the beast into drive and peeled out, causing a woman to scream and pull her stroller back onto the sidewalk from the curb.

I sank lower into the leather seat. "Slow *down*. And what the hell are you doing with a truck?"

Jade plucked a pair of bright pink Aviators from the top of her head and slid them over her eyes. This was when I noticed the new camel-colored suede duster she was wearing, with brass buttons and fringe on the shoulders, giving me *waaaay* too many Calamity Jane vibes.

"They rent them here."

"What? Trucks?" I set my purse on the floorboard, careful to tuck the Ziplock bag of pills out of my sister's sight.

"Yeah," she said. "Like rent-a-cars, 'cept trucks."

I frowned, settling into the seat. "Why would anyone rent a truck—why did *you* rent a truck?"

Jade shrugged, adjusting the rearview mirror, on which she'd already hung a furry pink rabbit's foot. "Thought we should try to fit in."

We exited the airport, and when she pulled onto a narrow two-lane road flanked by fields, she quickly accelerated to double the speed limit.

"You don't like it?"

"It's fine." I glanced back at the truck's bed. "We just don't need half of it."

Jade grinned with a mischievous wiggle of her eyebrows. "You never know."

Navigating the winding roads with the ease of someone who rarely drove, she tossed me a shopping bag from the back seat.

I caught it in midair. "Hey, keep both hands on that big ol' manly wheel of yours, all right?"

"Open it."

I lifted the bag, examining the bucking bronco printed on the side.

"I was bored," Jade said, ignoring my skepticism. "I did some shopping while waiting on you."

"At the OK Corral?"

"Nope. A store called Feed Your Need." She scratched her chin. "Wasn't exactly what I'd expected. Was hoping for wine, but nope. They literally sell feed. Like grain and shit, food to feed your cows, deer, and dogs and stuff."

Frowning, I pulled a sweatshirt from the bag. Green, with a big yellow tractor knitted on the front. "You're not serious."

"Yes, I am. We need to fit in here. These are normal

people clothes—you know, country-people clothes. I got this beaut there too." She motioned to her suede jacket that looked like it had been stolen from the set of *The Good, The Bad, and The Ugly*.

"Do I need to remind you that going undercover is kind of my thing?"

"How many designer labels did you pack, Cole?"

"None of your business." When she slid me the side-eye, I said, "*Fine*. Five. *Fine*. I'll wear the damn tractor sweatshirt. And what else . . ."

My jaw dropped as I pulled strings of black studded leather from the bag.

"*Assless chaps*? You got me a pair of *assless* chaps?"

"Every woman needs a pair of assless chaps. Trust me, I have three. Just so happens they're extremely popular here."

"Please tell me people aren't just walking around town with their asses hanging out . . ."

"Unfortunately, no. Figured you could wear yours over those skinny jeans you wear all the time." She glanced at me, her eyes narrowed. "What's wrong with you?"

I slowly exhaled, my grip tightening around the assless leather as I observed the mountains in the distance. When it came to my emotions, nothing got past Jade. Terminal illnesses and midnight airport-motel rendezvous, on the other hand . . .

"Just had a busy morning at the office, that's all."

I debated whether to tell my sister about my run-in with Robo-Cop, aka James Black, but decided against it. We needed to stay on topic. Focused. And something about the six-foot-plus Adonis kept pulling my attention to every place it shouldn't be.

"You need to delegate more work to Kareena," Jade said, serious now, reminding me of this for the hundredth time.

I scoffed and glanced out the window.

"Come on, don't be so hard on her. She looks up to you."

"Maybe I wouldn't have to be so hard on her if you'd come to work, you know, one day a year and train her yourself."

"I told you not to put my damn name on the letterhead."

"You and me." I flashed my sister a pointed look, my brows arched. "It's *always* you and me."

A moment of understanding passed between us. She dipped her chin in agreement, and that was that.

"Anyway," Jade said, "what's really your deal with Kareena?"

"She's just so damn nervous and jumpy all the time. Always second-guessing herself." I tilted my head thoughtfully. "You remember that time Linx chewed on Dad's computer cord, got electrocuted, went nuts, and got stuck in the chimney? Took us six hours to get her out because she wouldn't let us touch her? Kareena's like that. Just . . . a train wreck all the time."

"She's a recovering drug addict."

"Which is the only reason you had me hire her. Because you felt bad when you ran into someone we went to school with eons ago, who told you her entire sob story over lithium-sprinkled ice cream."

Jade chuckled. "That was a fun night. Give her more work, Cole. Seriously. Or hire another PI. Something's got to give. You're so damn stressed out all the time. Especially lately."

"I'll give her more work once she proves she can handle it and stops coming to work shaking like a damn chihuahua."

"Cole." Jade sighed deeply as if choosing her next words carefully. "In case you hadn't heard, word on the street is that you can be kind of intimidating. An uptight, stone-cold bitch, to be exact."

"I am not a bitch."

"Cole, you gave the girl a bottle of Beano and a can of Febreze for Christmas."

"Who flatulates openly in a small space—*every day*, Jade? I tried to break her addiction to kung pao chicken, but when that didn't work, I had to resort to dramatics."

"One, Wok This Way has the best crab Rangoon and kung pao in the city. Two, I'd bathe in that shit. And, three, I'm pretty sure flatulates isn't a word."

"Fine, passes gas."

Jade threw her head back with a cackle of sorts. "Why can't you just say it?"

"Say what?"

"Fart."

I visibly shuddered.

"Fart, fart, fart," she sang from the driver's seat while passing a logging truck in a no-passing zone.

My fingertips curled around the edge of my seat. "*Stop*, sister, and slow down. *Jesus*. And it's a disgusting word."

"No, it's *the* word." Pulling one hand from the steering wheel, she gestured flamboyantly, needling me while almost giving me a coronary. "The word for *flaaaatulence*."

I waited until we were safely back in the right lane to continue. "Incorrect. It's a word only freckled, buck-toothed twelve-year-old boys use when referring to flatulence."

Jade shook her head. "You're hilarious."

"I just don't like her. I don't know why, I just don't. Get off my ass about it."

"You don't like anyone."

"I don't like you right now."

"And I don't like you deflecting. You had a busy morning,

that's nothing new. Now tell me what else is going on. What's really got you extra bitchy today?"

As I shifted in my seat, the cab grew quiet.

"I'm just ready to get this done," I said quietly, keeping my gaze ahead.

"Impatience is your worst enemy, and it'll be your downfall if you're not careful, Cole. If this trip doesn't pan out, we'll come back. Don't push it."

No. There was no coming back. My time was literally limited. This was it, whether Jade realized it or not. But I bit my tongue, stuffed the bag holding the sweatshirt and chaps onto the floorboard, and pulled a folder from my purse.

"You locate him?" I asked, referring to the task at hand.

Jade nodded, the jovial mood between us suddenly turning dark.

"Did you make contact?"

"No. Not without you—as per your request, my dear sister."

I nodded, flipped open the folder, and pulled out a map. "So. Broken Ridge, Montana. An hour away, right?"

"Right. Two closest towns are an hour in either direction. Broken Ridge is at the bottom of a valley between two huge mountains, literally out in the middle of nowhere. Population six hundred thirty-seven."

"*Jesus.* Where are we staying?"

"A bed and breakfast smack dab in the middle of town."

"No hotels?"

"One. A motel that's one termite away from crumbling to the ground. You ever had bedbugs?"

"Gross. No."

"I have. Never again. Also, the bed and breakfast is across the street from the bar your boy owns."

"Creed's Tavern."

Jade nodded. "Opened at four."

I glanced at the clock, noting it was 5:37 p.m.

"You already eat?" she asked as we passed a McDonald's.

I shook my head. "Not now. Let's check in at the B and B and regroup. We'll go from there."

Thirty white-knuckling minutes later, I peeled my fingers away from the oh-shit handle and swallowed deeply, thankful the spit that had pooled into my mouth hadn't turned into vomit. Making the vow to never let Jade behind the wheel of a truck again, I loosened my seatbelt as we slowly crossed into the town limits of Broken Ridge, Montana.

Population: Shoot-myself-in-the-head.

Jade wasn't kidding. The town was nestled between two massive mountains, both tall enough to touch the clouds.

A single two-lane road split the center of town, a row of small quaint stone-and-log storefronts lining either side. Behind them, the immediate and severe slope of the mountains. The town operated under a partial shade, if not from the mountains, then from the towering firs and maples that lined them. Painted with the bright colors of fall, the nature surrounding the town was postcard perfect. Broken Ridge reminded me of a shrunken version of Aspen, Colorado.

It was warm, welcoming, and also my worst nightmare, because there was nowhere to run or hide. It was the type of town where everyone knew everyone else's business. Everyone was "family." I often wondered what people who lived out in the middle of nowhere did to make a living. I guessed I was about to find out.

And Jade was also right about her choice of vehicle. There wasn't a single car, motorcycle, taxi, or anything that didn't have four-wheel drive as far as the eye could see. Big trucks, small trucks, four tires, six tires, loud trucks, louder trucks.

Despite its small size, the town was bustling with activity.

Men in cowboy hats, some wearing overalls, and women in muck boots and straw hats. Flags swayed lazily from the storefronts. Hay bales decorated the front of a busy leather shop. Brightly colored flowers in hand-painted pots lined the sidewalks. A balding man in a pearl-button shirt adjusted an American flag outside the barber shop, which was surprisingly packed with people.

Jade slowed. "There it is."

My focus zeroed in on the wooden sign that read CREED'S TAVERN.

My pulse picked up as I braced on the dash and leaned forward, watching a trio of Wrangler-wearing cowgirls push their way inside the two-story log cabin bar.

"Not sure how late he's open," Jade said.

I tore my gaze away from the neon signs blinking in the windows and glanced at my notes, though I didn't need to.

"Leo Creed closes Creed's Tavern at midnight on the weekdays and one on the weekends. He personally stays until closing every night. Sometimes until past three on the weekends." I shuffled the papers, pulling the blueprint of the building from the stack. "Looks like an apartment on top, maybe?"

"His?"

"Not sure. If so, not every night. Seems he goes somewhere else on the weekends."

"How'd you verify this?"

"Security cameras from the coffee shop across the street."

Jade gave me the side-eye. "You hacked in?"

"Got a problem with that?"

"No, ma'am."

"Good." I refocused on my notes. "The tavern only has one security camera in the back."

"What'd you find there?"

"Nothing. He's only turned it on once over the last few days."

"Any inside?"

"Don't know. Not on, anyway."

"We're here." Jade flicked on her turn signal and barreled into a narrow slanted parking spot under a blazing-yellow maple near the end of the main road. One front tire slammed into the sidewalk, earning us a few disapproving glances from the couples passing by.

I frowned at the combination coffee shop/bakery/bookstore in front of us.

"This is the B and B?"

"No, the B and B is back there, beside it." Jade gestured to a courtyard overflowing with manicured trees and bushes. She turned off the engine and grabbed the key. "Get your shit."

After attempting to rub off the scratch my Louis Vuitton luggage put on the side of Jade's rental truck, I joined her on the sidewalk. In contrast to my matching luggage set, Jade had a backpack the size of a Volkswagen Beetle strapped to her back, and ironically, a clutch the size of a Tic Tac box in her hand.

I couldn't help but grin. In her effort to fit in, Jade had done exactly the opposite, sticking out like a movie star in this one-horse town, with her pink Aviators, suede duster, and knee-high boots. God, I loved the woman.

Men did too.

Flinging my purse over my shoulder, I adjusted my wrinkled trench coat, then yanked the luggage onto the cobblestone sidewalk and joined my rock-star sister—me in my boring trench coat, white long-sleeved tee, skinny jeans, and designer sandals, and Jade in all her glory.

Whispers carried on the wind behind us. I held eye contact with a man and woman gawking at us as if we were aliens from another planet.

Ignoring the glances we drew, we bulldozed our way down the sidewalk, our chins up and shoulders back, no bullshit. Places to go, people to see.

I followed Jade to an ornate black iron gate between two heritage buildings, their once-red brick walls now spotted and faded to a dusky pink. Withering vines snaked through the gate, spiraling up the trees in the courtyard beyond the iron fence, whose leaves created a thick canopy overhead.

I glanced over my shoulder as Jade pushed through the gate. Keeping my head on a swivel, I followed her closely down the pebbled pathway, dragging my luggage behind me. The path curved to a wooden staircase that led down to a large courtyard fully enclosed by the brick buildings.

Black iron tables and chairs circled a massive fountain in the center. Dozens of potted plants and flowers lined the walls, heavily shaded by the trees above. A bright red door gleamed under a small balcony. It reminded me of an upscale spa or oasis.

"Not bad, huh?" Jade glanced over her shoulder.

"No, it's beautiful. Nice work."

"No bedbugs. Says right there on the website." She winked, strolling to the red door just as it swung open.

A striking young woman with fiery red hair and shimmering cat-like eyes greeted us with a smile. "Miss Archer, Miss Archer." She nodded to us both. "Welcome."

"Thanks, Ruby," Jade said, apparently already familiar with the woman. "We're a bit early."

"No problem at all." Bypassing Jade, who clearly had her single backpack under control, Ruby took the luggage from my hands.

"Thank you, Ms. . . ."

"Galean. I own the building."

"It's beautiful."

"Thanks," she said, scanning the lines of the walls with a judgmental eye. "I've put a lot of work into it."

"I can tell."

Letting herself in, Jade disappeared past the red door as if she owned the place too.

"Come on in." Ruby jerked her chin, pulling my suitcases up the small step. "I just put on a pot of coffee for you both. Honey and cream, right?"

"Right."

I followed the red-haired stunner inside, my stomach instantly growling at the scent of fresh-baked cookies. Not chocolate, not sugar . . .

Jade stepped into the entry, a nut tumbling off her chin onto the expansive Persian rug that ran along the hardwood floor.

Macadamia nut cookies—our favorite.

Jade winked, licking her lips, and I grinned. Small blessings.

Ruby set my luggage next to the wall and turned to us. "So, this is the main room. Feel free to use it at your leisure."

She gestured to a sitting room bathed in warm golden light from various stained-glass lamps. The walls were lined with built-in bookshelves, fully stocked, between arched windows that overlooked the courtyard. A cozy couch and loveseat centered the room, facing a fireplace. A self-serve bar and coffee station sat in the back corner.

"We call it the library. Feel free to read any or all of the books you'd like, just remember to put them back in place. Took me a week to alphabetize these bad boys." She smiled. "You're the only two staying here for the week, so it's all yours."

She pivoted to the left, pulling our attention to a small breakfast nook. Just then, a short, stocky, balding man wearing a white chef's coat, black slacks, and cowboy boots pushed out a swing door that I assumed led to the kitchen.

"And this is Chuck."

Ruby made the introductions. The man's hand was as rough as sandpaper and as firm as a bear trap.

"Chuck will be your chef during your stay. He's here from six thirty to eight thirty in the mornings, eleven to one for lunch, and six to eight for dinner. That's it. If you miss those times, he'll leave something wrapped for you in the fridge, or feel free to rummage around the kitchen as if it's your own. The bar is located in the library—wine, liquor, beer, juice. All included in your stay. If you're aiming for local taste, I've left the menus of a few diners on Main Street. If you're looking for a bar, Creed's Tavern is right across the road. Local hot spot."

Ruby walked to the base of the staircase and gestured upstairs.

"Two bedrooms up there, separated by a full bath. One has a balcony overlooking the courtyard, the other overlooks Main Street."

I shot Jade a quick glance. We didn't need to draw straws. The one overlooking Main was mine.

"There is another bedroom around the side of the building, not accessible from here. Considering you booked the whole building, feel free to use it as you wish as well. I'll replace the towels twice a day and the bed linens once. My number and cell phone are on the table in the breakfast nook. If you need anything at all, feel free to call or text anytime."

"Where do you live?" I asked.

"About four miles west of here, in the mountains. Takes me about ten minutes to get here if you need something."

I nodded. Jade had already left the conversation and busied herself perusing the bar in the library.

Ruby smiled. "Keys are in an envelope on the table over there, and Chuck will begin dinner shortly. Do you ladies need anything else from me right now?"

"No, ma'am."

"All right then, I'll see you all tomorrow. Enjoy Broken Ridge, if you don't die of boredom first," she said with a wink.

From the bar, Jade glanced over her shoulder and our eyes met.

We both knew that death might come to us there in Broken Ridge, but it certainly wouldn't be in the form of boredom.

13

Colette

It was just past midnight as I pushed out the iron gate and stepped onto the sidewalk under the dim glow of a streetlight. It was a cold, dark night, colder than I'd anticipated. The mountain air was thinner, sharper than I was used to. The kind that cuts through your clothes and chills you to the bone.

As expected, the one-horse town was dead. Not surprising, considering everything seemed to shut down by eight o'clock. It was so different from the world I knew. The only place in town that was open was Creed's Tavern, across the street.

An eerie stillness engulfed me as I took a moment to scan my surroundings.

Not a soul, not a single car passing through. The storefronts were dark, the small-town shop owners finding no need to deter potential criminals, likely due to the fact the most common offenses in the area were drunk driving and the rare domestic dispute. The potted mums and pumpkins had been pulled from the sidewalks, leaving nothing but the occasional leaf tumbling by.

I immediately felt like an exposed lab rat, on display for anyone who might be peeking through their windows. How could anyone live like this?

I tugged my scarf tighter around my neck and paused, glancing around for my sister. When I didn't see any sign of her, I pulled my phone from my pocket and checked her location, verifying she was still in town.

Sometimes I wondered if Jade knew I tracked her and simply didn't say anything about it, understanding that I just needed to do it for my own sanity. Kind of like how she'd patiently listened to the case notes I reviewed over dinner, which included Plan A, Plan B, and Plan C. I didn't need to go over them again with her—Jade was the type of woman you only needed to explain things to once. I did it simply for myself.

After that, Jade had ventured out, in all her suede glory, while I took watch. The window from my bedroom granted an unobstructed view of Creed's Tavern, something I assumed wasn't lost on Jade when she rented the place.

The sound of my heels clicking on the cobblestones echoed through the cold night air, and I wondered what the lonely men of Broken Ridge did for entertainment.

There were no airport motels close by. Trust me, I'd checked.

I was surprised when my pulse rate picked up, nerves sending my heart into overdrive. I didn't like this. I wasn't used to being nervous.

My hand slipped under my gray wool peacoat to the knife in my jeans pocket. Fingering the hilt, I reminded myself to relax. I had the plan laid out. A, B, and C, and even alternate contingency plans aptly labeled A2, B2, and C2.

Nothing could go wrong.

I stared across the street at the bar, a dim glow from its windows pooling onto the cracked sidewalk in front of it. Neon signs flickered from the two front windows, and an OPEN sign flashed above the door. There were no heavy thuds of bass or muted sounds of laughter carrying on the wind. No, Creed's Tavern wasn't that kind of bar. It was the kind that locals went to when they wanted to get away. To be alone, or to forget.

I glanced at my watch. I was early. I shouldn't have left my window yet.

Why am I so jumpy?

I lowered onto a bench hidden in the shadows near the bed and breakfast and watched the bar. This was something I did before any announced drop-in. Read the room. Feel the energy. Become the character.

Minutes passed.

An old man pushed out the front door, stumbling down the sidewalk and disappearing into the shadows. A recent widower, still adjusting to the torture of being alone, I guessed.

Another glance at my watch.

A pair of headlights in the distance caught my attention, coming straight toward Broken Ridge.

I leaned farther into the shadows and squinted at the two yellow dots, wondering who was traveling through the mountains in the middle of the night.

Little did I know that the person behind the wheel was the one contingency I hadn't planned for.

14

Leo

I swear I could feel her before she walked in, as smooth and hot as the glass I was wiping down, fresh from the dishwasher.

I glanced at the clock as the front door creaked open. Twelve forty-one a.m.

Just nineteen minutes—*nineteen fucking minutes*—to closing, and she walked through my door. Nineteen minutes, and I would have been home free.

It had been a slow Friday night. My last patron, an Army vet named Chap, left thirty minutes earlier, and I'd turned off the overhead lights before the old man was even halfway out the door. Locals knew that meant I was closing down, regardless of the time.

Something about the click of this woman's shoes told me my late-night visitor wasn't a Broken Ridge local. And something about the intent behind the quick stride told me she wasn't a midnight wanderer looking for one last drink.

The words "you've got ten minutes" were a second from

rolling off my tongue when I turned and faced the dark silhouette crossing the bar.

Her height and those long, thin limbs backlit by the blinking neon signs were the first things I noticed, followed by her hair, a mass of long, thick blond strands fanning over a silk scarf that reminded me of the old black-and-white movies.

But it was her eyes that rooted me in place, ice-blue under long feathered lashes that could make a man forget his name. My grip tightened around the glass I'd forgotten I was holding.

Suddenly, the time of day—or morning, I should say—didn't bother me in the least. The fatigue from another twelve-hour shift after months of sleepless nights had nothing on the rush of adrenaline those eyes gave me. The ten-minute warning I had on the tip of my tongue disintegrated, along with the ability to form a complete sentence.

Her focus locked on mine as she drew closer, illuminated in a peachy hue by the reflection of neon lights in the mirrored wall lined with liquor bottles.

The gray coat she wore moved seamlessly with her, hugging her curves as if tailored specifically for her body. Same for the dark skinny jeans and sky-high heels.

A total opposite, I mused, considering my uniform for the evening—a black T-shirt, worn jeans, and a pair of cowboy boots two years past their prime.

Though the woman was probably well-kept by a rich man twice her age, she appeared to be in her thirties. Which was a good thing, because checking her ID was the last thing on my mind.

The sharp look in her eye suggested she'd lived long enough to know how to take care of herself. The naivety of youth had escaped her long ago. No girl in her twenties was capable of such a fervent stare, hypnotizing and potent with a kind of confidence that demolished anything that stood between her and her goal. And there was no question—her goal that night was me.

I felt drawn to her immediately, a deep-seated connection that I didn't understand at the time. She'd been something to me once, in another life, maybe. Maybe the afterlife.

I actually thought these exact words, standing there gawking at her, which was hilarious because the afterlife was something I'd never considered until that moment. Someone with sins as heavy as mine usually didn't.

"Mornin'." I slid the warm pint glass onto the counter, narrowly missing the edge.

"Evening," she said, her voice as elegant as the package.

I nodded to the clock on the wall. "Not anymore."

"As long as it's still dark outside, it's night." Unfazed by the silence or emptiness of the bar, the woman dropped her leather purse on the bar top and slid onto a stool.

I walked to her like a gnat to a fluorescent light, knowing now this was her intent. "Can I get you something to drink?"

"Tequila."

I couldn't hide my surprise. "Tequila?"

"If you want my money, yes. Top shelf. Please."

Of all the drinks on the wall behind me, tequila was the last one I'd expected this city girl to ask for. And dammit if I didn't feel a tingle of lust shoot straight to my balls.

Definitely not a local. Definitely not an idiot.

"On the rocks?"

I didn't need to ask. Of course this woman drank her tequila on the rocks. After confirming this, I stepped to the shelves, despite the whisper of a warning not to turn my back on this one.

My mind racing with this new twist in the evening, I poured from my most expensive bottle, one that I rarely offered to anyone. One that I only drank from once a year. Once a year, to forget.

As I passed her the highball glass, she eyed the clear liquid as if deciding if the quality suited her.

It did.

Plucking a Corona from the cooler, I decided not to remind the woman that I closed in ten minutes. Instead, I popped the top and took a sip, leaning against the counter.

"You must have a forgiving boss," she said, nodding to the longneck in my hand.

"I am the boss."

Her perfectly sculpted brow arched. She liked this. And I liked that she liked this.

"You own the place?"

"Yes, ma'am. Going on eleven years now."

"Eleven years . . . long time." She sipped, eyeing me over the rim. "What's your name?"

"Leo."

"Leo what?"

"Creed. Yours?"

"Cole."

"Cole what?"

"Just Cole."

"Like Cher?"

"Something like that."

"You're from out of town."

"What gave it away?"

"The four-inch heels."

"Only four inches around here? Boy, am I in the wrong place."

The corner of my lips tugged to a grin. "Women around here wear six on the weekends, two for church. Never four."

"Noted. So, four says I'm from where, then?"

I tilted my head thoughtfully, studying the picture of perfection in front of me. "City girl. East Coast. White-collar job. The boss, I'd guess."

I watched her take another sip, deeper than the first, and wondered if I was making her uncomfortable. No . . . I didn't think much made this woman uncomfortable.

After setting down the glass, the woman only known as Cole pulled a folded piece of paper from her designer bag. The mood in the bar instantly shifted.

"You're right about the city." She unfolded the paper and pushed it forward, her eyes never leaving mine. "Do you recognize this woman?"

Like a car squealing to a stop, my heart froze and my blood turned cold. "You a cop?"

"Nope."

That tickle of warning intensified as I glanced at the blurry picture of a woman standing against a wooded backdrop that appeared to be a trailhead of sorts. Pulled from a security cam, if I had to guess.

"Nope."

"You sure?"

"Why don't you tell me what's going on here, Cole."

"The woman in the picture is Sarah Kay. Went missing from Butte two weeks ago."

"That's unfortunate." My gaze narrowed. "And you're not a cop?"

"Nope."

"A detective?"

"No, sir."

Sir. Never had a single word been so loaded with condescension. And God, I loved it. I wanted to hear her say it between my sheets, between my legs.

"What are you then?"

"I'm a private investigator." She returned her focus to the image. "Miss Kay's family called me a week ago after the local police failed to determine their daughter's whereabouts. The case went cold. It seems she vanished into thin air. You're sure you don't recognize her?"

This time, I didn't bother looking at the paper she was pushing forward again. "Should I?"

"Perhaps. Sarah Kay was last seen in your bar fifteen days ago."

I blinked, my mind skipping with incoherent thoughts. "Are you sure?"

She dipped her chin.

"Am I a suspect or something?" I asked, a bit too quickly.

"Not that I'm aware of. She was last seen at this exact location, which is why I'm here."

"Wait a second—why are you the first person questioning me about her then? Wouldn't the cops have come by already? Why didn't they?"

She lifted her drink and sipped, slowly this time.

My eyes narrowed, I set down my beer and folded my arms over my chest. "I see. The cops haven't come by because you're the only person who knows this particular piece of information. Am I right?"

Her brow cocked with an aloofness that suggested she wasn't going to confirm or deny this obviously confidential information.

"So, that's it, isn't it? Okay. What else have you got?"

"That." A pink tongue trailed over her lips, pulling every shred of my attention to the tiny dimple down the middle of the bottom one. "That's what I've got. According to my source, Sarah Kay was last seen here."

"Who's your source?"

"Have you never seen a true-crime show, Mr. Creed?"

Mr. Creed.

Mr. Creed . . . As I pull her hair, she could call me Mr. Creed.

"Is that a no?"

"No. I mean yes—never reveal your source, I know." I glanced at her purse with the paper now tucked safely back inside. "Two weeks ago, you say?"

"Fifteen days."

"Well, like I said, I don't recognize her, although that's not saying much. I get a lot of folks through my bar."

"Locals?"

"Not just locals. Travelers. Wayward wanderers. You'd be surprised how many people come through our little town."

"Are there any locals who might have been here that night that I could speak with?"

"I can give you a few names."

A moment passed as she stared at me, as if waiting for me to say more. I stared back, wondering what her game was.

Cole looked upward, to the corner, where the wall met the ceiling. I followed her gaze.

"Is there only one security camera in here?" she asked.

"Only one right now."

"Do you have footage from fifteen days ago?"

"I'll have to check. I forget to turn them on from time to time."

"Do you think you remembered fifteen days ago?"

"I'll have to check." A moment settled between us. "If I did, I should have the footage. It's an app. Records continually once I turn it on."

"How long does it save the video?"

"At the twenty-four-hour mark, the camera erases and starts over, sending the video to a file on my computer, where it stores in a log for thirty days before deleting them."

"Great. I'd like to see the day of, a few days before, and a few days after. Assuming you had the camera on, of course."

I picked up my beer, the cold glass shocking my heated skin. "Okay. I can do that for you."

"Now?"

"Tomorrow."

Cole tipped back the tequila, draining the glass in one smooth swallow. Then she grabbed her purse and stood. "Tomorrow, then. Same time?"

"Sure."

"I'll see you tomorrow, Leo."

And with that, the mystery woman sauntered out of my bar into the black night, leaving me speechless and my heart beating a bit too quickly.

15

Colette

Fourteen years earlier

"Mom, not *there.*" I snatched the bouquet of lilies from my mother's hands and placed them three inches to the left. "*Here.*" Now each bouquet was exactly eight inches apart.

My mother smiled at me, a beam of late morning sunlight catching the little gold specks in her eyes. "Cole, baby, what would I do without you? The whole world would fall apart."

I remember that moment as if it were yesterday. Sometimes at night, I can still hear the soft tone of my mother's voice, the lilt of her Southern accent. Sometimes, I can even smell the scent of her rose perfume on the air. I picture that smile so often, I could draw it blindfolded. Her rosy pink lips, that little gap between her front teeth that my father loved so much.

The whole world would fall apart.

If I had only known then.

"I'm here, I'm here, I'm here!"

My mother and I turned to see Jade barreling down the grassy hill, a dozen colorful balloons whipping wildly behind her, one escaping without her notice. Her new-to-her rusted Volkswagen hatchback loomed behind her, parked square in the middle of two parking spots, literally down the center of the yellow line. Sometimes I wondered how my sister passed her driving exam.

The sunlight sparkled off the handful of foil-paper crowns she carried in her other hand, which read HAPPY BIRTHDAY across them. Their obnoxious neon-pink color matched the shade of lipstick Jade had chosen for the occasion.

Mom laughed, and her blue eyes twinkled as they usually did anytime Jade was around. She always reacted differently to my little sister than she did to me. The two shared a lighthearted kind of love that I'd yet to experience. Jade gave her a happiness that I never could.

When my mother spoke to me, she was always more serious, her gaze intent and focused. With pride, I think. Something had made her push me, test me, groom me just so. Mom always coached me more than she laughed with me, perhaps because I'm not funny. I wish I were, but that extroverted eccentricity went to Jade.

I was the smart one. Always aced the tests. While Jade was dancing to the latest pop song in her room, I was reading or studying in mine. Never satisfied with myself, I was driven by an incessant need to be better. Making my mother and father proud became my purpose in life, laying the groundwork for the neurotic perfectionist I'd grown into.

I quickly became known as the serious sister, the one

with a resting bitch face. The one who had to have straight As because anything less was unacceptable. Had to be the best at everything. Had to *have* the best of everything. Because doesn't that a worthy woman make?

I'd always admired my mother, her work ethic, her ability to raise four headstrong girls and still wake up with a smile on her face.

A smile I'd give anything to see again.

"Dad's five minutes behind." Her chest heaving, Jade stumbled to a stop in front of us, a waft of vanilla-scented perfume strong enough to singe your nose hairs following seconds later.

Jade had changed since receiving her driver's license. She was more . . . just *more*. Reckless, I think. I saw her less and less, and I didn't like it.

Jade rolled her eyes. "He said he got stuck in traffic, but I think he got caught up at work. Again."

Likely so.

My father, David Archer, was an emergency medicine physician, an exalted position in most areas of the country, but a hellish job in the South Bronx. Mom worked as a receptionist at the hospital where he got his first job. They met, fell in love, and married a year later.

A few years after I was born, my father opened a walk-in clinic to meet the dire need of additional facilities in the area. He was overworked and grossly underpaid for what he did. Between fighting the insurance companies and dealing with patients who either didn't have insurance or couldn't pay their bills, my father was basically running a free health care clinic.

It wasn't until age fourteen that I realized we lived paycheck to paycheck, my father struggling to pay the mortgage on the tiny townhouse we called home. That next day, I got a job as a dishwasher at the café across the street. I was paid in cash, and left everything I earned under my mother's pillow every Friday night.

It was never spoken of—until I turned eighteen and worked up the courage to tell Mom that I wanted to go to college. My first year's tuition was covered by the four thousand dollars my mother had set aside for this very reason from my wages. She said she'd always known I'd be the one to do big things.

Sometimes these days, I wonder if I let her down.

Jade's eyes rounded as she took in the table. "Oh my *God*, it's beautiful."

"It was Cole's vision." Mom nodded to the table. "She did all the work."

I surveyed the party I'd been planning for months. Literally every detail, including the location, color palette, food, flowers, and decorations. I'd checked the weather incessantly, every hour, for the three days leading up to the event. I'd had Plan B and C outlined in a notebook I kept under my car seat. Rain or shine, I'd planned for it. And shine it did.

It was a glorious autumn day in New York, cool, crisp, not a single cloud in the brilliant azure sky. I'd chosen a park near our townhouse for the location of my littlest sisters' birthday. Twins, Presley and Anna, sixteen on that day.

The party was scheduled to start at ten o'clock in the morning, late enough to avoid the early morning joggers, but early enough to avoid the riff-raff that showed up for pick-up basketball games that started around lunchtime at the courts adjacent to the park. This time of the morning was the only time of day I considered safe in our neighborhood.

The picnic table I'd chosen was nestled between three

shade trees, one yellow, one red, and one orange. I'd been the first to arrive, removing the litter and sweeping the dead leaves from the concrete platform that would be perfect for family pictures.

Jade and I quickly strung balloons from the branches, while our mother sprinkled glitter down the floral center display I'd spent the evening stringing together.

Always glitter with Mom. No matter what age.

We turned as a trio of beeps sounded behind us, and watched Dad pull into a parking spot, shaking his head at Jade's inability to park between the yellow lines.

Presley barreled out of the front seat, followed by Anna from the back, their blond curls bouncing around their shoulders, curled and styled exactly the same. Though Presley wore much more makeup than Anna, as usual, and to my parents' dismay. Both wore skinny jeans, sweaters, and nude Payless wedges.

I remember thinking how alike they were, especially on that day. Completely identical, if not for the small birthmark on Presley's cheek.

My little sisters. I'd helped raise them since birth.

Dad jogged unsteadily down the hill in a thinly veiled effort to exude ample energy, but the circles and bags under his eyes told a different story. He greeted my mother first, with a kiss, then turned his attention to the stars of the day, Presley and Anna.

Together, we celebrated under the trees, singing, laughing, eating the twins' favorite breakfast of sausage-and-cheese burritos, which Jade had ordered from the café across the street. Hash browns and fruit were thrown in for free because she's, well, Jade. And the grand finale, a triple-tiered strawberry shortcake Mom and I had spent the morning baking. Presley's favorite.

After songs had been sung and strawberry decadence consumed, the twins were presented with their gifts, one small box each. Inside was a key fob that opened their new car. A pre-owned black Audi with over eighty thousand miles on it, parked just out of sight, that they would share until another could be bought.

I'll never forget how happy they were on that day.

An hour later, the evidence of the party was cleared away and the leftovers packed up. Mom and Dad left to go back to work, leaving me in charge, as always.

Not unexpectedly, the twins only had one thing in mind—taking their new car for a joyride. Though both had passed their driving tests and had driven plenty of times over the last year, I wasn't comfortable with it. When I offered to go with them, it was clear that the neurotic control-freak big sister wasn't allowed. Jade offered, because she was cooler than me. Still, no.

I crossed my arms over my chest, sensing more to the request than to cruise the neighborhood. "What's going on?"

Anna shot Presley a glance, to which she quickly responded, "Nothing." It was the only answer that undoubtedly meant "something."

"Where are you guys wanting to go?" Jade asked, stepping next to me to join forces.

There was a moment of hesitation, then both twins spoke at the same time.

"A friend's house," Anna said, just as Presley blurted, "The mall."

My eyes narrowed on them. "Which is it? The mall or a friend's house?"

"Both. Mall first, then a friend's house." This from Presley.

"Whose friend?"

"Ours. Some friends of ours want to celebrate our birthday."

"Who are these new friends, and why don't I know them?"

"They go to a different school."

Jade cut me a glance. Dating "between schools" was something the most popular girls did.

"No," I said simply, and this was met with snorts and whines.

"Come on, Cole." Presley pushed, the rebellious of the two. "We're sixteen now. We're not babies anymore. I'm so sick of you treating us like we're still in diapers."

"We'll be home by ten," Anna said.

"No."

Jade cleared her throat. *Damn her.*

Still, I stayed strong. "*No.*"

Presley cocked her hip, folding her arms over her chest. "I'm going."

"I said no. You're—"

"Eight," Jade said. "Be home by eight."

The twins looked at me, waiting with bated breath.

Something in my heart tripped as I stared back at them.

Instinct . . . I know that now.

16

James

Present day

There's something therapeutic about Montana air. A crispness that you feel deep in your lungs when you inhale, almost like a medicine that clears your sinuses and head, and cleanses your soul. It was my first morning in weeks breathing air that wasn't perfumed by exhaust, cigarettes, or Chanel N°5.

After a layover in Chicago, I'd landed at the Billings airport late in the afternoon, where Dad was waiting at the curb. We drove straight to his house, where we shared a dinner of two racks of baby backs and an ice-cold six-pack. After a good talk that reminded me of the beautiful simplicity of home, I jumped in the truck I drove in high school that Dad never could part with—a black F-150—and headed north.

It was just past midnight by the time I arrived in Broken Ridge. Not surprisingly, the town was shut down, which meant my hunt for Colette would have to wait until morning. So, I drove into the mountains, parked in a clearing, and . . . just sat.

That night, I slept under the stars. Out in the middle of nowhere, in the bed of my truck, and loved every fucking second of it.

I'd awoken to the sounds of birds chirping, to a cool, silky breeze against my skin, and a blazing orange-and-black butterfly resting on the tip of one cowboy boot.

Home.

It had been too long, I decided that morning. Much too long.

With one elbow hanging out the window, the other resting on the steering wheel, I made my way down the mountain, feeling the most refreshed I'd felt in a long time. Then I thought of Colette and laughed at the thought of her sleeping in the bed of a truck in the middle of the woods. A woman like that would probably consider camping her version of hell.

Or would she? Why did I feel like there was so much more under that prickly facade she wore like a shield in her office?

I glanced at the open folder sitting on the passenger seat, the pages flipping in the wind. A handful of photos peeked out from beneath a faded map, a pair of ice-blue eyes staring directly at me.

What was it about this woman that intrigued me so much?

Maybe it wasn't her, I considered. Maybe it was nothing more than simply coming across a blond bombshell after spending weeks cooped up behind a computer screen.

Sex. Maybe that's all it was.

I tried to remember the last time I'd had sex. When I

couldn't, I decided it had been way too long for that as well, and that this was something I needed to remedy immediately.

I yanked a Slim Jim from the bulk pack I'd purchased at the airport and bit off the top, chewing ferociously as I stared at the town ahead, my brain trying to dissect the woman who had captivated my thoughts for the last twenty-four hours. Trying, for the hundredth time, to calculate the odds that this woman was somehow connected to *two* separate cases the DEA was investigating.

One: Her connection to Avery Bell, the rumored mistress of notorious drug lord Enrique Salazar. Although the private investigator didn't admit to her assistance in Ms. Bell leaving the country, her eyes said it all. And she was right—there was no way I could get a warrant based on my hunch alone, but I knew in my gut that Colette knew Salazar's mistress much better than she'd let on. I wanted to know everything about that relationship, including if Avery Bell knew Mr. Salazar's current location.

Two: Leo Creed, a thirty-two-year-old drifter whose name I saw mentioned in the stack of papers on Colette's desk. *This*, combined with her connection to Salazar, was what had me booking a last-minute airline ticket across the country.

What the hell does Colette Archer have to do with the man who could be responsible for destroying my family?

Dirtbag Leo Creed had been connected to one of the biggest fentanyl busts in the Midwest, ten years earlier, in my hometown of Billings. Though never formally linked to the bust, Leo was rumored to be associated with a few of the dealers, and therefore forever burned into my brain. The DEA had been interested in him for years. I'd kept tabs on him and his misfit brother, Dylan. Based on his criminal record, I could only assume Dylan had his hands in the same illegal activities as his brother.

Birds of a feather and all that shit.

The connection between Colette and Salazar's mistress was clear. Avery had sought Colette's services in fear she was being followed. It wasn't a stretch to imagine Colette using her fancy computer science degree to whip up a fake passport and assist Avery out of the country.

This all made sense to me.

What didn't make sense was what the hell Colette wanted with Leo Creed. Or could she be after his delinquent brother, Dylan, maybe?

And why include her sister? Dragging her to a small Podunk town in the middle of nowhere? Why now?

Again, what were the freaking odds that the woman was connected to two separate DEA cases? There was a link there, somewhere, and I couldn't help but wonder if that link could reveal Enrique Salazar's location, and therefore redeem me from my mistake at the Harlem raid. *That* was enough for me to board the plane and track the mysterious smoke-show that was Colette Archer.

The assessment Colette had made of me in her office wasn't too far off. I was no longer the top dog, and no, I didn't like it. I didn't like to lose. Didn't like to *fail.*

I tossed the empty jerky wrapper on the floorboard and clicked on my phone to call my office.

"Blaze here." The buzz of a fax machine was audible in the background. Of course my overachieving assistant was at the office on Saturday morning.

"Did you pull together the information I asked for?"

"The information you asked for at midnight last night?"

"Four hundred and twenty minutes ago? Yes."

A second passed. "No. Sir. It's on my list. I'll have it to you by the end of the day."

"Move it to the top spot on that list. I need—"

"You're breaking up, sir . . ."

I glanced at the bars on my phone. Only two. Shoddy cell reception in Montana was something I'd used to my advantage as a teenager. But I had a feeling this trip was going to require a more reliable network.

"Where are you?" Blaze asked over the rapid clicking of keys, probably tracking my company phone. "Wait . . . what the hell are you doing in Montana?"

"Weekend retreat."

"I thought you were supposed to be—"

"Putting together eighty-seven reports for our Monday morning meeting?"

"Exactly. Are you sure—"

"I need the Archer report within the hour, Blaze. That's the purpose of this call, not for you to climb up my ass."

There was a brief pause while Blaze mulled over trying to convince me that my impromptu decision to travel cross-country when my job was on the line wasn't a smart one.

"The report, Blaze," I said, interrupting his thoughts before he could speak them. "I need it now."

"Okay. So, to confirm, you're wanting me to quote, dig deeper, into Colette Archer?"

"I want anything you can pull up on her. Check for police records, bank accounts, anything. I want to know where she's traveled in the last few months. Her regular hangouts, where and how she spends her money. Same for the family—the sister and parents. Everything you can get. I want to know if she prefers red or white, and if the carpet matches the drapes. Within the hour."

"Yes, sir."

I didn't need to ask him to pin her current location because I already had. The one hotel in Broken Ridge had no vacancy, booked with leaf peepers who had traveled to the area to catch a glimpse of the fall colors. My only other option was a bed and breakfast that I learned, much too easily, was booked out by two sisters.

I clicked off the phone, then tossed it in the passenger seat as I rolled into the one-horse town known as Broken Ridge.

Something in my soul stirred as I passed the shops that lined the main drag, the mountains soaring behind them. It was the type of town where Mother Nature was just as much a citizen as the people. Life was slower there, the people more laid-back and centered, but no less hardworking than the dwellers in the city that never sleeps. The difference was, in this part of the country, power was measured by the calluses on a man's hands, not the hours he spent behind a desk.

Work was different here. Life was different.

It stirred me. Deep inside, like there was something here that I was missing, that I'd been yearning for.

I just didn't realize it was going to come in the form of a woman.

I slowed as I passed the black iron gate to the bed and breakfast where Colette and her sister were staying, then made a U-turn at the end of Main Street and pulled into a narrow slanted parking space in front of the bakery adjacent to the B and B.

Turning off my truck, I settled in to wait. Nothing like fieldwork, good old surveillance, to get the blood pumping.

God, I missed it.

17

Colette

Jade peered over my shoulder out the window. "How long has it been there?"

I slowly lowered the corner of the sheer curtain. "Eight hours."

"Eight hours?" My sister gawked. "Seriously? That truck has been parked there since ten this morning?"

"Eight, Jade. Since eight this morning. Jesus, did you sleep through kindergarten?"

Jade innocently lifted her hands, one gripping a Miller Lite, the other a cupcake from the bakery next door. "Sorry, my fingers are busy." She winked, then nodded to the truck parked below. "As are his, I'm assuming, considering I've been walking around my room naked half the day."

"No, whoever it is has an unobstructed view of my room, but only a sliver of yours above the balcony." I slid her a grin. "And we all know a sliver isn't enough to see *all that*." With my index finger, I indicated the lines of my sister's beautifully curvy body.

"Amen to that, sister." She winked again with a confidence I'd always admired. "You sure it hasn't left?"

"Yes. When I went out for a walk at seven, the spot was vacant. When I got back, it was there."

"And you've been watching the entire time?"

"Pretty much, between catching up on work."

Jade plucked the laptop from my lap. I tried to snatch it back, but she held it up in the air, out of my reach, like an ornery child.

"Give it back," I said, in the same manner.

"Cole—*no.* You didn't get in until after one in the morning last night. When I peeked in here at four, you were sitting on your bed, working. You jogged at seven this morning, and haven't left the window or your laptop since. Did you sleep at all?"

"Jade—"

"Don't lie to me, sister."

"No. I didn't sleep."

Groaning, I scrubbed my hands over my face, mentally cataloguing the number of pills I'd taken over the course of the evening. I'd started doubling up on my pain pill, and something else that had a side effect of boosted energy. An interesting combination, no doubt.

"I've got a big case I'm working on. Senator Samson, insurance fraud, gold-digging wife. It's a whole—"

"Distraction. It's a whole distraction, Cole." Jade sighed, then handed me my laptop. Disapproval mixed with concern pulled her face. "You're different. Something's up."

"Yeah, this." I dramatically gestured out the window to the truck, whose driver had been watching us all morning.

"No, it's more. You're unnaturally stressed, even more than usual. You're emotional."

"I am not."

"You are."

I took a deep breath, shifting my gaze to the bar across the street. Secrets were hard to keep—the kind I was keeping, anyway. As the days dragged on, the heavier the weight felt on my shoulders. I felt emotional, and I hated it.

Jade put her hand on my shoulder. "We have one thing to focus on here. One. Is that right, sister?"

"That's right," I whispered, but it was a lie.

"Then set everything else aside, including work."

I scoffed.

"*One* thing," she snapped. "Okay?"

Finally, I nodded.

"Good." She tossed my laptop on the bed, and we refocused out the window on the truck.

Jade took an aggressively large bite of her cupcake and peered closer, hovering just above my head, her lips smacking and jaws feverishly working the cake like a horse devouring a carrot.

"Did you get me any?" I asked as my stomach growled.

"Two German chocolates. Downstairs." A crumble of strawberry tumbled onto my shoulder as she added, "Weirdo."

"*Hey*. Mom would roll over in her grave if she heard you say that."

Jade grinned, and for a moment we were swept back to Sunday afternoons and Mom's coconut cream pies—the only dessert Jade wouldn't touch with a ten-foot pole. My sister dipped pineapple chunks in jalapeño ice cream but couldn't stomach coconut. And I was the weirdo?

A minute passed as we studied the barely visible silhouette in the blacked-out Ford F-150, both wondering the same thing.

Are we being watched?

"Did you get the tag number?" Jade asked, licking the frosting from her fingers.

"Not yet."

"You're sure he's been in there all day?"

"He or she, and yes. Whoever it is hasn't left their vehicle since exactly eight oh four."

"Gross."

"What's gross?"

"You have to wonder where the guy's relieving himself."

"Do you remember that time we drove to Grandma's and I made you pee in a Styrofoam cup?"

"Because you didn't want to miss that documentary on Mata Hari?"

"You mean a World War One secret double agent who moonlighted as an escort? A woman who singlehandedly was able to pull top-secret information from some of the richest and most influential men in the world while servicing them in her bed, only to turn around and sell that information to the French government? Murdered execution-style shortly after? Yeah, I held my pee for nine hours for that, so I know it's doable. And why are you so certain it's a guy?"

"The frame is too big." Jade took a swig of her beer. "Shoulders are too broad. It's not only a dude, it's a large one."

I narrowed my eyes, a little warning bell going off in my head. One that I couldn't quite define.

"I don't know. I've met some pretty large women in my life, Jade."

"*Plus size.* God, you're a bitch."

"Take it easy, Gloria Steinem. I meant tall." Tearing my gaze away from the truck, I pivoted, fully taking in my sister for the first time. "Uh . . . whoa."

Wearing a fringed leather vest over a skintight Henley, ripped skinny jeans, knee-high boots, and a boho bandeau around her long blond hair, my sister looked fifty years late for Woodstock. Her hair was down in that sexy, beachy wave she could always perfect, while mine, on the other hand, lay limp. A pair of round rose-colored glasses covered her eyes.

She opened her arms, swaying the fringe. "You like?"

"Where are you going?"

"Work."

My brow arched. "Already?"

"Just some preliminary research."

I narrowed my eyes. "I don't like you going without me. You know that."

"I also know that you're going to die of a heart attack before you're forty if you keep worrying about everyone else but yourself, Cole. I'm not doing anything dangerous. Yet. I promise. Just gathering intel."

"You don't even know what intel means. Listen, just steer clear of the F-150 plus-size he/she. I don't like him/her. Not until we determine who he/she is."

"I promise."

"Seriously. Promise?"

"*Promise.* Jeez." It was her turn to scan me from head to toe. A wry smile tugged at her lips. "The country looks good on you." She nodded to the boyfriend jeans I'd thrown on in an effort to dress down the cashmere sweater I'd slipped into.

"I'm not wearing the chaps, Jade."

"Give it a week."

"We're not going to be here a week," I snapped back, acutely aware of the desperation in my voice.

Jade didn't miss it either, and it wasn't a good color on me.

I cleared my throat. "I want to be back in New York by Monday. Two days, tops."

My sister smiled, something in her eyes expressing doubt at my ability to reach that deadline, and she was right. "You heading to Creed's Tavern?"

I glanced at the clock. "In a few hours."

Eight, to be exact. I had eight more damn hours to kill until my midnight appointment with Leo Creed. Eight hours of watching Mr. Ford F-150 watching me.

"He's quite the ladies' man, I hear."

"Leo? How did you hear that?"

"I listen."

Leo's image flashed in my head, the rough, bad-boy persona that drew women like moths to a flame.

Not this woman.

"Sure you don't want me to come?" Jade asked with a concerned look in her eyes I didn't like. It felt like she was doubting me. No, I didn't like it at all.

"I'm sure."

Jade nodded, downed the rest of her beer, and grabbed her beaded bag from the accent chair in the corner.

I took another glance out the window, then refocused on my younger sister. "Just research, okay? And keep your eye on that truck. Stay away from it."

"Okay, okay."

She started to turn, but I lurched forward and grabbed her arm. "One at a time, Jade. We do this *together* . . . one at a time."

Her face hardened.

A moment passed as we stared at each other. Finally, she dipped her chin and lifted her fist. I released her arm, pressed my fist against hers, and together, kissed our knuckles.

"Dinner tonight?" she asked over her shoulder as she strolled to the door.

"What? I'm sorry. I was hypnotized by all the fringe swaying around that plus-sized ass."

She laughed. "Dinner, then."

"See you in a few hours. I love you."

"Love you too."

With a flick of a wave, I watched Jade descend the staircase, trying to ignore the knot twisting in my stomach.

I closed my eyes and inhaled deeply.

One at a time, sis. One at a time.

Exhaling, I slid on the new Birkenstocks I'd picked up at the leather store a few doors down, then tucked the usual items into my pockets—phone, credit card, driver's license, and switchblade—then added a zip drive and a compact mirror. Sitting on the edge of the bed, I looked at the window, the sheer curtains swaying in the breeze, and pictured the truck below.

Mr. Ford F-150 felt like a wrench working its way into my carefully crafted plan. A last-minute discovery of one more piece to a puzzle that was almost complete.

My pulse picked up at the thought that I was missing something. Something that I had no control over. It was a feeling I wasn't used to. Control was my *life.*

I thought of my sister's words. "*You're emotional.*"

She was right, and things always went awry when I didn't have control.

Angered by this rush of insecurity, I strode across the room, slid open the sheer curtains, squared my shoulders, and presented myself in front of the window.

Colette Archer here. Come and get me, motherfucker.

18

James

I wasn't surprised that I hadn't received a call or an update in the twenty-four-plus hours since Colette Archer promised to contact Avery Bell and inquire about Enrique Salazar's whereabouts. I was surprised, however, at the number of times since then I'd checked my calls, texts, email, and junk folders.

This pissed me off, and gave me more resolve than ever to figure out this woman and the game she was playing.

I knew she knew that I, or *someone* in a truck, was watching her, and therefore assumed she'd been watching me. But the moment Colette presented herself in front of the window, like the unveiling of the killer in the final act of a play, I knew she was making a statement—intended for the man in the black F-150.

She meant it to be a moment.

She didn't, however, mean for it to confirm that my being there was affecting her. Bothering her, stressing her out.

And this, I decided, was her weakness. Not money, *this* was the secret she was guarding so fiercely.

This worked to my advantage. I'd built a reputation on my ability to extract secrets from even the most loyal of men. However, capturing and waterboarding this woman wasn't an option, so I needed a plan to approach her, gain her confidence, and get what I needed.

Contemplating this, I wiped my greasy hands on my jeans and mindlessly pulled another slice of triple-meat pizza from the box sitting on my passenger seat. I'd ordered the pizza the moment I saw Colette's sister return from her afternoon walk, knowing that this distraction would be my only opportunity to get food and take a piss. I'd also convinced Kristy, from Pioneer's Pizza, to throw in a few beers and a bag of candy for an extra twenty.

Best stakeout I'd had in a long time.

Even though a Saturday afternoon in Broken Ridge moved at the pace of a drunken turtle, I wasn't bored sitting in my truck. It felt good to be out of the office, out from behind a damn computer. To be following up on a tip that could be the turning point in a huge investigation, despite the fact I was technically no longer on the Salazar team.

I was more focused, something to do with the fresh air coming through my cracked window, and the nature around me. I felt clearheaded, ready to take on the tall, slender silhouette that kept peeking through the second-story window of the bed and breakfast.

Colette was the opposite of her sister, who practiced some sort of naked tai chi in front of her window for the world to see. Beautiful woman, and I have to be honest, I was surprised my attention didn't shift to that Archer sister. Or my hand to my pants, for that matter, considering how long it had been since I'd last had sex.

But there was something about Colette that snagged me and didn't let go. Something about the juxtaposition of her prickly, callous behavior and the vulnerability—sadness—behind those blue eyes.

Her sister would probably be a blast in the bedroom, while Colette would probably make me wash my hands and brush my teeth before touching her. The room would have to be just so, the temperature to her liking, the lighting dim enough to hide any imperfections in her skin. Colette was probably allergic to KY and required some organic lube special-ordered from Switzerland or something.

Yep, that was Colette, while Jade probably preferred a strobe light, chocolate syrup, and a mirror over the bed. Still, Colette was the one who held my attention.

She was going to be a challenge, not that the other sister wouldn't be. I just got the vibe that the challenge from Jade would include brass knuckles. Colette's inner torment was hidden much deeper, carefully concealed under layers of designer clothes and secrets. She was an enigma I wanted to solve, a challenge I wanted to meet head-on.

I wondered, at that moment, if that was simply all it was with her for me. Maybe Colette was nothing more than a fun game, a carrot dangled in front of a very bored horse who was craving anything that didn't include Excel spreadsheets and dress shirts. Whatever it was, I couldn't get the woman off my mind, not since the moment she demanded I leave her anally retentive clean office while bullfrogs croaked behind her.

Colette Archer. My new game.

I tossed the crust into the box and chugged the Gatorade tucked between my thighs as I glanced at the clock. Almost five p.m.

After checking my email again, I considered calling

Blaze one more time for that update I'd demanded earlier in the morning. I think there were only two remaining cuss words and phrases I hadn't used in my last voice mail to him. One that I was pretty sure was illegal in most parts of the world.

I needed to know more about Colette Archer and her family immediately.

This dance needed to begin because I had a job to get back to. And I wasn't going back empty-handed.

19

Colette

A simmering, amped-up vigilance I hadn't felt in years gripped me as I made my way through the courtyard, my focus locked on the black F-150 peeking through the bushes that lined the sidewalk.

Slanted beams of late-afternoon sunlight cut through the thick canopy of trees, sparkling in the crisp, cool autumn air. I glanced up at the sky, a brilliant sapphire blue speckled with fluffy white clouds.

Five in the afternoon, and still, the truck hadn't moved. I was surer than ever that whoever was behind the wheel had a purpose. They shouldn't be there—I felt it in my gut. Something wasn't right, and it was throwing me for a damn loop.

A gust of wind swept past me, cutting through the cashmere and straight to my bones. My entire body vibrated with a weird, wired energy, like a subliminal warning deep in my soul. Going undetected in the small country town of Broken Ridge wasn't nearly as easy as in the city.

I felt exposed. Vulnerable. It was a feeling I wasn't used to.

A woman and man in their mid-sixties held hands as they strolled past the bed and breakfast, smiling in comfortable silence. They wore matching cowboy hats and fitted Wranglers, the denim of choice in Broken Ridge. The couple fit together like two pieces of a puzzle.

I thought of my mom and dad, and how they would love Broken Ridge. But thoughts of the past made blackness quickly replace the light.

Pushing open the iron gate, I lifted my chin and strode across the sidewalk, keeping one eye on the mystery truck. I could feel the mystery man watching me, an omnipresent scrutiny like an army of ants slowly climbing up my legs and spreading over my body.

In that moment, I considered aborting the plan. Turning around and booking Jade and me a one-way ticket home.

I pressed on, though, the devil winning that battle as I forced common sense aside. This was happening. Hell on earth wasn't going to keep me from my—*our*—goal.

With my head on a swivel, I crossed the street, focused on the reflection of the truck in the shiny pole ahead of me. Still, no movement. As I stepped onto the sidewalk, I slid the compact mirror from my pocket, and while pretending to check my makeup, watched the truck in the reflection.

I wondered why he wasn't following me.

Dabbing my lips, I kept my gaze on the truck, thankful I'd opted for the loose-fitting boyfriend jeans and leather sandals. Easier to run if needed. Plus, I wasn't getting nearly as many looks from the passersby, although I wasn't sure if that was a good thing or a bad thing.

I replaced the compact next to the switchblade in my

pocket just as the OPEN sign flickered to life over the front door of Creed's Tavern. Right on time.

After a quick glance over my shoulder—still nothing from the truck—I pulled open the thick wooden door.

The bar was empty. I slowed my pace, quieting my steps, taking a moment to study the tavern, so different in the light of day.

Under the shadows of night, the bar had a saloon feel to it, pulling the patrons into the comfort of an old Western movie. In the daylight, the bar resembled more of an Irish pub, warm and welcoming. The moody melody of a classic blues song played softly in the background.

It was obvious that ample time, money, and effort had been put into renovating the space. Painting, adding, changing. Leo Creed took pride in his bar, and I wondered if it was because it was all he had. I also wondered where the hell his brother, Dylan, was.

I glanced from corner to corner, my gaze lingering on the single security camera above the door that led to the bathrooms. No red blinking light to indicate it was on.

Just then, the door to the cooler swung open, and our eyes met instantly.

Balancing several cases of beer in his arms, Leo froze in midstride as the door slapped closed behind him. For a moment, surprise flashed in his eyes, or was it fear? Just as quickly, his expression morphed into that crooked smile I remembered from the night before.

"You're early." His voice was deep and gravelly as if he'd only recently awakened.

"Papa always told me to get a jump on the day."

"Papa, huh?" Leo slid the cases of beer onto the counter. "Is there a country girl somewhere under all that cashmere?"

He walked around the bar, a grin on his lips and a twinkle in his eyes. A zing of excitement purred through my body, a cat and a mouse finding each other at a lonely airport bar. Except this was no one-night stand, I reminded myself.

The fresh scent of soap preceded him as he met me in the middle of the bar. His dark, shaggy hair was combed back, still wet from the shower he'd obviously just stepped out of. He was more alert than the evening before, the golden flecks in his deep brown eyes sparkling as he gave me the once-over.

"Your jeans are too big," he said with a smirk.

"It's the style."

"Not around here."

I grinned as we quickly fell into the same flirty banter we'd left on. Leo had charisma, and I could see why women flocked to him.

He shoved his hands into his pockets. "I didn't expect you until tonight."

"Turns out it only takes an hour to wander through every shop on Main Street."

"And now you're bored."

"Exactly."

"No high-speed car chases or what other excitement private investigators find themselves in on a daily basis?"

"Not around here." I winked, mocking his earlier sarcastic response. "Although I'm hoping you can change that. Were you able to pull the camera footage?"

His attention darted down, to the left, then quickly back to me as he shifted his weight. "I spent some time on it last night."

"And?"

"And I don't see your girl, Susan—"

"Sarah. Sarah Kay."

"Sorry. Yeah, Sarah Kay. I don't see her in the footage."

"So the cameras were turned on the day she was last seen here?"

"The date you gave me, yes."

"Can I see the footage myself?"

He hesitated, and I got the vibe he was weighing whether to trust me or not. "I haven't pulled the surrounding days yet. Thought you weren't coming by until after midnight tonight."

"I'll take what you have now."

"Of course you will." His eyes narrowed with a playful smile. "Follow me, then."

I was led through a narrow door past the freezer that led into an office the size of a bathroom, and smelled about the same too. No windows, the room was dimly lit by a single floor lamp in the corner. Dozens of boxes littered the dingy tile floor. A corkboard cluttered with bills, orders, and notes hung behind a small metal desk with a computer and a phone. A ripped leather chair was pressed against the wall. In the corner was a small mini-fridge—his own, I guessed. And in the other corner was a door even narrower than the one that led to the office.

"Where does that door lead?" I asked as Leo slipped behind his desk and clicked on the monitor.

He looked up, his face bathed in the blue glow of the screen booting up. "Upstairs. My apartment."

"You live in a bar. I'd hate to see the color of your liver."

He laughed. "Yep, quite the life, I know. I have a cabin in the hills I go to on the weekends, but stay here mostly."

"Who's this?" I leaned down and peered at a small

framed photo covered in dust, haphazardly placed on the corner of the desk as if obligatory more than anything else.

"My brother." A sharpness suggesting the two weren't close colored Leo's tone.

"You look like twins."

His hand stilled on the mouse for a moment before continuing to maneuver through the files in his computer.

"Are you two close?" I asked.

"Used to be."

"What happened?"

Leo peered at me from under thick dark lashes. "Family stuff."

Private stuff, he meant. And I was pushing it.

Nodding, I turned away.

"Okay." He clicked a few keys. "Where do you want me to send the files?"

I pulled the zip drive from my pocket, and our fingers touched as he took it. Our eyes met. A shot of electricity as hot as lightning zipped up my spine.

Leo cleared his throat and slid the drive into the computer, then dragged the file over to copy into it. "So . . . how long are you here for?"

"Not sure," I said, perusing the stacked boxes that lined the room. "Do you have the receipts from the days surrounding Sarah Kay's disappearance?"

His laser-sharp eyes met mine. "You'll have to get a warrant for that, as I'm sure you already know." He grinned, softening the not-so-subtle message that was intended to remind me he was no fool.

Got it.

I stared at the boxes as the files loaded onto the drive.

"Here you go." He pulled the drive from the console. "The day she was supposedly last reported being seen here."

"Thanks." I slid the drive into my pocket. "And the days before and after?"

The bell to the front door jangled, followed by laughter from a group of tourists.

"I've gotta . . ."

I nodded. "Busy."

"Right. If I don't get to it tonight, I'll do it Monday," he said. "I've got some things to do tomorrow."

"How about I swing by your place after you get off work that night?"

"That'll be after one o'clock in the morning."

"I don't sleep much."

"For some reason, I believe that." Leo crossed his arms over his chest, assessing me, and I stared back, a small smile on my lips. "Fine. Monday night, one fifteen a.m. The front door will be locked, so go around back. There's a staircase that leads to my apartment."

The front door chimed again. An old man shuffled in, carrying a Styrofoam spit cup in one hand and the newspaper in the other. He slid onto the seat at the end of the bar, his seat, I guessed. The trio of tourists were perusing the beer menu.

"That's Bart. A regular."

"Seems thirsty."

"Always is."

I dipped my chin. "Better get at it, then. See you soon, Leo."

I felt his gaze on my back as I strode across the bar, nodding to the old man as I passed. The zip drive burned like fire through the pocket of my jeans.

Taking a deep breath, I pushed out the front door and into the sunny autumn afternoon, my attention immediately refocusing on the truck—now with the dark silhouette of a man leaning against the tailgate.

I stopped cold.

The videos were going to have to wait.

20

Colette

"What the *hell* are you doing here?"

I stormed across the street, ignoring the honk of a trailer-towing dually that narrowly missed the heel of my Birkenstocks. Too bad.

James Black rolled an obnoxiously large sucker from one cheek to the other, a grin spreading across those full, succulent lips.

I hated everything about him at that moment. The way he casually leaned against the tailgate, one foot resting on the hitch as if he didn't have a care in the world. The way he'd replaced the ill-fitting suit he'd worn to my office with a thin gray T-shirt that stretched across a massive chest that should have an *S* painted in the middle.

I hated the way his khaki tactical pants hugged a pair of thighs as thick as tree trunks, and the way his scuffed combat boots made me envision him tossing me over his shoulder and carrying me to safety from the barrage of bullets behind us.

Most of all, I hated the tickle of butterflies that erupted in my stomach and danced when our eyes met.

I mentally kicked myself for not considering the possibility that the man in the mystery truck could be him. Of course it was the stubborn, brash DEA agent who wanted something from me.

James Black, the contingency I hadn't planned for.

A breeze blew past us, ruffling his mussed hair and rippling the thin cotton across his body, showcasing—what else—that perfect V of a waist. Everything about James was different from the man I'd met in my office.

What was once a short-tempered, combative white-collar asshole was now a rugged mountain man of sorts with a lethally confident disposition and a mischievous sparkle in his eye. The man was one with the jacked-up truck behind him and the bevy of colorful leaves that slowly fluttered past him.

Unlike me, James Black fit like a glove in this small country town. We were polar opposites.

"Well, fancy seeing you here," he said in an obnoxious Southern accent.

"This isn't the South, and you must mean *fancy seeing me through the window all damn day*."

James pulled the sucker from his lips with a loud pop and grinned.

I scowled at the spit-covered ball of sugar. "What is that?"

"A sucker."

"I know that. Why is it brown?"

"Root beer."

I jerked my chin back in disgust. "Who the hell buys a root-beer lollipop?"

"Someone who likes beer. And I'm pretty sure only

schoolgirls with ringlets call them lollipops." He tugged another from his back pocket and thrust it at me.

I snorted.

"I really debated it," he said, ignoring my disdainful expression as I stared at the candy as one might a can of sardines. "At first, I was going to go with strawberry, but then I thought, nope, too plain for someone like Colette Archer. Then I picked up the apple, and decided that was too simple for a woman who color-coordinates her earrings with her shoes. So I went with cherry-limeade—simple, sweet, but with a tartness sour enough to melt rocks."

I plucked the sucker from his hand and slammed it to the asphalt, where it shattered. "Why are you spying on me?"

He frowned down at the broken sucker. "I'm not. There were a bunch of Girl Scouts selling suckers, so—"

"Cut the bullshit. Why are you here?"

"Returning to my roots."

"What roots?"

"The kind that sprout manly men."

I made a show of looking around, searching for one of these manly men but coming up short. He grinned in response, seemingly amused with me, quite a contrast to the contempt that had radiated off him in my office the day before.

"I'm from Montana," he said to clarify. "A small town about sixty miles south."

"Sixty miles north of your hometown isn't returning to your roots."

"Did you contact Avery Bell and get me Enrique Salazar's location?"

"Not yet."

“I’m not leaving until you get me this information, Colette.”

“Then it just got pushed to the top of my to-do list.”

“Good.”

“You could have just called, you know.”

He spread out his arms, gesturing to the backdrop of fall foliage behind us. “And miss all this?”

“Why are you spying on me, Black?”

“Why are you spying on Leo Creed?”

“Who’s Leo Creed?”

James’s eyelids drooped in an unimpressed deadpan. He jerked his chin to the bar where he’d clearly just seen me exit.

“Oh,” I said flippantly. “Is he the owner of that bar?”

James rolled his eyes.

“Huh.” I flicked a strand of hair from my shoulder. “Didn’t realize that was his name.”

“Just like you didn’t when you visited him after closing last night too?”

I crossed my arms over my chest. “How did you know I was here?”

“Airline tickets on your desk.”

I narrowed my eyes as I put the pieces of the puzzle together. When James had barged into my office seeking information about Avery Bell and Enrique Salazar, I’d had airline tickets and printouts with Leo’s name stacked on top of a folder on my desk.

Bastard.

He winked. “You’re not the only one who knows how to investigate.”

“Investigate this.”

I flipped him the bird, something I hadn’t done since grade school, and the first of many surprising shifts in behavior that this maddening man brought out of me. Then I pushed past him, my Birkenstocks crunching on the busted cherry-limeade lollipop (my favorite kind) as I stormed onto the sidewalk.

"Tell me why you're spying on Leo," he called out.

Though I didn't hear his footfalls, I could feel him trailing behind me as my mind raced.

What was his interest in Leo Creed? What did he know about him? Why did he care about my interest in him? I wanted to know all this, but engaging with a federal agent was the last thing I needed at that moment.

"Leo's not the kind of guy you want to be digging into, Colette."

"It's Miss Archer," I snapped over my shoulder. "And I have a feeling you and I have very different definitions of digging into someone."

"You might be right. How about you demonstrate yours first, and I'll grab the handcuffs from—"

"You're twelve years old, you know that?"

"I'm not the one who called a sucker a lollipop."

"Who says I'm digging into this Leo Creed guy?"

"I do. And I might be good at PI work, but I'm really bad at patience. I'm not going to play this game with you, Archer."

"I'm not going to play *any* game with you, Black—cuffs or not."

"We'll see about that. Why won't you tell me about Avery Bell, or why you've got an interest in Leo Creed? Or is it his brother, Dylan, you're really after?"

I stopped at the black iron gate that led to the courtyard of the bed and breakfast and spun around. "Avery Bell was a client of mine. And I told you, I take client confidentiality very seriously."

"And I take ensuring that no woman ever needs to seek a new identity in the first place very seriously."

Colette folded her arms over her chest. "I hear you're no longer on the Enrique Salazar case."

"Hacking is illegal, you know."

"So is stalking."

He stared at me, looming over me in a way that told me I was stuck with him. James Black wasn't going to leave me alone until he got what he came for. After all, he'd flown more than two thousand miles to get under my skin—or "dig into me," perhaps.

"Listen, if I give you information on Avery Bell, what's to say the Feds won't lead the cartel right to her?"

"I really hate your lack of faith in the US government."

"I hate your lack of ability to bring down the cartel."

I'd hit a nerve with that; I saw it in his eyes. James Black didn't like to lose, and I'd just made him more determined than ever to get what he needed from me.

So, I did what I always do when things get a bit too sticky with a man. I turned my back on him and walked away.

21

James

I waited, watching the sway of her slim hips as she stomped across the courtyard that led to the B and B.

I can read desperate when I see it, and Colette Archer was one unplanned moment away from losing the self-control she clung to with bloody, manicured fingertips. She was a woman on the edge, and the scariest part was that I don't think she realized it. Maybe because her entire focus was on me and ensuring that I knew I wasn't welcome.

Colette was desperate, and I knew from experience that desperate people snapped. I didn't have to wait long for hers. I could practically see the smoke fuming off the top of her head the second before she spun back around in a whirl of fury.

"James Black, I'm going to call the cops if you don't leave town," she said through clenched teeth, her unwillingness to back down from me igniting a carnal attraction deep in my soul.

"Miss Archer," I said from behind the gate. "I don't think you realize the magnitude of your situation right now. I can officially link you to two separate DEA cases. That alone is enough for me to do more than surveil your 'vacation.'"

Fire sparked in her eyes as she glowered at me, probably internally warring between wanting to know the information that I had, but questioning my validity. That distrusting brain of hers was telling her to keep moving, to ignore the bait I'd carefully laid in front of her.

Colette lost that battle, and with a huff, stomped back to me with flushed cheeks and fire in her steps. "You said two cases?"

"Yes. Enrique Salazar, courtesy of Avery Bell, and now your boy, Leo Creed. He's been on our radar for years."

She blinked. She didn't know.

Very interesting.

I flipped open the latch on the iron gate and stepped through it, closing the inches between us. "Fentanyl, Miss Archer. A synthetic opioid a hundred times more potent than morphine. The deadliest and most desired drug on the black market today. Leo Creed is associated with some very dangerous fentanyl dealers."

Her gaze shifted in the direction of Creed's Tavern, those little wheels in her head turning a mile a minute—as were my own. If Colette's connection to Creed wasn't drug-related, then what was it?

"When?" she asked. "When did he first reach your radar?"

"Ten years ago."

"Is there an open investigation on him now?"

"I'm not at liberty to discuss that with you. Something like client confidentiality, you understand," I said with a wink.

Her nostrils flared, a cute little tell seconds before she would lose it. A moment passed as we studied each other, and I got the feeling she was wondering how she could use me. Because that's the type of woman Colette Archer was. The type to bulldoze her way over someone to get what she wanted. Especially men.

"It's going to be like this, then?" she snapped. "You won't share what information you have on Leo Creed until I share information on Avery Bell?"

"I don't see this as anything other than two officials sharing information to better the community. It's not as complicated as you wish it were, Miss Archer."

"You don't know complicated until you've spent a little time with me, Black."

A breeze drifted past us, sending a strand of hair dancing across a face as sharp as granite, but her eyes were filled with sadness. *Tortured* was the word that filtered through my head. The woman was a tortured soul. Lost.

I wanted to kiss her in that moment, to make her forget whatever was controlling her, if only for a minute.

"Everyone has a complicated past, their own story." I reached forward, tucking the wayward strand of hair behind her ear. "It's only as bad as you make it. You either accept it or let it eat you alive. That's *your* decision."

She pushed away my hand and looked down. The pain inside her was so palpable that I could feel it in my soul. Then, without another word, she slowly turned and walked away.

I stepped forward as carefully as a hunter might approach a wounded prey. "Colette—"

"Do you always chase women like this, Mr. Black?" she spat out over her shoulder.

I stopped. The woman was wounded, but still very much alive.

"You're no average woman, Ms. Archer."

I watched her storm her way through the blooming greenery that enclosed the courtyard, streaks of sunlight casting angry slashes against her back. Between the trees, I watched her place her hand on the doorknob—and hesitate. Turning, she scowled at me with a savage fierceness that reminded me of the women we'd find caged and chained in the caves overseas.

She opened her mouth to say something, but seemed to think better of it.

"Good evening, Colette," I said as leaves danced between us, across our line of sight. "Be safe. Make sure your sister remembers to lock the door behind her when she gets back."

The look Colette shot across the courtyard nearly set my hair on fire.

And damn if my dick didn't give a little kick.

22

James

Colette didn't emerge from her room the rest of the night, or the following day. And I was bored off my ass.

Her sister, on the other hand, had been in and out of the bed and breakfast—wearing a new outfit for every adventure, by the way—perusing the shops and mingling with the locals and tourists like a normal human being.

What the hell was Colette doing cooped up in that tiny space? Her nails? Her hair? Plotting global domination? Not calling me with information about Avery Bell or Enrique Salazar, that's for sure.

A part of me wondered if she'd found some alternative exit from the B and B that I wasn't aware of. Although, according to the blueprint of the building I'd dug up, there was none.

So, what was she doing in there?

It was driving me crazy, along with the fact that my assistant, Blaze, wasn't answering my calls since I'd left him a message informing him that I wouldn't be back in the office on Monday, and that I'd decided to cash out some of my vacation days.

I wasn't going to return to my new job empty handed. I needed Salazar, which meant I needed to know everything about Colette. With each passing hour, the creature seemed to become more and more complex.

Last night at eight p.m., the owner of the B and B had stopped in for exactly seven minutes to change out the towels, based on the basket she'd carried in her arms, then made her way to Creed's Tavern for a drink. I made a mental note to have Blaze check on her too.

Around eleven that night, Colette's sister ventured out for the fifth time that day, her ear pressed to a neon-pink phone with flashing lights. Two hours passed, and I was beginning to grow concerned for her as well. But I couldn't keep my eye on both sisters. Hell, I had a feeling Colette was all I could handle.

Taking a swig from the Corona I had resting on my knee, I glanced at the clock—1:07 a.m.—then back at the building, where a dim glow shone from Colette's window.

Still awake.

I glanced around, up and down Main Street. The full moon cast long shadows across the two-lane road, like fingers reaching desperately for its prey. The woods at the base of the mountains were bathed in a silver glow, the tops of the massive peaks a glimmering white. Beautiful, if not for the feeling of doom deep in my gut.

I checked the rearview mirror just as the OPEN sign flickering above Creed's Tavern turned off. A second later, my attention was pulled to a shadow moving in the courtyard ahead of me. My gaze darted to Colette's window, where I saw her silhouette move.

I sat up, a rush of adrenaline surging through my veins. I quickly scanned the street again—no new cars—then refocused on the courtyard, my gaze darting from tree to tree, bush to bush, searching the shadows.

Again, I saw it, movement ever so slight from one tree to the next. Definitely not someone leaving the B and B, but someone sneaking into it. It wasn't Jade, I decided, because why would she need to conceal her return to her room? I glanced up at the light glowing from Colette's room, and something in my stomach twisted.

I set the beer in the cupholder, my hand automatically sliding to the Sig Sauer on my hip.

After turning off the automatic interior lights, I slowly opened the truck door and slipped out. The night was still, cold, and eerily silent. There was no way I could close the door without being discovered, so I gently pushed it closed the best I could. My heart pounded as I slipped into the shadows, hugging the row of buildings.

Closing my eyes, I took a second to get my bearings, allowing my senses to adjust to the darkness, shifting my focus to hearing just as much as sight. I silently edged along the wall to the iron gate that led to the courtyard, where I paused and listened.

Nothing.

After another glance over my shoulder, I silently slipped through the gate, not bothering to close it, and disappeared into the shadows. Whoever had been there seconds before was there no longer. I was sure of it. My pace quickened as I searched the courtyard, looking for tracks or any sign of the intruder.

A spine-chilling scream broke the silence, turning the blood in my veins to ice.

Pulling the gun from my belt, I sprinted across the

cobblestone courtyard to the entry of the B and B. The red door was locked.

Fuck.

I darted around the side of the building where vines hugged a trellis that climbed the length of the brick. Holstering my gun, I gripped the brittle wood structure and began climbing, mentally bracing myself for impact when the thing would surely splinter from my weight. The trellis led to a window in the second bedroom—Jade's, I assumed—now missing a screen.

Climbing inside, I pulled my gun, my eyes adjusting to the pitch darkness. Not a single light flickered in the room, not a television, a radio, nothing. Either the lights had been turned off or the electricity cut.

I sprinted down the short hallway and entered the second suite just as a loud thud shook the windows, quickly followed by the sound of dead weight falling to the floor—a body being thrown against the wall. I knew this sound well.

A quick shuffle was followed by the violent noise of hand-to-hand combat—hard punches against bones, slaps against skin, swift inhales and exhales. I followed the muffled grunts to the bathroom, where, bathed in the moonlight streaming from the bathroom window, two silhouettes were engaged in a vicious fistfight.

"Colette!" I raised my gun, though I didn't know which silhouette belonged to her.

"James!" Her panicked scream was feral. Terrified.

My adrenaline surged into overdrive as I tried to discern which body was hers.

Colette's attacker took advantage of her momentary loss of focus, slamming her into the wall. Something liquid splatted across my face, the moment the moonlight caught hers.

I saw nothing but her in that moment.

Lunging across the room, I threw my body between Colette and her attacker, steeling myself for the brunt of the attack at my back. Instead, the room suddenly went quiet.

"Colette." My voice was low as I desperately ran my hands over her body, checking for wounds.

She was naked, I could tell, and wet. With blood or water, I wasn't sure.

23

James

"Colette. Say something."

"James." Panting, she whispered my name, desperately grasping for me.

"I'm here. Right here."

I wrapped my arms around her trembling body and pulled her close. The smell of vanilla and coconuts engulfed me as my hands ran over slippery wet skin. Soap. Not all blood, thank God.

My pulse roared in my ears. I wanted to calm her, help her to stop crying, but I knew I needed to check her over. Could she have been knifed? Shot? Could she have broken bones?

"Are you hurt?"

She didn't respond, simply nestled deeper into my chest as if she wanted to climb inside.

Experience told me that every second mattered, and I needed to ensure she was okay.

After gathering her like a baby in my arms, I slowly

lifted Colette off the floor and grabbed a clean towel from the stack. A groan escaped her lips as I lowered her onto the white bedspread, glowing under the streaming moonlight from a nearby window.

After quickly covering her naked body with the towel, I guided her against the stacked pillows. She winced with the movement, and white-hot anger shot through my veins.

"Colette, I need to check you, make sure you're okay. Is that all right?"

Keeping her eyes closed, she froze, her only movement the quiver of her lower lip.

She didn't fight me when I demanded to look her over. She was in shock and scared. Colette had been caught off guard in the shower when someone killed the lights and attacked her.

I started with her back, my anger exploding to nuclear proportions at the lumps and bruises already beginning to form across her skin. Her spine had taken a hard hit, probably by the corner of the wall, and I could only imagine it hurt like hell. Angry scratches, swollen and bloody, ran down her neck and arms. A bad one traversed the side of her cheek, which would possibly leave a scar.

Although she looked like she'd been in a car accident, there didn't appear to be any life-threatening wounds.

With that tiny piece of comfort, my mood shifted from unbridled rage to a simmering fury. I snatched a washcloth from the bathroom, wet it, then grabbed a few ice cubes from the mini-fridge in the corner. After securing the ice in the towel, I gently placed it on her lower lip that was already doubling in size.

Her hand swept mine as she took the makeshift ice pack. She looked embarrassed, needing space.

Unable to stand still, I turned and began pacing, trying

to give Colette the time she needed to gather herself. The room was so silent, I could hear the heavy inhale and exhale of her breath.

I felt like my head—and heart—were about to fucking explode.

"Okay . . . what happened?" I asked as softly as the adrenaline roaring through my body would allow.

Her throat worked a hard swallow. "I was in the shower . . . and suddenly the room went black. At first I thought there was some sort of electrical problem, but then the shower door swung open and . . . someone lunged inside after me."

"Did you see them?"

"Not a damn thing." Her jaw clenched. "I was washing my hair. Between the darkness of the room and the shampoo stinging my eyes, I was almost blind."

Yet she'd fought, blind and wet, as she was attacked in her most vulnerable state.

My heart slammed against my rib cage, adrenaline surging through my veins at the thought of what I was going to do when I found the asshole who did this to her. I had to force myself to focus.

"We fell out of the shower and fought until you came in."

"Did they have a weapon?"

"Not a gun. If they had, I'm sure I wouldn't be here right now."

"Neither would your attacker." I began pacing again. "Too loud. A gunshot in this small town wouldn't go unnoticed. Not having a gun was on purpose, I'm sure."

"They had me, James." Fury shone from her eyes like fire.

James.

Something about what had happened had erased the formality between us, the tension. Whether due to the fact that she was literally naked in front of me, or that I'd just saved her life, in that moment, we were one. It was us. A kind of take-it-or-leave-it moment.

And I took it. Hard.

"They had me," she said again, trembling with anger. "Had me on the floor."

"Colette, stop."

I sat on the edge of the bed, wanting to scoop her up until she stopped blaming herself and could think clearly again. I wanted to hold her, kiss her, tell her everything was going to be okay. But true to form, I froze when it came to anything that resembled emotions or real intimacy.

I placed my hand over hers. "You were completely caught off guard, wet and blind. You—"

"It's no excuse," she snapped. "I know how to fight. I'm . . ." She shook her head and turned away. "I'm off."

"Off?"

"Yeah. Off my game. I'm not myself."

"Why?" I asked, hoping she'd open up even more.

"It just feels like everything's off. My mind, body, everything."

"Because you can't control everything."

She blinked, staring at me, and something deep inside me flickered to life, an instinct.

Tell me, I thought. *Give me your pain.*

But Colette looked away.

I exhaled. "So you're off, okay. Well then, let's focus on finding whoever the hell just tried to kill you so it doesn't happen again. All right?"

She nodded.

"Tell me who here in Broken Ridge wants you dead."

"No one knows us here. Me or my sister."

"Leo Creed knows you."

"Leo Creed was not my attacker."

"How do you know that?"

"Whoever it was wasn't as tall as him."

"But you said you were blind—"

"And I said I know how to fight. I've been taught how to read an attacker. This person was around my height."

"You're tall."

"Not well over six foot, like Leo and his brother."

I scrubbed my hand over my mouth, already not liking this. Of course it wasn't Leo, because that was too obvious and too easy.

Suddenly, I stilled, my stomach dropping to my feet. "Did you make contact with Avery Bell?"

Colette dipped her head. Then her eyes slowly rounded, as she undoubtedly came to the same conclusion I just did.

Fuck.

I surged off the bed and resumed pacing. "I need you to tell me *everything*."

"I made contact this morning."

I spun around. "This morn—"

Furious, I closed my eyes and ran my hands over my face. I needed to get a damn grip. What was it about this woman that ignited so much emotion in me? I rolled my wrist, indicating that she continue.

"I called a number that only she and I know. She answered on the first ring."

"What did you say?"

"I asked how she was doing, and if she was safe. She said things were good, and that she had a job and had rented an apartment on the beach. I asked if she'd had any contact with the past, meaning Enrique . . . Her silence was answer enough."

"So, despite you helping Avery leave the country, she ran back into the arms of a ruthless drug lord."

"It happens in abusive relationships more than you'd think, James."

"It's bullshit is what it is."

"It's an addiction like drugs, money, fame, or anything else. Some people can't let go, despite the fact that it's literally killing them."

Memories flashed like a horror show behind my eyes. Heat rose up my back as I imagined Colette's face instead of my mother's. My insides started shaking.

"I asked where he was," she said softly, pulling me back from the past.

"What did she say?"

"She froze up."

"Froze up?"

"Yeah."

"*Fuck.*"

When asked about Enrique, Avery Bell froze up and then probably went directly to him, or his associates, and told him that Colette Archer, *private investigator*, was asking about him.

For me—Colette had done this *for me,* at my request. And then she was attacked. *Because* of me.

"She lives in California now, still under the identity I supplied her with. I really don't see her telling him, James. She and I developed a friendship, a mutual respect. She was so scared, truly wanted out—"

"It's not a coincidence!" I shouted, snapping at her like a child. I took a deep breath, then cleared my throat. "It's not a coincidence," I said again in a much calmer tone, hoping to simply erase the outburst. But it was never that easy. "What aren't you telling me? You're still keeping something from me."

"Do you just expect me to tell you my entire life story?"

"No, but I think you've got something big that you're hiding from me."

"Just like you think Enrique hopped on a flight from wherever he's hiding and attempted to eliminate me tonight?"

"It's not unfathomable. It could've been one of his men. And there was plenty of time for Avery Bell herself to catch a nonstop flight from California and do it for him."

"No." Colette vehemently shook her head. "No way."

"Why? Threats against someone they love make people do crazy shit."

"No. I just don't see it."

"Just like you didn't see your attacker come into the bathroom."

"Fuck you, James."

I was angry. At her for not telling me everything, and at myself for putting her into this mess. I was being an asshole.

Truth? I'd never felt so much emotion before that night. And I didn't like it, didn't know how to deal with it.

I should have known better than to get Colette involved in my hunt for Salazar. It was a rookie mistake.

Off her game? Colette was throwing me off mine, and I couldn't allow it. Because everything in my gut told me whoever attacked Colette that night hadn't gone far.

Colette had been lucky.

And I, of all people, knew how quickly your luck could run out.

24

James

Colette's skin was ashen, the bedside lamp casting ghostly shadows under her puffy, red-rimmed eyes. At my urging, she had remained on the bed where I'd placed her, but had forced herself up to a seated position, sitting cross-legged on the white comforter, her adrenaline not yet allowing her to relax.

A towel draped her bare shoulders, another wound around her torso, and yet another rested across her lap. She hadn't dressed yet, despite a visit to the bathroom where I heard the shake of multiple pill bottles. It concerned me, but now was definitely not the time to discuss anything that wasn't an immediate threat.

After making certain the windows and doors on the top floor were locked, I'd found the fuse box and turned the power back on, then checked every inch of the downstairs, ensuring everything else was locked and nothing was out of place. The intruder had one thing in mind—Colette. They had probably scoped out the location first, mapping the quickest route of access to her bedroom, via the trellis.

If I'd been a second later . . .

If no one had been watching out for her . . .

I'd never felt such a strong protective instinct, almost animalistic as I stared at Colette on that bed, battered, bruised, and scared, though trying to hide it. The tornado of fury that funneled within me at whoever had hurt her only meant one thing—the woman had gotten under my skin. And at that point, I didn't care anymore. I didn't want to assess it, to try to talk myself away from her. All that mattered was that I kept her safe.

I'd figure everything else out later—like her sister, who barreled into Colette's room like an M67 grenade.

The door burst open, slamming against the wall. I spun around and will never forget the look in Jade's eyes as she leaped through the air at me like a crazed animal.

She intended to kill me. There was no doubt in my mind. And she might have if her sister hadn't screamed for her to stop.

The tension in the room was palpable as I shifted to my toes in an offensive position, between the sisters, keeping one eye on the one who obviously thought I was Colette's attacker.

"Stop, Jade!" Colette barked in a gritty voice. "*Stop.* He's safe."

Safe.

I laser-focused on Jade, attuned to every twitch of her eyes, every move of her fingers, poised for a fight. Although I was at least a full foot taller than Jade, she eyed me back with a fearless ferocity that immediately earned her my utmost respect.

"Jade. Calm," Colette said, her voice fading to a whisper.

Finally, Jade relaxed her stance and nodded. I dipped my chin and did the same.

Jade rushed to her sister's side, and I was impressed by the younger sister's composure.

"You okay?" Her voice was sharp enough to cut glass. "I saw the screen in my room was gone—are you okay?"

"Yes. Yes."

"Is that your blood on the towel downstairs?"

Colette glanced at me, and Jade followed her gaze.

I nodded. "I cleaned her up."

Jade refocused on her older sister. There were no tears, no sympathy. Once she was sure her sister was physically okay, Jade demanded a replay of the evening, from both Colette's perspective and mine. She sat stoically as we delivered the update.

All signs pointed to someone wanting to silence Colette after inquiring about Enrique Salazar's location, but nothing felt concrete. There was more to the story, and I didn't like being shut out.

"Someone needs to talk here. I need to know exactly what's going on," I said, pacing at the foot of the bed.

Jade glanced at Colette, obviously weighing what to tell me. This pissed me off.

Focusing on Jade, I said, "Your sister could have died tonight. Tell me what the fuck is going on. What does Leo Creed have that you want?"

"Information," Colette said quickly, before her sister could speak.

"On what?"

"A missing girl."

I frowned. "Tell me everything."

"Her name is Sarah Kay, age nineteen, from Butte. She told her friends she was going for a drive and never came back. No sign or trace of her anywhere. The case went cold."

"Then why are you picking it up?"

"Her parents live in New York, where she was born and raised. They'd heard of my firm, called me up, and I accepted the case. Here I am."

"Bullshit."

"You don't believe me?"

"No. And I'm two fucking seconds away from calling the cops about what happened tonight." To prove it, I pulled my phone from my pocket.

"*Stop.*"

I froze, cocking a brow.

"I'll give you Enrique Salazar."

"How?"

Colette looked at Jade, then nodded to the door. After shooting me a glance laced with warning, Jade exited the room, quietly closing the door behind her.

"I know one of his secure locations," Colette said. "Only a few people know about this spot, including Avery Bell."

"You're going to give me his location? Just like that?"

"Yes."

"What do you want in return?"

"Your discretion."

My eyes narrowed. "You want me to keep what happened tonight—your attack—a secret."

"Yes . . . and for you to leave town immediately."

"Why?"

"That's my business."

"Your business almost got you killed tonight, Colette."

"No different from yours."

I jabbed my fingers through my hair, and with a guttural groan began pacing again. "You could have *died.*"

"So?"

I stopped and spun around. "So? How can you say that?"

"Everyone dies."

"You got a death wish, Colette Archer?"

She looked down, and that instinct, that red flag, roared to life again as her lids dipped low over red-rimmed eyes.

Exhaling, I wrapped my hand around the back of my neck and stared at the woman, half-naked, bloodied, bruised, but somehow no less dignified. Colette had a strength and ruthless tenacity that I admired.

I crossed the room, then sat on the edge of the bed. She glanced at me. We didn't say anything for a moment as I contemplated the current situation.

Finally, I said, "No."

"No?"

"No, I don't agree to the deal. I'm not going to leave."

"Then I'm not going to talk."

"Listen, I don't know your story or the type of men you've had in your life, but no man worth anything would leave a woman he knew was in imminent danger."

My mother's face flashed through my mind, and a knot caught in my throat.

"Are you saying that you're willing to forgo getting information on Enrique Salazar just to ensure my safety?"

"Yes."

Surprise flickered in her eyes, and I wondered how deep her distrust in men went.

"But hear me, Colette. I'll find out what you and your sister are hiding. I can promise you that. For now, you keep your information because I'm not leaving. You, Colette Archer, are stuck with me until I see you safely home."

"You can't do that."

"I just did."

She grabbed my forearm, a feral panic flickering in her eyes. "You don't understand. You'll—"

"I don't have to understand. I just need to keep you safe."

"You're going to regret this, James."

I removed her hand from my arm and held it in mine. "I'd regret walking away more, and that's the absolute truth." Because I'd made a vow long ago to never leave a woman in need again.

"You're crazy," she said in a breathy whisper.

I leaned forward, nearly nose to nose with her. "Then I've met my match."

The door opened, shattering the moment between us.

Jade stepped inside, her patience cashed out, and she began crossing the room. "What's the plan? I—"

"No." I stood, cutting her off. "She needs to rest, sleep. It's enough for the night."

There was a break in Jade's stride as she considered her sister, now leaning against the pillows, her eyelids heavy and mouth downturned as if it simply took too much energy to lift her lips.

I jerked my chin to the door, and Jade followed, meeting me in the hallway.

I lowered my voice. "You'll stay up all night?"

"You'll keep watch outside all night?"

"Yes, ma'am."

"Then yes, sir."

I took one last look at Colette, her eyes now closed.

"All night," I told Jade before stepping onto the staircase.

"James," she whispered.

My hand on the rail, I paused and turned.

Jade stared at me a moment, then dipped her chin.

She didn't need to say it.

25

Colette

One year earlier

I can still smell the lilies Jade brought that evening, their familiar scent carrying on the autumn breeze. Sweet. Fragrant. Innocent.

A candle and two martinis separated my sister and me at the Manhattan rooftop restaurant we met at every Friday night, rain or shine, good day or bad. We never missed our Friday-night date, regardless of work, men, or travel. We made it work, no matter what. One time, Jade had an interview in DC and was delayed overnight. I flew to Virginia and met her at her hotel for our Friday-night date.

We *never* missed it.

That night, though, was different.

Despite the warm temperature and clear sky, the atmosphere was dark, the energy between us gray and haunting.

After having our usual dinner—a poppyseed chicken

salad for me and a bacon cheeseburger for Jade—we settled back against our seats, wondering who would address the elephant in the room first.

She did. It was always Jade.

Guilt, I assumed. Guilt had changed my sister by that time, changed her into someone I had to relearn how to deal with, to communicate with. Guilt had transformed a young, bright-eyed, optimistic, ambitious, beautiful young woman into a dark, martial-arts loving, ass-kicking tattoo artist who wandered aimlessly through life.

Guilt had taken over my sister's life and turned her into a totally different person. As it had done for me too, just in a very different way, I guess.

She'd worn all black for the evening, with a pair of leather skinny pants that turned every head—male and female—as she'd walked in. A low-cut blouse clung to her generous breasts under a faded jean jacket she'd likely made from scraps of old jeans she no longer fit into.

We'd both lost weight over the years. Me more than Jade.

I, on the other hand, had come straight from the office wearing a black pencil-skirt suit. Black blouse, black jacket, black heels. It was an all-black kind of night.

Jade drained her martini, set it down, and flicked her hand to the waiter, who hadn't taken his eyes off our table all night.

"Another, Miss Archer?"

"Two," she said, nodding to my half-empty glass. "And two bowls of strawberries with vanilla ice cream on the side —and whipped cream. Extra whipped cream. A *lot* of whipped cream."

"I'm sorry, ma'am, I don't think we have any fresh straw—"

"Find some then. We'll wait."

The waiter blinked, then nodded. "Yes, ma'am. I'll see what the chef can do."

I flashed the poor waiter a smile and a wink, a subliminal *Don't worry; I'll triple your tip.* He dipped his chin and scurried off, undoubtedly trying to figure out where to get a basket of fresh strawberries in the middle of October.

We didn't speak, waiting for the bartender to bring our fresh drinks before ripping off the Band- Aid and exposing the wound that had never healed.

Once the vodka was delivered, we sipped simultaneously.

A few minutes passed with me staring at the city horizon, and Jade slowly circling her finger over the top of her martini glass.

"Twenty-nine. Can you believe they'd almost be thirty years old? *Fourteen years*, Colette."

"It's been thirteen years. One year until fourteen. Not fourteen yet."

I don't know why, but this felt significant to me. Like fourteen set everything in stone. I thought of this mark in my life like most women thought of their fortieth birthday, a milestone that no one wants to remember. One that most women had been dreading since birth.

My fortieth would have nothing on one year from today.

My gaze shifted to a pair of blue eyes staring into my soul.

"You're so fucked up, Cole," she said thoughtfully.

"No, I'm not."

"Yes, you are."

"Most people wouldn't consider someone who single-handedly started a seven-figure-a-year company from scratch to be fucked up."

"Tell that to Elon Musk."

I didn't laugh. Instead, I tightened my grip around my martini glass. "When are *you* going to get a real job, Jade? Put down roots somewhere?"

I expected her trademark smartass, witty response to deflect from the topic that I always waited until two martinis to bring up with my little sister. Usually, she didn't take the question well.

That night was different. In fact, so different, she answered me directly.

"I don't know, Cole . . . I don't know. My jobs pay the bills, but . . ."

I waited through the silence. Jade always came back around to the point. She just needed time.

"But I don't want to be a sixty-year-old tattoo artist slash martial arts instructor."

"Do they even have sixty-year-old martial arts instructors?"

Her brows arched. "You've never met Bo. She'd flip you on your ass and tie your hands behind your back before you even realized your Louboutins were flying through the air. Almost seventy years old, and the woman is absolutely terrifying."

"Let's not become Bo, Jade."

She laughed, but it didn't reach her eyes.

"Work for me," I said—for the umpteenth time.

"No," she said—for the umpteenth time.

"Why? You're one of the best private investigators I've ever had the privilege of working a case with. And you already own half the company anyway."

"I still hate that you did that."

"You and me, Jade. Because it's you and me."

And because I wanted to ensure my little sister was set

up for life, but she didn't need to know that. Every decision I'd made in the last thirteen years revolved around ensuring Jade was taken care of if anything happened to me. In one way or another. Nothing could pull me away from my little sister, not wild horses . . . not even death.

Jade was mine. Mine to take care of, mine to protect. Whether in human form or not, I would spend infinity protecting my sister.

"Well, I don't want to work in a stupid office," she snapped defensively. "You know that. And besides," she said, pissed now. "Don't think I don't know that the only reason you started your firm was to create a beard for what you really love to do—hacking. Tell me, how long did it take to hack into the FBI's database?"

I shifted uncomfortably in my seat.

"A few weeks? Years? Don't think I don't wonder if you got what you were looking for. All the time—all the fucking time—I wonder if you got the information."

"And yet you've never asked."

Not once. Not one single time did my sister ask for the information I risked my life to find. And find it, I did, and I had every word of those two files memorized.

"And you've never asked why I haven't."

We stared at each other, a knot catching in my throat. Because we dealt with the past differently. I know that now.

"Anyway . . ." Jade sniffed, picked up her martini, and took a deep swallow.

I did too. "I can teach you how to hack, you know. Computer science. Give you something useful to do with your time that doesn't involve split lips and broken bones."

She shook her head. "No. That's your thing. You're the smart sister." She winked, then sighed. "I've thought about . . ."

"What?" Something about her tone had me leaning forward.

"I've thought about becoming a cop."

"*What*?" Heads turned at the shocked squeal that came out of me.

Her eyes met mine with that defiance I loved so much about her. "Yeah. A cop, Cole. And working my way up to become a detective, maybe eventually the FBI."

"What the—"

"In their sexual crimes unit."

My blood went cold. "No." I had to physically restrain myself from surging out of my chair and shaking her. Hard. "*No*, Jade. The answer is no."

"You can't tell me what to do, Cole. Regardless of what you think, you are *not* my mother."

No, I wasn't our mother. I wouldn't put a gun in my mouth and pull the trigger the same week our father died of a heart attack. A heart that never healed back quite right, he'd said, the day before he was found dead in the janitor's closet at his clinic, clutching a photo in his hand.

"And how dare you tell me what I can and can't do with my life, anyway." Jade took a deep sip of her martini, and I wondered how many she'd had before meeting me. "Who the hell are you to judge me, Cole? When are you going to quit whoring yourself out in some sick, twisted way to get affection?"

I stilled, and again my grip tightened around the stem of my martini glass. Slowly, I began counting backward in my head, although I couldn't make it past four before my thoughts started swirling.

Does she know about my late-night trips to the trashy airport motel? Has she followed me?

We stared at each other like two boxers in a ring.

"How many men have you had sex with in the last ten years?" she asked, her eyes narrowing.

A mad cackle burst out of me as I lost my cool.

"Fine. The last *year.* How many men, Cole?"

"Why are you so interested in what I do behind closed doors?"

"Because I've seen the fucking condoms you keep buried in your purse and in your car. In your bathroom trash can, in the kitchen trash can. I know exactly what you're doing when it takes you thirty minutes to return my call or text on a weekend night. And if I had to guess, you actually pause to check the text while riding your poor victim of the night."

I surprised myself by not exploding. Instead, I stilled, her words cutting me like a knife.

She was right to call me a whore. I didn't know what my number was in the last thirteen years, ten years, last year, or the last six months.

"At least I have male interaction," I said in a cool, measured tone. "Have you even had a date in ten years, Jade? Let a man touch you?"

I sipped, and she sighed.

"We're so fucked up, Cole."

"It's because we never got closure."

Her eyes met mine, and I stared back, my pulse quickening. It was time. I felt it.

"We're never going to get over this, Jade. You know that, right?"

She didn't nod. She didn't need to.

I reached into my purse and pulled out an envelope. It felt like fire in my hands as I placed it on my lap. There was no going back after this. But the thing is . . . we'd never even gone forward.

As if my arm moved on its own, I slid the envelope

across the table, exposing what I'd spent every night of the last thirteen years working on. The gritty deals of the information I'd gathered, and the plan I'd put together to commence exactly one year from that day. The weapons we'd use to get it done.

I watched my little sister open the envelope, my heart exploding with violent pumps of blood.

An agonizing two minutes dragged by as Jade read the details of my plan. When she looked up at me, I knew.

She's in.

And it only took a terminal diagnosis for me to finally have the guts to put the wheels of my plan in motion.

26

James

Present day

At three in the morning, Broken Ridge reminded me of the deserted towns we'd cross in northern Iraq, buildings and homes completely intact but deserted due to the surrounding unrest.

Haunting.

After two perimeter checks of the bed and breakfast—one to ensure Colette's attacker wasn't waiting in the shadows, and another to search for any signs or tracks that might lead to where he or she were hiding out, I walked down Main Street, mentally cataloging every detail of the buildings, every vehicle, every storefront. Creed's Tavern was closed down for the night, not a light on anywhere in the building.

Though Colette, Jade, and I were operating under the assumption that the attack was somehow related to Colette's communication with Avery Bell, I couldn't shake the feeling that Leo Creed was somehow tied into everything. But how? The only common thread between him and Enrique Salazar was the drug fentanyl. Both were known dealers, though one much more infamous. Did they know each other? Work together, maybe? And what the hell did the Archer sisters want with him?

It was then that a more sinister thought hit me. Leo had something of value to Colette, something she fiercely protected and wanted to keep off the radar of law enforcement.

Could Leo Creed have Avery Bell? Holding her captive? For Enrique Salazar, maybe?

Colette had mentioned she and Avery became friends.

Or, if the story of the missing woman were true, could Leo be holding Sarah Kay captive? It was an interesting thought, and one that I needed to unravel over a stiff cup of coffee.

At four o'clock in the morning, after ensuring Colette was in no immediate danger, I made my way back to my truck. While keeping my eye on the B and B, I pulled out my phone.

"Where the fuck have you been?" I snarled into the phone when Blaze answered.

"Sleeping."

"Bullshit. I've been calling you for two days."

"I've been busy. Got pulled into a fire."

"You have no idea the heat you're going to feel from me if you don't have what I asked you for."

"You know it's six in the morning here, right? On Monday morning."

"Yep, and I know you've been at your desk since four."

He hesitated because I was right. "So . . . you're taking some vacation days, huh? In Montana?"

"Where's my report about Colette Archer?"

"It's not r—"

"Give me what you have now. CliffsNotes."

"CliffsNotes is going to be tough."

"Why?"

"Let's just say there are a lot of skeletons in the Archer sisters' closets."

"What do you mean?"

Papers rustled in the background. "I'll start from the beginning. To recap, you asked me to dig up anything I could on Colette Archer; her sister Jade Archer; and their parents. Travel history, criminal records—"

"Get on with it, Blaze."

"Colette, raised in the Bronx, born to David and Marlie Archer, is the oldest of four sisters—"

"Wait. Did you say *four*?"

"Correct. Colette is two years older than her sister Jade, and three years older than her twin sisters, Presley and Anna. Both deceased."

"Deceased?"

"Yep. According to the Soundview police report, both girls were murdered on the night of their sixteenth birthday, almost exactly fourteen years ago today, which would be their thirtieth birthdays."

My head spun as a million tiny pieces started to come together. "Murdered, how? What happened?"

"According to multiple reports, transcripts, and interviews I spent an hour scouring through, the story goes something like this. On the twins' sixteenth birthday, the family had a party for them at a nearby park—"

"Who was there?"

"Family only. Colette, Jade, and their parents. After the party, the twins took their new car to the mall, then met up with some friends at a house party. According to records, these friends—Bryan Carter, Joey Flores, and Brock Adams —were not model citizens, to say the least. Drinking, drugs, petty theft, the whole nine yards. Bad guys. The records show everyone at the party decided to get tattoos, this confirmed by the manager of the tattoo shop they went to. Afterward, they went back to the house. According to the confession—"

The confession.

"—drugs were offered, and everything got out of hand. Anna and Presley were raped repeatedly, strangled in some sick BDSM act, and eventually died from asphyxiation. The ME report claims they both had large amounts of alcohol and GHB in their systems. Both girls were also"—he cleared his throat—"sodomized."

My lips parted in shock and I glanced up at the window, where a slender silhouette stood, backlit by a dim golden light. Although I couldn't see Colette's face, our eyes met directly. I knew it. Goose bumps ran like ants over my skin as if she somehow sensed I'd just found out about her past.

The curtains fluttered, and the silhouette moved away.

I blinked, refocusing on the call. "What happened to the guys who did it?"

"They were just seventeen years old at the time, but Bryan Carter and Joey Flores were tried as adults, convicted of second-degree murder, and sentenced to forty years in prison, where they are both still currently serving their sentences. Before you ask, yes, I confirmed this."

"Only second degree?"

"Their attorney argued that the boys didn't mean to actually kill the girls. It just got out of hand."

"But they fucking meant to rape them." My fist clenched

around the phone. "You mentioned three guys. What about the third guy, Brock Adams?"

"He was at the party but didn't rape the girls, just watched. He was referred to as one of three watchers in the report. The other two weren't identified."

"Watchers? Fucking sick fucks. And let me guess, they also didn't call the cops."

"Bingo. Did nothing to stop it. He was charged as an accessory, his fifteen-year sentence reduced by ten after providing a full confession and ratting his friends out."

"Where is this Brock Adams now?"

"Not sure."

"Find him."

"Will do." There was a brief pause as Blaze made a note before continuing. "The trial went on for months, gained national attention. Colette and Jade's father died of a heart attack shortly after the sentencing. The mother found out she had breast cancer soon after and committed suicide, leaving Colette and Jade without any living relatives. Colette was nineteen and legally adopted Jade, only seventeen at the time. They've been inseparable ever since."

I was so dumbfounded by what I was hearing, I hadn't realized I'd quit speaking.

"In terms of financials, Colette Archer is worth an estimated three point six million dollars—solely due to the success of her company, Archer and Archer, Inc.—which she spends mostly on charitable giving, shoes, handbags, travel, and trips to the spa."

"What travel?"

"Not much. In the last six months, Colette has only left New York three times. One, a solo trip to meet a client in Virginia, and the other two with her sister. One trip to

Miami, and one to Lake Placid in upstate New York last week."

"What's in Miami?"

"A fifteen-thousand-dollar bill at the Mandarin Hotel. Girls' weekend, best I can surmise, based on the number of cocktails consumed."

"And Lake Placid?"

"Another weekend getaway with her dear sister is my guess."

"What charities does she donate to?"

"Various breast cancer charities and RAINN."

"What's rain?"

"RAINN—Rape, Abuse, and Incest National Network. It's the largest anti-sexual-violence organization in the nation."

Breast cancer research for her mother, and an anti-sexual-violence advocate for her twin sisters. There was a lot more to Colette than met the eye. Little did I know what Super-Blaze had in store for me next.

"Though I should note, there are some . . . expenses that stood out to me."

"Like what?"

"Colette Archer frequents the Mahalo Motel a few miles from LaGuardia Airport."

I frowned. I was familiar with the Mahalo Motel, a hot spot for drug deals and other closed-door activities. Definitely not Colette's scene—or so I thought.

"How frequent?" I asked.

"Almost every single weekend."

My stomach rolled.

"According to her transactions, she goes to the bar, sometimes only ordering one drink, sometimes picking up someone else's tab too . . ."

My heart started to pound.

"And this is always followed by a motel room rental. By the hour."

My heart stopped. I was speechless. The thought of Colette being either a hooker or a whore exploded in my head like a nuclear bomb.

"I'll send you everything in a report," Blaze said. "You can go through it at your leisure . . . you know, on your flight back home this morning."

"Right."

"James?"

"What?"

"Considering your recent reprimand and current standing with Clancy, I feel the need to advise you to cancel your *vacation* and stay as far away from these sisters as possible. I don't know why you're awake right now or why you're in Montana, but I know it's not a vacation. And I get the feeling you're doing anything but relaxing."

"Blaze—"

"No, *listen*. These sisters have a damn dark past that involves the Feds, and you're on thin ice as is. You're asking for trouble, brother."

"One, I am not your brother. Two, until I'm either fired or get transferred, you take orders from me, not the other way around. Do you understand?"

"Sir."

"Good, because I've got two more for you. Look up Sarah Kay, nineteen years old, born and raised in New York, currently residing in Butte, Montana. She's gone missing, reportedly last seen in this area two weeks ago. Confirm that. I also want you to send me everything we have on Leo Creed."

"Leo Creed . . . the Montana fentanyl bust, right?"

"Right. I want to know if there are any connections between him and Enrique Salazar."

"Holy shit, dude. You are *off* that case. James, you're going to get fired—"

I killed the call, tossed the phone across the cab, and stared up at the silhouette in the window as my stomach rolled.

What the hell had I gotten this beautiful, innocent woman into?

Because she was innocent . . . right?

27

Colette

They say one minute of hand-to-hand combat is physically more exhausting and taxing on your body than a forty-five-minute jog. However, that statistic doesn't include the mental and emotional toll from engaging in violent combat, and it certainly doesn't take into account a body that is already fighting for its life.

After the attack in the bathroom, my body felt like a wet blanket while my brain was spinning on overdrive. I'd taken double my pills, including an extra one for pain.

I'm slightly embarrassed to admit I'd never been in a physical altercation before that night. In the Bronx, where I grew up, fighting was a common resolution to problems—between both men and women. By the fifth grade, I'd seen more fistfights on the playground than most saw in their entire lives.

It never sat well with me.

Watching two intelligent human beings resort to intentionally causing others physical pain in response to conflict affected me deeply. It was like watching two animals using the only thing they considered of value, their ability to hurt, instead of their ability to think through a problem. I vowed to never be one of those animals.

Jade had gotten into a fight once in eleventh grade—with a boy. My sister met heartthrob Quincy Hull in the alley between the gym and the cafeteria at the prearranged time of three fifteen, and she proceeded to break Quincy's nose in two separate places after learning he'd forced himself on Christy Botner after she'd had too much to drink. It was the talk of the neighborhood for weeks.

Unable to bear the constant chastising from his friends for being beaten up by a girl, Quincy dropped out of school and was never seen again.

I had a long talk with my sister that night, and to this day, I believe Jade thinks she did the right thing. As much as I hated to admit it, I understood.

Needless to say, Jade quickly became the most popular kid in school, while I remained the nerdy girl who used her brains and wits over her fists.

This difference between us was never more evident than the night I was attacked in the shower.

Jade had changed out of her boho floral dress and into a pair of leggings and running shoes, a more appropriate wardrobe for the ass-kicking she was going to lay down if anyone stepped through my bedroom door.

We'd stayed up into the wee hours of the morning, discussing and analyzing the attack, then weighing our options.

Though the attack had shaken Jade to her core, she didn't show it. My sister had an uncanny way of hiding her emotions, tucking them away under lock and key so she could analyze a situation dispassionately. Black and white.

Facts and figures. She tried to hide it, but I could see it in the flush of her cheeks, the tremble of her hand. If James hadn't promised to keep watch outside, she would have been on the hunt, and very likely ended up beaten to a pulp like me.

My sister was almost as protective as she was vengeful. Almost.

Jade agreed with James that all signs pointed to Enrique Salazar. But I wasn't so sure.

After every second of the night had been analyzed and dissected, Jade turned off the light and began her watch on the other side of my door, insisting I get some rest.

Despite the cocktail of medications, I couldn't sleep. Instead, I found myself sitting by the window, wine in one hand, bloodied tissue in the other, watching the man who saved my life circle the building over and over, ensuring nothing else happened to me that night. Finally, he climbed into his truck, and I watched him as he watched over me.

I couldn't tear my gaze away, my emotions ranging from hostile loathing for the man who wouldn't leave me alone, to an exigent desire to be close to him. Flames of interest, lust, slowly licked through my core in a way that was impossible to ignore. I'd never had a man treat me the way he did, stand up for me—and *to* me—the way he did. Shield my body with his, willing to take a bullet for me. Give me those goddamn butterflies the way he did.

I couldn't remember the last time a man held my interest the way he did.

The dreamy image of James's face was the last thing I saw before finally falling asleep sometime after six in the morning, knowing that I wouldn't have been able to if he hadn't been watching over me. The power in that fact made me almost as uncomfortable as the fact that he could wreck everything for me.

I slept through most of the day. I was beginning to feel sicker, weaker, the cancer likely spreading and taking its toll.

When I awoke sometime past two in the afternoon, my first thought was not of the attack, but of James. Despite feeling like I'd been run over by a Mack truck, I hurried to the window and was comforted when I saw his truck.

Nerves bubbled up and I began to pace, finding myself digging through my pills. After eating a handful of tablets and splashing cold water on my face, I attempted to start the day.

Gripping the banister for support, I slowly descended the staircase, pausing midway at the muffled voices coming from the library. I recognized one as my sister's voice.

Frowning, I tiptoed down the remaining steps and peeked around the arched doorway.

"Morning, sunshine." A shit-eating grin brightened Jade's face as she looked up from the laptop she was hovered over.

My receptionist/office manager Kareena Bashar shot to her feet like a child with her hand caught in the cookie jar, her brown eyes widening as she scanned the scratches and bruises that covered my arms and legs.

The look I shot my sister drained every ounce of energy I had, but Jade only smiled.

"Colette . . . are you okay—"

Jade yanked at Kareena's sleeve, cutting her off and pulling her back down to the chair she'd been sitting in.

"Kareena's here for the next few days to focus on work so you don't have to. So you can focus on our *vacation*, sister."

My mouth dropped open and my gaze flicked back and forth between Jade and the employee that I absolutely despised. Of all the things I'd expected to wake up to that morning, Kareena was not one of them.

Jade quickly continued before I could explode into a million little pieces. "Kareena will be staying in the third room on the far side of the building, and will be at your beck and call for anything involving work, including the Sarah Kay case. She'll be available for you to drop in and check on all things Archer and Archer, Inc. when your neurotic, control-freak ass can't stop thinking about work."

"*Jade—*" The sudden rush of blood to my head surely wasn't healthy under the circumstances.

"Colette," my maddening sister said sharply, interrupting me. "You have more important things to focus on."

Kareena nodded feverishly. "That's right. Jade told me you've been too stressed. She turned on your out-of-office email response, and I'm going to pick up where you've left off on the Samson case. I've already—"

"*Absolutely* n—"

"It's *settled*, Colette," my sister snapped in a tone that reminded me of our mother. "Work is going to be the death of you if you're not careful."

The subtext to her warning hit me hard.

Jade was right. Aside from James, work had been my biggest distraction. And the last thing I needed to be at that moment was unfocused.

Knowing she'd won that battle, Jade nodded, then stood. "Appears you could use some coffee while you sit down and review the Samson case notes with Kareena before she retreats to her room."

Biting my tongue, I stared at the woman who'd flown two thousand miles to help me out, and decided I still hated her.

28

Colette

"Son of a bitch."

"Need some wine?" Jade launched a bottle of red through the air as I turned from the window.

I caught it in midair, considered, then tossed it back. The last few days, my medications had taken me on a bad trip that swung from vomiting every few hours to being absolutely ravenous but unable to eat. My body truly was a wonderland. And not in a John Mayer kind of way.

"No," I snapped back. "I need that bastard to quit watching us."

"You mean the bastard who saved your life?"

"He didn't save my life."

Jade snorted. "Take the wine." She launched it back. "And maybe a Xanax to help with this vile mood you're in."

It was just past eleven, a cold, clear night. My entire body ached like an infected tooth, while the persistent headache was like two machetes piercing my brain. My back hurt too, a new pain.

James Black had yet to leave the front of the bed and breakfast. He was right—I was stuck with him, and this fact was leaving me with all sorts of mixed emotions.

I'd spent the afternoon in and out of Epsom salt baths to alleviate the dull, aching pain pulsating through my body with each heartbeat. The attack had left me more sore than it had given me bruises, and barely able to move.

When I wasn't soaking, I was pacing or lurking outside of Kareena's room, checking in on my cases when Jade wasn't watching. True to form, my assistant was eager to please, working like a madwoman so I could relax on my "vacation."

"Forget about him," Jade said, sipping her wine.

I regarded my sister across the bedroom. Her bare feet were kicked up on one end of the loveseat next to the bed, her head resting on the other, a mug of wine balancing on her stomach as she stared at the wall as she usually does when she's lost in thought.

The TV remained off. Neither of us watched TV much.

It never ceased to amaze me how the woman could relax in the most stressful situations. I, on the other hand, was a train wreck who had been contemplating a quick trip to the local motel more times that I cared to admit. I needed to blow off steam. Refocus.

I needed something.

"Forget about him?" I said, more curtly than intended. "How can you say that? I'm supposed to meet Leo for the security footage of the days surrounding Sarah Kay's disappearance in two hours. Do you understand what we're about to do, Jade? If by telling me to forget the federal agent watching us, you're suggesting we should reschedule this whole thing, you are fu—"

Jade kicked her feet to the floor, deftly balancing her

mug, and narrowed her stare on me. "You need to take a deep breath, Cole. You're emotional. I don't like it. And I'm not saying we should reschedule this trip. It's happening—a jacked-up federal agent watching us or not. Kareena is handling everything work-related, so you need to forget that too. *Focus.* You'll figure this out as you always do. I'm one hundred percent sure of that. Don't let this guy get under your skin so damn much . . ."

Her head tilted, then her eyes rounded as a massive grin spread across her face.

"Wait . . . you *like* him. Oh my God." She popped off the couch like a jack in the box, not spilling a drop of wine. "You *like* him."

"No." I turned to face the window, but was spun back around by the sudden vise-like grip on my elbow.

"I'm right, aren't I? Of course I am. James Black is hot as shit. And you *like* him."

"You've lost your damn mind, sister. I can say with complete honesty that I don't like him. In fact, I despise him."

"But you're *attracted* to him. Admit it."

"No, I'm—"

"Go invite him in. Poor guy's been out there all night. The man saved your damn life, Cole, and has spent the last twenty hours checking the perimeter of the building to make sure you're safe. He deserves more than your hatred. Go . . . bake him a cookie or offer him coffee, or dinner, or a drink. Put on the assless chaps. Do something domestic for a change."

"I'm not having this conversation right now."

"Fine." She dropped my arm and spun on her heel, heading for the door. "I'll go invite him in myself."

"Take one more step, and I'll tell the world about how you peed your pants on the zip line."

She froze, then turned and jabbed her finger into the air. "Humans don't have wings for a reason, Cole. We aren't meant to fly."

"Why won't you admit you're terrified of heights?"

"Why won't you admit you're attracted to Thor down there?"

I gasped. "He totally does look like Chris Hemsworth, doesn't he?"

"Spitting image, I'm telling you."

I sighed. "Listen, my feelings toward this man are totally irrelevant right now. He needs to leave."

Jade pushed past me, flipped open the curtains, and put herself on full display for the man. She frowned, jerking her chin back. "What the hell?"

"What?" I nudged her to the side and peered around the curtain.

James Black had left the confines of the cab and was lying on his back in the bed of his truck.

"Is he *sleeping* there?" she squeaked.

I glanced up at the starlit sky, checking for rain. Because that was what mattered at that moment—that my stalker didn't get wet.

"The motel is booked." I'd called. Trust me.

"I can't believe he's sleeping in the back of his freaking truck. We've got a damn couch downstairs." Disapproval flashed in Jade's eyes as she glared at me. "I'm going outside."

"No." I slipped into my Birkenstocks and grabbed a throw from the bed. Flinging it around my shoulders, I strode across the room, cutting off her exit. "Stay. This is my problem. I'll deal with it."

"You can't deal with *everything*, Cole," she yelled to my back as I jogged down the staircase.

My brain was telling me to stop, assess, calm down. But between my aching ribs and pounding headache, I didn't listen, which should have been my first red flag that I was, in fact, losing it.

I pushed out the door, stomped across the courtyard, and shoved past the metal gate, sending it popping on its hinges.

As usual, Broken Ridge was a ghost town. Not a single person, dog, or black bear sniffing around the trash cans. Only Creed's Tavern, dimly lit across the street.

I stomped up to the truck. "What the hell are you doing?" I barked, leaning over the side of the bed of the truck.

James didn't even flinch, almost as if he'd been expecting me. With his eyes closed, ankles crossed, and hands threaded behind his head, he said, "Trying to get a few minutes of sleep."

"Here?"

"The motel is booked, and an unruly pair of surreptitious sisters reserved the entire bed and breakfast."

"That's a big word for someone who sleeps in the back of their truck."

"That's a lot of attitude from the woman who would be dead if not for the man in the back of this truck."

Sighing, I rolled my eyes. "Why don't you go to the next town over or something? Surely, there are rooms there."

"That's an hour away. Don't feel like driving an hour just to sleep."

"This is better than that?"

Finally, his eyes opened. He turned his head and looked

at me, his green eyes twinkling in the moonlight like a panther on the hunt. Alert. Ready. Intrigued.

Interested.

"Not much is better than this." He returned his focus to the sky. "See the Big Dipper?"

I looked up, taking a moment to find the formation in the million stars twinkling around a bilious moon, seemingly so close I could climb a tree and touch it.

For a moment, I was awestruck at the sheer size of the sky, of the power of the moonlight illuminating the world below. It reminded me of seeing the ocean for the first time, the power of the vastness that disappeared into the horizon so many miles away. I felt small, just as I had then, underneath the infinite space above me. Humbled, as I'd been then.

It was then that I heard the silence, or perhaps listened to it for the first time. The beautiful sound of nothing, except it wasn't nothing. It was the cool breeze rustling through the brittle leaves of the trees that lined the street, the crickets singing under the moonlight, the sound of nature in the mountains behind us, the spicy scent of fall in the air.

It was as if I'd been transported to another world.

"Hungry?" he asked, and my nose detected another scent.

Pizza.

My gaze followed the mouth-watering aroma to a cardboard box tucked under the toolbox of his truck. My stomach audibly growled, reminding me that I hadn't eaten since the day before.

But I really didn't have time to eat. I needed to think, plan, assess . . .

I glanced at the bed and breakfast, where Jade stood in the window, making obscene gestures with her hands.

I quickly looked back. "What kind?"

"Triple meat, extra cheese."

"How long has it been sitting there?"

"Can't remember."

I looked back over my shoulder at Jade's bare white ass pressed against the window. "Sure. I'll take a piece."

He sat up as I stepped to the tailgate.

As I gripped the gate, two strong hands slid under my arms and lifted me into the air. James's head was next to mine, that alpha-male scent awakening a carnal desire I hadn't felt in a very long time. Different from stalking my prey at a back-alley bar.

This wasn't a need for release . . . this was lust.

I tucked my legs as he lifted me over the tailgate. My heart fluttered as I was lowered lightly onto the bed of the truck, though it took me a minute to find my footing.

"Hang on." He slid an obnoxious manly plaid travel pillow across the bed. "Sit."

I lowered myself onto the pillow, crisscrossing my legs and tugging the throw tightly around my shoulders, cursing myself for not thinking to pull on a pair of boots. But then a flannel blanket was draped over my lap, its earthy colors matching the pattern on the pillow. I recognized the set from the leather store where I'd purchased my sandals.

A napkin with a slice of pizza was set in front of me, along with a bottle of some sort of imported lager I'd never had, the amber-colored glass catching the moonlight with a sparkle.

An impromptu midnight picnic under the stars.

Where the hell was I?

29

James

Colette was uncomfortable. Exactly where she needed to be for me to begin chipping away at that armor she hid behind.

Colette Archer reminded me of a Russian spy I once had the pleasure of interrogating in an underground bunker beneath the dunes of the Syrian Desert. For four days, the man withstood my team's tactics, never once wavering. A loyalty to his cause that, quite honestly, I admired. Both he and Colette caused me great headaches, both seeming to have a death wish of sorts. Both uncaring if they died—something else I admired.

But there was only one difference between the Russian spy and the woman sitting beside me that night.

Stoicism.

Where the spy had unwavering control over his emotions, Colette radiated a kind of desperation that made me uneasy. She was a woman at the end of her rope. Where the Russian spy had a dispassionate vacancy behind his eyes from years of being brainwashed, Colette Archer showed ice-cold resolve. The kind of courage and vigor granted only to those with pasts as horrific as hers.

I wanted so badly to convince Colette to release the pain from the past, the pain from losing her sisters in such a brutal way. The perpetrators had been locked up, still serving their sentences and rotting away in prison. Justice had been served, and she had to accept that and move on with her life, instead of allowing it to torture her, to eat her alive.

Losing whatever battle Colette was fighting wasn't an option, and that ego was going to be her downfall . . . unless she'd let me under that armor first. I just had to find the right buttons to push, at the right time.

And considering the woman was eyeing me with the suspicion of a feral lynx, that time was not now.

But I would get there, somehow, some way, because the only thing I needed more than to find the person who attacked Colette was to understand why this woman spent her weekends at the Mahalo Motel. Though I'd tried to come up with every excuse in the book for her, there was only one reason a woman rented a motel room for one hour.

"Eat," I said curtly, forcing myself out of a thought that made me want to drive my truck into a lamppost.

Be present, I reminded myself, my years of military training kicking into gear. Not a difficult task, considering the woman in front of me was, without question, the most stunning creature I'd ever laid eyes on.

Colette studied the triple-meat pizza in front of her with the same suspicion she'd been eyeing me with since the day we met.

I watched and waited, then eventually lost patience. Grabbing her slice, I bit off half in one bite, then flopped it back down on her napkin. "See? Not poisoned. Eat . . . and try to relax while you're at it."

The battle in her head wavered and finally she gave in, devouring the food like a starving POW. It was quite possibly the sexiest thing I'd ever seen in my life.

Fighting a grin, I took a slice, even though food was the last thing on my mind.

Admittedly, I know little about the idiosyncrasies of a woman, but one thing I do know is that they don't like you to watch them eat. I'm assuming this has something to do with the whole obsession with weight thing, which is absolutely ridiculous. But at that moment, I'd have done anything to keep Colette mowing down that pizza like a damn bushhog.

"So, who's the brunette?" I asked, although I'd recognized the Archer and Archer, Inc. receptionist immediately when Jade had led her into the B and B. Undoubtedly, she was a member of Colette's team to help with the Sarah Kay case that seemed about as solid as the marinara sauce dripping from her chin.

"A pain in my ass."

"That's no way to talk about someone who works for you."

After chugging half her beer in one go, Colette picked up another slice. "If you already knew who she was, why did you ask?"

"I wanted to see if you'd tell me the truth."

"Because everything is an illusion, a lie, a distortion of the truth when it comes to me?"

"Had that bottled up, didn't you?"

She rolled her eyes, chewing feverishly.

I tossed her another beer from the cooler and stealthily replaced my slice into the box. Colette downed the rest of the beer, swiping the dribble from her chin with the back of her sleeve.

Who was this enigma of a woman sitting in front of me? How many secrets did she have? And how many of those secrets involved men in sleazy motels?

More importantly, why did I care so much about that part?

I regarded her closely, lost in her pizza and beer, wrapped like an Eskimo in her throw and the blanket I'd purchased on the off chance she'd visit. A neon-pink toenail peeked out from under the flannel.

I grinned. "Nice Birks."

She frowned, swallowing the huge bite in her mouth. "Oh." She kicked out her foot. "These things." She scowled, examining the leather strapping her foot.

"Yes, *those* things, otherwise known as one of the most popular sandals in the world."

"Jesus tends to have that effect on crowds."

"I'm pretty sure they didn't have Birks in twenty A.D."

"I heard someone in the store refer to them as *Jesus shoes*."

"Well, that person is incorrect. The actual Jesus shoe was designed by a Brooklyn-based company who transformed a pair of Nike Air sneakers into a four-thousand-dollar commodity by inserting holy water from the River Jordan into the sole."

"You're joking."

"Nope. But in your defense, people do call Birks Jesus cruisers or sandals . . . or Jandals, even."

"I'll stick with my Loubs, thank you very much."

"Of course you will."

"What's that supposed to mean?" She tipped up beer number two.

"It means you value labels more than good sense."

"Ouch."

"Yeah, my thoughts exactly. Ever seen a hammer toe?" I shuddered, then took a swig of my beer. "Where does this love of fashion come from?"

"The Bronx."

"Didn't know they had many designer stores in that area."

"They don't. That's the point."

"Ah. So you grew up poor and now grip onto material things with bloody fingertips as if having a closet full of three-thousand-dollar suits proves you're worthy of a life outside barred windows. That's such a disappointing cliché, Colette."

"I'd say the same of you, Jarhead James, in your khaki tactical pants and combat boots, if not for our first meeting in my office."

"And what did that meeting tell you?"

"That you are the exact opposite of the white-collar stereotype you presented yourself as. Correction, *poorly attempted* to present yourself as."

"What gave it away?"

"The pleated fronts."

My brow cocked.

She grinned. "They don't make pleated fronts anymore."

"Huh."

"See? How does that feel?"

"If you're expecting me to be offended, I'm far from it."

She leaned back, releasing her weight—and a touch of that amped-up vigilance—against the side of the truck bed. Sinking into her buzz, I noted, pleased by this. Those icy blue eyes squinted as she assessed me, sweeping up and down my body in a way that made my dick stir. Buzzed or plotting . . . now I wasn't sure which.

"You're different here. Almost like a completely different man."

"How so?"

"More . . . relaxed. Confident."

"Unlike you in those Birks."

She scowled down again at the Jesus cruisers.

"Maybe you should give it a chance."

A perfectly sculpted brow arched as she met my eyes with a smirk. "The Birks, you mean."

I grinned. "Yes, the Birks. Of course that's what I meant."

A moment passed as we smiled at each other, electricity crackling between us.

"Here." I opened my palm.

"What?"

"Give me your foot."

She pulled back her chin, horrified by this request.

"Relax. I'm not asking for your credit card. Give me your foot."

"You're so annoying."

"In my natural habitat or in my pleated fronts?"

"Both."

"Damn. Give me your foot, you weirdo."

"Fine." Her leg sprang out from under the blanket with such force, I'd be missing my head if I'd been leaning down. Intentional? Absolutely.

I picked up her sandaled foot. The corner of her mouth twitched.

"Ah, we're ticklish, I see." I tightened my grip when she attempted to jerk away.

"Don't you dare . . ."

"Okay." I mocked her before lifting her foot in the air,

playfully examining the sandal. “There is no way, Miss Archer, you can convince me that these shoes aren’t more comfortable than your red bottoms.”

“There’s no way you can convince me that you know what red bottoms are.”

“I do. Cardi B told me all about them.”

The laugh that exploded out of the woman caught me by surprise. A full-blown, head-tipping-back cackle. It was officially the best part of my day.

“I didn’t take you as a rap music kind of guy.” She wiped the tears from her eyes.

“I’m not, but that woman fascinates me.”

“You’re not alone, I promise you that.”

“I had to google what it meant. As you can imagine, I was very disappointed.”

Chuckling, Colette took another sip of her beer and set it down, a twinkle in her eye now. She was enjoying herself, although she’d never admit it.

“As I was saying,” I refocused on her foot in my hand, “the Birkenstock is hand-crafted in Germany with a cork sole that uses the heat from your body to mold to your exact foot structure.” I slipped the shoe from her foot and froze. “Jesus, Mary, and Joseph, where the *hell* is your pinky toenail?”

She jerked her foot back, recoiling with a loud groan. “I have a pinky toenail, thank you very much.”

“Do you? Where is it?”

“It’s there. I just don’t—*can’t*—paint it because it’s kind of small.”

“It looks like a damn little smokie.”

“You’re an ass.”

“It’s the heels, I’m telling you.”

She scoffed, looking away.

"Jesus, woman, wear these Birks, get your nails back. Or slather them in BBQ sauce and let me have a go at them."

Her brows arched. "Tempting."

"Is it? Do we have a foot fetish, Miss Archer?"

Blushing, she looked away.

Bingo.

"Good to know."

"Your lips are getting nowhere near my feet, Agent Black."

"Then you probably should avoid the barbecue sauce."

"Gross. *Fine*," she said. "I'll go pick me up another pair of them there Birks, and maybe a corn pipe and a pair of Crocs while I'm at it."

"I'd pay money to see you in a pair of Crocs. And with a pipe, for that matter."

"Yeah, how much?"

I tipped up my beer, sipped, then winked. "Not nearly as much as I'd pay to see you in those assless chaps."

Her jaw dropped. "Do you mean to tell me while I was getting my ass kicked in my bathroom last night, you took the time to notice the pair of chaps hanging out of my suitcase?"

"Hard to miss—the brass snaps sparkled in the moonlight. Thought it was a weapon."

"Well, now I know why I'm so bruised," she muttered, running her hands over her arms.

"I'm semi-joking, and we talked about this. You were caught off guard. Give yourself a break. And by the way, what I did see was nothing short of impressive. Where did you learn to fight like that?"

Colette took a deep sip of her beer. "My sister."

"Why doesn't this surprise me?"

"I know, right? She's a martial arts instructor, although her true love is judo."

"Ah. Otherwise known as the 'gentle way.'"

"Don't tell her that."

"This makes sense then."

"What makes sense?"

"Why you were getting your ass kicked."

"Has anyone told you that you need to work on your people skills?"

"More than I can count. Judo, otherwise known as the gentle way, is the only self-defense technique in the world that doesn't involve kicking, punching, or striking. You were defending your body by blocking hits, not fighting back. But still, it was impressive. If you would've tried to attack back, there would have been no contest."

She meditated on this a moment.

"One of the five rules to self-defense is to strike first. If you know a fight is unavoidable—like when your attacker lunged into the shower—you strike first. Your goal is to immediately destabilize your attacker. Instead, you went into defensive mode."

She nodded. "Yeah, I guess I did. Strike first," she said softly, her expression hardening.

"Always. Strike first, fight back. Two million women are assaulted every year, Cole—can I call you Cole?"

"I think so."

"Good. Two *million* women, mostly by men. If you're smaller than your attacker, always use their body weight against them."

"How do you know all this?"

"I know a lot about a few things. Like how that faded bruise on your cheekbone isn't from last night."

She blinked, resembling a deer caught in the headlights. A secret exposed.

Three slices of pizza and two bottles of 9.1% alcohol later, and I'd found my *right time.*

"Who hurt you, Colette?" I asked, diving in. "Not last night . . . last *week.*"

Like a turtle retreating into its shell, she pulled her knees to her chest and looked down.

My hands curled into fists as I watched her, a possessiveness I'd never felt before slicing through my chest and gripping my heart. I was suddenly desperate for her to open up to me. And in desperation, I lost my cool.

"Did the Mahalo get a bit out of hand last weekend?"

Her gaze shot up to mine. "What did you just say?"

I stared at her, my jaw clenched so tightly that pain shot up the sides of my head.

"I fell," she said, fixing a fierce look on me as if daring me to question it. Defensive? Abso-fucking-lutely. "That's it. That's all there is to know."

"I know about your sisters, Colette. I know tomorrow would have been their thirtieth birthday."

If she was surprised, she hid it well. Her jaw twitched in anger. "What else do you know, Agent Black?"

"I know what happened to them, and that both your parents died shortly after, and that you adopted Jade."

"That's all?" she said, mocking me.

"I'm sorry."

"For being so blunt?"

"No. For your losses."

"Well." She shifted. "Yes, you would be, just as everyone else is. They're sorry, but they don't know what to do or say other than give Jade and me glances full of pity every time we walk into the goddamn room. Do you have any idea what it's like to grow up with people treating you like you're broken, like you're defective?"

"I do." I took a swig of my beer. "My mom killed herself, just like yours."

Colette stilled, her eyes rounding.

"Got addicted to drugs after my dad left her. Began selling her body for meth after she'd emptied out the family savings account. I confronted her about it, and an argument broke out. When she threatened to kill herself, I walked out . . . something that I regret to this day. I shouldn't have left her. She needed someone, and I was there. I should have never left."

"What happened?"

"I found her the next morning, dead on her bedroom floor. She'd taken five milligrams of pure fentanyl straight into the vein. Her entire secret stash. Five thousand micrograms of the most potent street drug out there. I was sixteen. Finished high school with all those looks you're talking about."

Tears glistened in Colette's eyes. "I'm so sorry. I . . . I understand."

My eyes met hers. "I know."

"What did you do?" she whispered. It was a question that only someone who understood such loss would ask.

"Became a cop right out of high school, something to funnel the rage constantly flowing through my veins. One of the first cases I worked involved your boy, Leo Creed. A huge, multicounty fentanyl bust."

"Ah. That's why you hate him so much."

"Yes. For all I know, his connections fed my mother's addiction. Hell, she might have bought the drugs that killed her directly from him."

Colette nodded, again with understanding.

"After that, I joined the Marines. Killed a bunch of people."

"And then you went to work for the Drug Enforcement Administration. Cop, military, federal agent. Why?"

"Why what?"

"Why jump around so much?"

I looked away, pondering the question I'd asked myself so many times before.

"You're searching for something, James." She regarded me closely in a way that felt like she was staring into my soul. "Fulfillment. Happiness. You thought you'd find both by joining the fight on drugs to avenge your mother's death . . . but you didn't."

When I didn't respond, she grabbed my arm.

"Did you, James? Did you? Have you found happiness? Contentment?" A childlike desperation shone in her eyes, as if she were waiting with bated breath for the right answer. The answer that would ease the pain that blackened her soul.

But I didn't deliver.

"No," I said, staring into those wide blue eyes. "No, Cole. Not yet."

We stared at each other as a moment stretched between us.

"We're chasing ghosts," she whispered.

I regarded her closely. "Mine led me to a six-by-six cubicle and pleated fronts. I hope yours don't take you down the wrong path too, Colette."

She pulled back, my words seeming to have an impact on her. "Do you miss the life you had?" she asked softly.

"In the military? Yeah. The outdoors, the action, the adrenaline."

"Sounds like you're at a crossroads then."

It wasn't until that moment that I realized I was. I had absolutely no idea what my future held, just that I wasn't happy where I'd found myself.

Leaving the comment hanging in the air, Colette surprised me by lying back against the bed of the truck. "It is pretty out here," she whispered.

I lay back beside her, and together we stared at the endless black sky above. I don't know how long we lay there together in comfortable silence, watching the stars twinkle and the moon rise higher in the sky.

Until she finally spoke again.

"I have cancer."

30

James

I will never forget that moment for the rest of my life.

The way my heart stuttered before it quit beating. The way the entire world seemed to stop spinning. My body's physical reaction to Colette's three-word confession reminded me of the life-changing moment when I looked down at my mother's dead body—indescribable emotion for a woman . . . that I loved.

A full minute ticked by as the weight of her admission settled around us like cement slowly pouring from a truck. In my career and my life, I'd dealt with more injury, death, and life-altering news than the average person. But this news hit me like a tidal wave.

"What kind of cancer?" I asked, and my voice cracked.

"The terminal kind."

I propped up on my elbow, looking down at her, and our eyes met. A moment passed between us, one that made my heart stumble again and a knot form in my throat.

"Melanoma," she said, then shifted her gaze to the stars as if breaking eye contact somehow made the news less devastating.

I didn't know much about cancer, but I knew melanoma was a skin cancer, a result of getting too much sun, and was one of the fastest spreading cancers. I also knew, if caught late, the prognosis wasn't good.

"When were you diagnosed?"

"Fifteen days ago. My sister doesn't know."

I stilled and blinked, unable to hide my shock.

A sad smile crossed Colette's face. "I know. I just . . . I don't want Jade to have to go through it all. You know, they say stuff like this is actually harder on the patient's loved ones than the patient themselves."

"Then, who's taking you to treatment? Who's taking care of you?"

Colette turned her head away, and my stomach dropped.

"Colette . . . you are getting— " No. There was no way. "What kind of treatment are you getting?"

"I'm not."

I shot up to a seated position.

"*Don't*," she said sharply, her gaze meeting mine like the swipe of a machete through the air between us.

"You're not seeking treatment?"

The fight was back in her as she started to push herself up to a seated position. I reached out to help, and she viciously swatted my hand away.

"*That*. That is the second reason I'm not telling anyone. *That's* why I'm not getting treatment, James. I don't need your fucking help to sit up, and I don't want you to feel like you need to help sit me up. I *hate* the attention, the pity."

"I'm sorry, I—"

"Listen." She pulled her legs into a crisscross and began

picking at the edge of the blanket. "What I have is not curable. Period. All treatment will do at this point is prolong my dying. No thanks."

"But there *is* treatment. How do you know it would only prolong death? Maybe it could cure you. You have to try—"

"*Stop*, James."

I closed my mouth, biting my tongue, and took a deep breath to slow my heartbeat. I couldn't fathom Colette not giving treatment a chance, and worse, making that decision alone. Making a decision to die, all by herself. I thought of my mother, and how she'd made that decision, although in a very different way.

If I'd been there for her . . .

If I'd somehow been there for Colette . . .

But I was, I realized. I *was* there, right then, for Colette.

"I've spent most of my adult life obsessed with the what-ifs," she said thoughtfully, "constantly worrying about the past, the future, what could be, planning for the worst-case scenario. Well, it happened. Here I am. The worst-case scenario literally happened. And as fucked up as it sounds, it's almost a relief. Like a weight off my shoulders. Like, literally things could *not* get worse." She barked out a humorless laugh. "The worst has happened. And for some crazy reason, that realization is freeing."

"But that's no reason to accept death."

"It sure makes it easier."

"Easier, because this way you have control."

Frowning at this epiphany, she considered it.

"By choosing to accept the outcome of what the statistics tell you is going to happen, you're taking control by simply accepting it. On the other hand, if you decide to try treatment, everything is suddenly out of your control. Your life, literally, is in someone else's hands."

Colette blinked, digesting the comment, obviously one she hadn't thought of before.

"What about your sister? Jade?" I asked.

"I told you, I don't want her to go through all this. I don't want to cause her any more pain. We've been through a lot."

"I mean treatment. Why not try it for her?"

"Not now."

"Why?"

"Because . . . we have other things to focus on. I can't be going through treatment." She shook her head. "You don't understand."

"Then tell me, and I'll understand. Tell me why you're here in Broken Ridge . . . what it is that you're up to."

Colette sighed and lay back down in the bed of the truck. She stared at the stars, her eyes heavy, her cheeks flushed from the buzz of the alcohol. She had no fight left in her.

I lowered myself, turning toward her on my side and propping up on my elbow.

"Do you have any siblings, James?" she said finally.

"A younger brother. In the Navy. Followed in my footsteps."

"Do you worry about him?"

"Every goddamn day."

"What would you do if something happened to him?"

"I'd be devastated."

"Devastated," she whispered, a twinkle of a tear in her eye. Then, in a voice so small I could barely hear it, she said, "You have no idea, James."

I was overcome by the instinct to wrap her in my arms and hold her. To let her cry, let her release the millions of pounds of responsibility and blame she carried around every day. The fear she must have, wondering what happens at the end of this life.

Instead, I kissed her.

31

Colette

I saw stars.

In the sky, behind my eyelids, and in my soul, tiny bubbles of light burst to life as James Black kissed me into oblivion. For a moment, everything disappeared. The pain, the anger, the sadness, and the hurt. He and I, and *that* kiss, were the only things that existed.

He. A power so strong, that with only the touch of his lips, he could singlehandedly dissolve my focus, my purpose, my entire existence at that moment.

He. A power strong enough to destroy everything. For me, and for my sisters.

He. A man who had no idea that kissing me could end his career, and quite possibly his life.

What the *hell* was I doing?

32

Colette

I slid over the back fence of the bed and breakfast, landing silently on the soft grass, careful to avoid the brittle leaves that littered the tree line.

In a crouched position, I froze and listened. The world was as still and quiet as it had been when James kissed me senseless half an hour earlier. If not for my meeting with Leo that night, I would have never left James.

Sneaking out of the building without tipping James off had been difficult. I'd used the same trellis my attacker had used to sneak in, almost killing myself in the process. When I was sure James was unaware of my escape from my room, I pressed on, my entire body vibrating with anxiety. Anger. Attraction.

Need.

After James pulled away from our kiss—he was the one who had to do it, because I would have spent the rest of my life drowning in that kiss—I downed the rest of my beer, and with nothing more than a nod, jumped off the truck and disappeared into the shadows. I felt him watching me until I slipped into the safety of the bed and breakfast at midnight.

I knew he wouldn't leave me, as I'd asked, and the worst part was that I also realized that I was desperately clinging to that fact. The feeling of safety his presence gave me. I was torn between wanting him to leave and forget about me, and desperately wanting him to stay, scoop me up, and make love to me under the stars.

Not fuck. Make love.

Overwhelmed with emotion on the worst night possible, I felt like the walls were slowly closing in around me, pieces of bricks tumbling onto my shoulders as I was feeling everything other than what I should be at that moment. *Confident*.

Although I'd acted like I didn't hear him, I had heard James's smartass comment about the Mahalo Motel. I was embarrassed, humiliated that he knew about my weekend rendezvous. My dirty, disgusting little secret.

Did he judge me? And did I care?

I'd certainly never cared about the men I left lying in the motel room, buck naked and confused as hell. Just like I didn't care that the motel owner, MaryAnne, knew about my addiction. Didn't bother me one bit.

Why did it bother me that James knew? Why did he have such power over me?

The worst, though, was the sick feeling of wondering if James thought I was gross because of my cancer. Damaged goods, no longer attractive. A defective thing to avoid physical contact with, in case the cancer was somehow contagious. After all, no one likes sick people. Not when they know about the sickness, anyway.

At the time, I didn't know why I told James about my cancer.

I do now.

With the agility of a back-alley cat, I scaled a pair of dumpsters, pulled myself onto the roof of the bakery next door, and crept over the rooftops while keeping one eye on the bed of the black F-150.

James hadn't stirred. Likely still digesting a confession from a dying woman.

After putting a few buildings between us, I climbed down onto the sidewalk and crossed the street, heading back down the same side of the street as the tavern just as a man rounded the corner from the opposite direction, briefly stepping under a streetlight before the darkness engulfed him again. The silvery light of the moon illuminated a pair of broad shoulders under what appeared to be a long black duster.

Fear shot up my spine.

I quickly maneuvered deeper into the shadows, hugging the wall as I slowed my pace and eyed the stranger, his head down, shoulders slumped, hands in pockets, face hidden by the shadows. He was tall and substantial, not from fat but from muscle. I couldn't tell if the man had seen me or not, but something in my gut told me he knew I was there.

James's words echoed in my head as I assessed the enormous man walking directly toward me.

Make the first strike.

As he drew closer, I pulled the switchblade from my pocket. Flipping it open, I glanced at the truck at the end of Main Street, hoping to see James emerging from it. No such luck.

Steadying my nerves, I refocused on the potential threat walking toward me. If our paces remained the same, I estimated we would cross paths directly in front of Creed's

Tavern. My heart began to pound. Too much that night. It was just too much of everything.

I yearned for James, hoping to send some sort of subliminal message telling him that I might be in danger again. I wanted to glance at the truck again, but knew it would be unwise to take my eyes off the late-night wanderer.

I began counting each step, strong, steady, confident.

Closer, closer . . .

The dim glow of another streetlight caught the side of the man's face, and I recognized him instantly. My stomach plummeted. It was as if I was looking at Leo himself, but a taller, broader, angrier Leo.

The man was Leo's misfit brother, Dylan Creed, known only as Creed.

My pulse roared as we both approached Creed's Tavern.

Going with instinct, I kept up my pace, as he did, and we passed under the flickering neon signs of the bar. Leo's brother never looked up, never made eye contact, but I knew he knew I was there.

My skin ignited with adrenaline as we passed each other, as if I could literally feel the hostile energy coming off him in waves. Just as quickly as it came, the sensation left with him as if pulled in his wake.

Holding my breath, I kept walking past the tavern, listening to his footfalls fade behind me until I was sure he was no longer an immediate threat.

If Dylan wasn't going to his brother's bar, where was he going at this time of the morning? Pivoting, I glanced over my shoulder just as Jade slipped into the shadows outside the bakery.

Shit.

Damn, damn, damn.

Pocketing the switchblade, I ducked into an alley

between buildings. Jade was a smart, capable woman who knew what she was doing, I reminded myself. Still, I didn't like it.

Had James seen her? Was he following her now? Had Dylan seen her?

I decided at that moment that it had to end tonight.

My body began to tremble as I forced myself out of the shadows. Dylan was gone, as was Jade. And still no James.

Focusing on my breathing, I retraced my steps back to the bar. Instead of trying the front door, I took the shadowy alley around to the back, and up the wooden staircase that led to Leo's apartment. A dim light from an open window next to the door illuminated the small stoop. I ducked under it, unsure why.

I looked at my watch—1:19 a.m. Four minutes late.

Glancing over my shoulder, I said a little prayer for Jade, then refocused on the door in front of me with renewed resolve.

It *had* to end. Too many pieces were moving, being added, shuffling. Too many variables to consider, to ruin my plan.

As I raised my hand to knock, the door opened. Leo smiled broadly from inside, fresh from the shower, his shaggy brown hair wet and combed to the side. A spicy clean scent enveloped me, and my internal sensors zipped to life.

The man was attractive, no doubt about it.

I smiled, seamlessly putting on the mask I'd perfected over the years.

"Morning." He winked.

"Evening," I said with a smile.

Stepping back, he opened the door wide, giving me the once-over as I entered the apartment.

"Whoa . . ." His hand froze on the door. "What happened to your jaw?"

Leo leaned closer, examining the purple bruising that speckled my neck and jawline, courtesy of my intruder's ass-kicking the night before.

"I took an unfortunate stumble down the stairs of the B and B."

"I'd say so. You all right?"

"Fine."

"Okay." Frowning, he shut the door behind us.

Leo's home was exactly what I'd expected from an apartment over a bar. Enclosed in log walls, the space was small and minimally furnished, with a kitchen, a bedroom, and a narrow door that likely led to a bathroom-slash-laundry room. It was the bachelor pad of all bachelor pads.

"Nice place."

"Thanks. Saves me a drive to the cabin on late nights. That's my real sanctuary. In the woods, with the real Montana all around you." He took the leather jacket from around my shoulders.

It felt like a date, but it wasn't.

"I think I saw your brother just now."

His hands froze on the coatrack. "Did you?" He turned, suddenly laser-focused on me.

"I think so. Looked exactly like you, except taller and with tattoos."

"That's him." Leo's eyes narrowed. "Where was he going?"

I shrugged.

Leo frowned, turning his gaze to the window across the apartment that overlooked Main Street. "Was he with anyone?"

"No. Just wandering by himself."

Leo snorted, then shook his head as if this didn't surprise him. Then he dismissed the subject. "So, how long are you here for?"

"A few more days." I walked deeper into the apartment, studying the living room.

"You should come visit the cabin," Leo said to my back. "There's a river nearby. Good for fishing or canoeing. You know, get the whole Montana experience before you leave."

"I might take you up on that."

"I'll be there tomorrow." He grabbed a pen and paper from the bar that separated the kitchen and living room, scribbled on it, and handed it to me. "Directions and cell number."

I nodded and stuffed the paper into my pocket, my noncommitment lingering in the air.

"So, uh . . ." He rubbed his hands together. "You're here for the rest of the videos."

I turned away from the cheap landscape painting I'd been examining. "Yes. The days before and after Sarah Kay went missing."

"Right. I've got them on the computer. You have your zip drive?"

I nodded.

"Great. In here."

I followed Leo into the bedroom, to a desk in the corner that held a computer, several empty coffee cups, and candy wrappers. Glancing out the bedroom door, I could see the window that overlooked the small stoop by the back door.

"Were you able to pull all the footage?" I asked, joining him by the computer.

"Yes." He wiggled the mouse, awakening the monitor, and motioned for me to sit in a recently reupholstered bucket chair in the corner. "Everything you asked for, except for one day. Cameras were off for a bit."

The computer lit to life, a background image of a dog filling the screen.

"You're a dog person?" I asked, forgoing the offer to sit.

"Does this surprise you?"

"A bit."

"That's Simone." He began clicking through files. "A husky mix. Lost her a year ago."

"I'm sorry." When he didn't respond, I pulled the zip drive from my pocket. "May I?"

Leo glanced at the chair I didn't sit in, then stepped out of the way and nodded to the keyboard. "Sure. Go ahead. Those are the files, highlighted."

After sliding the drive into the console, I sat in the leather gaming chair. Leo didn't miss the opportunity to hover over me, putting one hand on the back of the chair, enclosing around me. He took control of the mouse while he leaned over my shoulder and transferred the files to the drive.

He was sweating, the cologne he'd sprayed on coming off his skin in a cloying musky scent that made my eyes water. I knew what was on his mind. All the signs were there.

I watched the hourglass turn on the screen. A little box popped up:

Downloading, 8 minutes remaining.

Eight minutes. My pulse picked up as I thought of all the things I could do in eight minutes.

As if he were thinking the same thing, Leo's hand left the

back of the chair and drifted onto my shoulder, a cold fingertip trailing the base of my neck.

Adrenaline kickstarted my heart, sending a flush of heat through my body. Slowly, I swiveled the chair, his finger sliding along my collarbone as I did so, and met his leer.

His finger trailed up my neck. I reached up, grabbed his hand, and pulled it to my breast.

A grin split his face as he leaned down to grip the armrest with his other hand, trapping me in place.

I closed my eyes, afraid I might reveal the true emotion swirling in my stomach.

33

Leo

The moment our lips touched, Colette grabbed my face and surged out of the chair, almost headbutting me in the process.

I staggered back, studying the wild, feral look in her eyes, unsure what the hell just happened. With a look so intense I could almost feel the heat, she grabbed my cheeks, burying her face into my neck as we tumbled onto the bed.

Jesus fucking Christ.

My dick inflated faster than a life raft as Colette trailed her tongue from my neck to my ear, then nibbled, shooting tingles to the already throbbing head of my cock.

I was in a dream, lost in this crazy moment with this crazy woman who apparently wanted nothing more than to fuck the life out of me.

And I was game for it.

I rolled her onto her back, shifting on top of her and taking control, my only reason for breathing at that moment to get my dick between this woman's legs as quickly as possible.

Colette's hands slid up under the back of my T-shirt, her nails clawing their way down my skin, the sharp pain sending a rush of animalistic desire through me.

I was trembling like a damn high school kid as I pulled her sweater over her head and yanked up her bra, exposing a pair of perfectly round tits with swollen pink nipples pointing right at me.

Fake. They had to be fake was all I could think as I filled my mouth with one of them while her nails shredded my back like a porn star on Ecstasy.

Fake—this *woman* had to be fake.

Because she walked right out of my damn dreams.

34

Colette

I imagined Leo's flesh ripping open as I raked my nails down his back, barely able to control myself. His lips felt like drops of acid, his touch an army of ants swarming over my body.

Memories flashed in my head like a horror movie as I turned my head—and saw *him* and his tall, menacing silhouette just outside the window, watching me. Watching *us*.

James Black.

Though his face was hidden by shadows, the abhorrence poured off him like waves of black tar . . . hot and thick, blanketing everything in its path. I could feel the fury, the judgment, the disgust.

The possessiveness.

My blood turned to ice, freezing my body, my breath, my thoughts. The look on James's face as our eyes met jarred me to my very soul.

I shoved Leo off me, sending him flying backward and

tumbling to the floor. Heat burned my cheeks as I yanked down my bra and scrambled off the bed.

"What the *fuck*?" Confused, Leo bellowed from the corner as I stared at the window.

Like a ghost, James was gone.

"Colette, what the *hell* . . ."

I recoiled as Leo approached, my gaze locked on the blackness beyond the window.

"Colette—"

"S-sorry . . . I'm sorry." I glanced at Leo, who was adjusting himself, then refocused back out the window. "I thought I saw someone outside. But no. No . . . it's nothing." I shook my head. "It's nothing."

Shit.

My skin burned with embarrassment and humiliation. Not caused by the confused man that I'd just thrown off me like a damn linebacker, but by being caught doing what I did best by the man I was falling for.

"Colette, are you okay?"

I cleared my throat, searching for my words. Any words at all. "I . . . I don't think I'm feeling well."

"Oh. Well, it's okay." Leo's stance relaxed. Sighing, he ran his fingers through his hair, obviously frustrated with the turn of events.

Still in only my bra and jeans, I hurried across the room and clicked the computer screen.

Download complete.

I yanked the drive from the console. "Thanks for this."

Leo simply stared back at me.

"I need to go. Can you . . ."

He tossed me my sweater from the floor. Once I was

dressed, Leo followed me into the living room, where I had to refrain from sprinting out the door. I wanted away from the bedroom, from him, from his apartment. From this damn godforsaken town.

I yanked my jacket from the coatrack, sending it teetering on its base. Trembling, I pulled open the door and stepped into the cold, dark night as the rack clattered to the floor behind me.

Obviously baffled, Leo lingered in the doorway, resting his arm on the frame above his head. "If you want to finish what you started back there, come by my cabin tomorrow night. I can promise you no one will be looking in the windows there. I'll be there late afternoon."

Already descending the staircase, I nodded but didn't respond.

"Night, Colette."

I felt Leo's gaze on me as I stepped onto the gravel lot behind the bar. My knees were shaking by the time I rounded the building, out of his line of sight.

Closing my eyes, I slammed my back against the cold log wall and took a deep breath to steady my pulse.

Fuck. Shit, shit, *shit.*

My eyes blinked open, searching for James.

Could I have imagined it, or had he followed me? Watched me like a sick fuck as I mounted Leo like an animal?

Did he hate me now?

Where was Jade? Dylan? Or had I imagined them as well?

Was I losing it? Was it the pills?

Ducking my head, I moved silently as I darted across the street, keeping my eyes on James's truck until I made it safely behind the black iron gate that led to the bed and breakfast.

Locking the latch, I turned, peeking at the truck through the bushes, waiting.

Waiting for what? For him to confront me? To tell me how disappointed he was with me?

Or to ask if I was okay and tell me he didn't hate me.

35

Colette

When I got up to my room, I looked out at Main Street. James was sitting in the cab of his truck, a large, looming silhouette staring directly at my window. I could almost feel the hostility through the glass.

My stomach rolled every time I pictured his face, watching Leo and me through his back window. Could I have imagined it?

I needed sleep.

After ensuring Jade was safe and double-checking the locks on the windows and doors in the bed and breakfast, I stripped down and stepped into a scalding-hot shower, where I scrubbed every inch of my body until my skin was red and raw, and cried until I had no more tears left.

With a towel wrapped around me, I pulled a chair next to the window, and from behind the veil of the sheer curtains, I made a solemn promise to myself.

Tomorrow is the day. No matter what—tomorrow it will be done.

With that thought, I settled back against the chair, spying on the truck until sleep pulled me under.

36

Colette

I awoke to a beam of sunlight glowing red through my eyelids. Blinking through the blinding light and the disorienting haze, I repositioned on the chair, my neck and back in knots.

Groaning, I pulled my legs out from under me, tingling with sleep, my knees cracking in protest, as the towel I'd fallen asleep in slipped to the floor. A line of dried drool cracked my face. My hair was tangled and matted to the side of my head from falling asleep in the chair with it wet.

I felt like *shit*.

Squinting, I slowly lifted the corner of the curtain. A bright orange orb peeked up from the mountaintops, vivid rays of sunlight pushing away the stars above. A line of thick, heavy clouds gathered in the distance, the promise of a storm to come.

I looked at James's truck, dark in the shadows. Still there, unmoved for days at this point. Again, my stomach roiled as

I pictured the expression on his face as he watched Leo nibbling my nipple.

Everything had gotten so out of hand. My plan was crumbling.

Squaring my shoulders, I gritted my teeth and reminded myself of the promise I'd made the night before.

Today is the day.

With that thought, I slipped on the first thing I could grab from my suitcase, a faded, oversize Grateful Dead T-shirt Jade had brought me from a festival, and pulled it over my head. Forgoing underwear or socks, I quietly pushed open the bedroom door and tiptoed across the hall to check on my sister.

Still asleep.

After checking the upstairs windows and doors, I padded downstairs with one thing on my mind—caffeine. The lights were off, the rooms were dark, the early glow of dawn yet to make it through the tangled canopy of the lush courtyard that enclosed the building.

The moment I stepped into the kitchen, the hair on the back of my neck raised. I stopped cold when I noticed the man standing in the corner, his back to me, his body concealed by shadows.

Definitely not the cook.

Spinning into action, I grabbed a kitchen knife from the counter, releasing a smooth swishing sound as it pulled from the wooden block. The silhouette turned the moment I lunged forward, wielding the knife like a weapon.

Before I could register what was happening, the blade was slapped from my hand, and in under two seconds, I was flipped around and bent at the waist, my cheek pressed against the counter, my arm behind my back.

I knew instantly who it was.

"What the hell are you doing here," I ground out, my voice raw.

"Apparently disarming a psychopath," James growled in my ear with a quick squeeze of my wrist before releasing me. "And way too easily, I might add."

I spun around. His green eyes blazed with anger, and it was no longer a question if he'd seen me with Leo the night before. Half-naked, tits in the air, all whore. I hadn't imagined it.

And the man was *pissed.* I couldn't talk—or fuck—my way out of this one.

My thoughts spun between him seeing me with Leo, and my confession of the cancer. In a single night, James Black had stripped me of my facade and seen me for who I really was. No more show.

Knowing he saw my flaws, both inside and out, I was gripped by insecurity.

A moment passed as we stared at each other, my expression one of defeat, and his of absolute fury. As screwed up as this sounds, I appreciated his response. Anger was better than pity. Anger meant that he considered my actions with Leo of greater importance than my terminal confession. It also meant that he saw me as capable, and I was. I wasn't gross and broken. Death on my doorstep or not, I was a worthy adversary, and James seemed to know that.

I pushed past him, clicked on the dim stove light, and beelined it to the coffee machine. Peering out the window, I scanned the dark courtyard for a moment, looking from lamppost to lamppost, studying the movement of the shadows in the breeze. Then at the tree line of the mountain in the short distance.

My hands shook as I poured the coffee grounds into the machine.

Say something, I internally begged of him. Say *something.*

We stood in silence, me watching the coffee brew, him watching me, the tension thicker than the scent of coffee permeating the air. He watched me pour the cream, the honey, and stir. I sipped, leaning against the counter as I met his gaze. I didn't offer him a cup.

"How did you get in?"

"Your sister."

My jaw dropped as my head twisted like in the *Exorcist* toward the staircase before my attention snapped back to him. "*What* did you just say?"

"Jade let me in. Last night. Or this morning, I should say."

"How? When, exactly?"

"You were in the shower." His tone remained as cold as ice, leaving no question as to how displeased he was with me.

My focus moved again to the staircase as a sense of betrayal settled in my stomach like a ball of grease. "Did you ask—no, why did she let you in?"

"Something about the man who saved her sister's life shouldn't be sleeping in the back of a truck. She offered me the couch in the library." He swooped down and picked up the kitchen knife from the floor, then pointed it at me. "And no, I *didn't* ask to come in."

"Liar."

"Funny, coming from you."

I ignored the jab. "Jade wouldn't let a stranger sleep on the couch."

James slammed the knife on the counter with such force that the clock dropped from the wall, shattering on the floor and making me jump. Losing the self-control he'd been barely clinging to, he surged forward, closing the inches between us.

Forcing myself to hold his stare, I quickly sat my coffee mug on the counter, sending piping-hot liquid splashing down my wrist. I didn't even feel it.

"I am *not* a liar, and I'm not playing this game with you right now. What the *hell* were you doing going to Leo's apartment at one in the fucking morning?"

"That's none of your business, James," I whispered, though my heart was pounding.

He grabbed my waist and pulled me to him. "Oh yes it is when you were under *me* only an hour earlier."

"That automatically makes me your territory?"

"Apparently not."

"That's right. I'm no man's property."

"You're reckless."

I jerked out of his hold and sidestepped him. "Screw you," I barked out, although I didn't mean it.

James's fury went far beyond possessiveness. He was worried about my safety, I knew that. But I didn't know how to react to this—to a man *caring* about me. More than just the right spot to get me off.

"Wait. *Shit.* Stop." He lightly grabbed my arm, a touch of desperation in his voice. "What were you thinking going to his room, Colette? I couldn't believe it when I saw where you were going last night."

I turned into his hold. "You followed me."

"I was less than a yard behind you every step of the way. On the rooftop, on the sidewalk, when you passed Leo's brother. When you almost had a damn panic attack in the alley. How many times do I need to tell you Leo Creed is a bad guy? He's dangerous. The guy is bad news."

"You have no idea what you're talking about."

"Cut the bullshit. You're looking for something here in Broken Ridge, and for some reason, you think Leo holds the key." James's eyes narrowed with fury. "I just didn't expect you to be willing to give him your pussy to get it."

The palm of my hand connected with his face so hard, it actually startled me.

I braced myself for the attack, but James Black didn't so much as flinch.

Before I could catch my breath, he cupped my face possessively in his hands, pinning me in place. Butterflies flapped wildly in my stomach. He leaned in, the reflection of the stove light twinkling in a pair of eyes as savage as a wildcat's.

"It made me fucking crazy seeing you with him, with another man. You're *mine,* Colette," he growled, inches from my face. "*Mine.*"

Our lips met with such force that my knees went weak. I was like putty in his grasp. His hands threaded through my hair, gripping the back of my head as he took me, greedily devouring me in a way that left no question as to who was in control. And to whom I did, in fact, belong.

The countertop was swiped clean behind me, cups, glasses, knives all clattering to the floor. I was lifted and set onto the cool granite, spreading my bare legs as he thrust himself between them as if he owned them, owned *me.*

James heard the creak on the staircase before I did. I jerked away as he stilled and hid my face from the doorway.

"It's my sister," I whispered. "We woke her."

I felt Jade, as I had so many times before, as she took in the scene from the doorway. A minute passed as she assessed my safety. Then I heard her quiet footsteps ascend the stairs, and the close of her bedroom door as she reentered, allowing James and me our privacy.

"*Shit.*" I shoved him back and jumped off the counter, smoothing the T-shirt that had ridden up to my waist.

Frustrated, James dragged his fingers through his hair and began pacing the kitchen, the early morning light illuminating his angry pivots.

"You're reckless—meeting him like that. Putting yourself in that position. You're tempting the devil." He turned, meeting my gaze. "Just like you do every weekend at the Mahalo Motel."

"How dare you judge me?" I stepped nose to nose with him. "Jade doesn't know what I do there. Do *not* say a word."

"Or what? You gonna hit me again?" He threw his hands in the air and turned away with a growl of frustration. "Why aren't you getting treatment, Colette?"

The swift change of topic gave me whiplash. That's when I realized the source of James's anger simmered much deeper than my visit to Leo.

"I told you why. It's pointless to prolong the inevitable."

He turned to me. "But what if it weren't inevitable?"

"It is."

"Maybe it's not. I . . ." He paused as if considering his words carefully. "I made some calls."

"To *who*?"

"Don't worry—I didn't mention your name. I spoke with my boss, George Clancy, who recently lost his mother to cancer."

"What kind of cancer?"

"The kind you have."

"Melanoma?"

"Yes. She passed away two months before clinical trials began on a breakthrough treatment specifically for melanoma."

My heart skipped a beat, a spark of hope shocking my system. An unfamiliar feeling before that moment.

"He gave me some numbers. I made some calls and eventually connected with a Dr. Tisevich at Johns Hopkins Cancer Center, the lead doctor on a medical trial currently underway."

My eyes narrowed. "You didn't just 'call him up,' did you?"

"It's a her, and yes, I did."

"How many people did you threaten along the way?"

A grin split his face, but the smile didn't reach his eyes. "Let's just say my name and number have been banned from several clinics, and my social media accounts are currently frozen for, quote, abusive use of direct messaging. Anyway, the treatment combines two proven immunotherapies—"

"Not chemo?"

"Right. Not chemo. This is a new immunotherapy treatment. So, here's how it works. While chemo targets the cancer cells directly and prevents them from replicating, immunotherapy actually works with your body, with your immune system to fight the disease. See . . ."

Energy flared in his eyes, and I realized this was what James had spent the entire day doing. And he was excited about it.

"When your immune system detects bad stuff in your body, like a virus, bacteria, or cancer, something called T-cells attack and destroy these foreign particles. The issue with cancer is that cancer cells hide from T-cells—until immunotherapy, that is. One of the drugs in this trial helps boost your active T-cells, making them more efficient and likely to find and destroy the cancer cells, while the other drug helps generate even more T-cells. So it's giving your body essentially two different ways to fight. These two drugs, given together, potentially work together to help your body fight the cancer. Maybe even cure it."

I inhaled deeply, not realizing I'd been holding my breath, and began pacing. "Potentially, as in experimental?"

"Yes, but promising so far. And you're the exact type of candidate they're looking for."

"Because my cancer is so advanced?"

"Yes. Dr. Tisevich is waiting for your call. She'd like to get started immediately." James picked up the coffee cup I'd abandoned on the counter and handed it to me.

I stopped pacing and accepted the mug. "Thank you," I whispered, avoiding eye contact because I didn't know how the hell to handle this situation.

"I want you to do it, Colette. I want to take you."

"No."

"Yes. *Yes*, Colette. What do you have to lose?"

"I don't need your help."

"Someone has to take you. You won't be allowed to drive. You'll probably be in Baltimore for a while. Let me—*I* will take you."

I stilled, actually considering it.

"Do it for your sister, for Jade."

I turned away and faced the window, blinking back tears.

It felt like my world was crumbling down around me. I was losing control of *everything*. Hell, I wondered if I'd ever truly had it. Nothing was going according to plan. My heart raced and my hands trembled.

The cup was taken from my hand as I was gently turned around. James lifted me into the air, two strong arms stabilizing me, pulling me in like a baby.

I nestled into that Superman chest, breathing in the comfort, the safety of his scent. I focused on the sound of his voice in my ear, soft and low, as he carried me into the library. I was gently lowered onto a chair.

"Look at me," James said quietly, kneeling at my feet.

I didn't. I couldn't.

"Cole . . . look at me, please," he said, slowly lifting my chin so I'd meet his eyes. "If you don't release whatever it is you're clinging to, it's going to be the cause of your death. One way or another, whether it be in a Mahalo Motel room by some random junkie's hand, or by whoever attacked you here in Montana. Release it, Colette. Whatever it is that you won't tell me, that I know ties to all of this . . . release it. Release it and focus on your health."

"The motel stuff doesn't tie to anything here."

"Yes, it does, Cole. Yes, it does."

"No, it doesn't. What I do there—"

"The sex."

"The *sex* is nothing more than a release for me, like booze or drugs. It's not much deeper than that. I promise. It's like my personal Xanax."

"No, it's not. It's allowing what happened to your little sisters to take over your life." He leaned closer, his chest against my knees. "Don't you see it? Your sisters were sexually assaulted, raped, and murdered. They died by sex."

"Where are you going with this?"

"You've heard of people doing what scares them the most over and over again until they no longer fear it? Do one thing that scares you every day until it's no longer a fear? Don't you see it, Cole? This is what you're subconsciously doing. You directly correlate sex to your sisters' deaths. Sex to you *is* your sisters' deaths. It scares the shit out of you, you hate it, and because of how damn stubborn you are to control everything, you won't accept this fear or the control it has over you. So you do it over and over again in a subconscious attempt to ease that fear. Thing is, you're slowly beginning to hate yourself in the process. You're punishing yourself because you blame yourself. It's all about your need for control. Like not seeking treatment for your cancer . . . control, control, control. The worst part of it all? I think you've accepted your fate because you believe it's karma for allowing your sisters to go to that party. I think that you think you deserve to die."

My heart stammered in my chest. He was right.

"You can't do this anymore. You're dancing with the devil, Colette. Look at me." He lightly tapped my chin. "It has to stop."

I turned my cheek, unable to hide the flood of tears any longer.

James was right. I was punishing myself in a screwed-up attempt to erase the past, and I hadn't even realized it. The guilt and fear were so crippling, they consumed me, over and over again until I fucked it away.

The sudden awareness of this hit me like a tidal wave.

Who was I? Who had I turned into?

Tears filled my eyes as a myriad of emotions swirled inside me. "You're right, James. It has to stop. It will stop. Tonight. Today is the day. It will be over . . . the thing I have to do . . . will be done."

"Today would have been your sisters' thirtieth birthday, right?"

"Yes. I . . . Listen, I'm going to give you Enrique Salazar's location, and in return, I want you to leave. Please." I forced out the words. "Salazar and his most trusted associates own a lake house in Burns Harbor, Indiana, on Lake Michigan, under the name of Mario Morales. They have a boat they use to travel to Canada where they have several border control agents on their payroll. That's where they fly in and out of to do their business overseas. That's where he is right now. You could have him arrested within the hour."

"Cole—"

I grabbed his hands. "You have to leave. You—"

"I'm not leaving you, Colette." James's jaw clenched, and his eyes glimmered. "I am *not* leaving you."

Thunder rumbled in the distance.

"You can't be a part of this, James. I won't ruin your life too. It's a big day—for me and for Jade. For my family."

He said nothing as he studied me for a moment. He didn't ask questions, didn't try to dig deeper, just stared into my soul. And for the first time in my life, I felt *seen*, understood in the most screwed-up way.

"A big day." He nodded as if deciding something, then stood up. "Then we'd better get a move on breakfast."

A wave of relief swept over my body.

I love you, I thought, but didn't say it.

Without another word, he took my hand and led me to the kitchen.

Just like that, James made me breakfast on the day that would forever change both of our lives. And to this day, I regret not mentioning the man I noticed standing in the shadows at the base of the mountain.

37

Colette

James had left Dr. Tisevich's contact information on the counter before retreating to his truck, where he'd remained all day, his face illuminated by the laptop glowing from his lap.

I wondered what he was doing. Working? Researching more about my condition? I became obsessed with it, peeking through the curtains every few minutes, between pacing the carpet.

Jade had spent the rainy day out and about, where she was socializing at the local pizzeria, attempting to get a bead on who had attacked me in my shower. Although something told me I was about to find out.

The man I'd noticed watching the bed and breakfast from a shaded spot in the woods had disappeared into the mountains, only to reappear the moment the sun went down.

I was ready.

Thick, heavy drops of rain pounded my shoulders, dripping off the hooded black sweatshirt I'd pulled on. Black skinny jeans, black boots, black mood.

Dusk loomed in the sky, a dreary, bleak gray lingering from the relentless rainstorm that had plagued Broken Ridge the entire day. I glanced at the woods behind the B and B, at the base of the mountain, shadowed by the weather. It was eerie. Haunting.

Staying low, I slipped from bush to bush, careful to stay outside the glow of the flickering lampposts that dotted the courtyard. After a quick glance over my shoulder, I gripped the side of the brick wall and pulled myself over, landing silently on the muddy, wet ground beneath it. Freezing in a crouch, I listened, hearing nothing but the drum of the rain, drowning out any hope of being alerted to movement from whoever was watching me from the woods.

I swiped the rain dripping off the tip of my nose, feeling the weight of my clothes sink around me as they became saturated with rainwater. Not ideal if a quick escape was needed.

Slowly, I pulled the switchblade from my pocket, hunkered down, and jogged along the back wall, putting distance between myself and the man. My plan was to stalk my watcher from the side, undetected, and hopefully learn his identity. That was the goal, anyway.

I had about ten more minutes of light before the world went completely dark.

Tugging down my hood, I cut across the short dip in the terrain and slipped into the woods that marked the bottom of the steep mountain. Blackness engulfed me, the rapidly diminishing light and rain stealing what little visibility I had.

My pace quickened as I slipped stealthily through the trees. In the distance, the lights from the bed and breakfast twinkled against the growing darkness, and I estimated I was about ten yards from where I'd seen the figure.

I stopped, listening. Nothing.

Where the hell did he go?

Squinting through the curtain of rain, I scanned the woods in a futile attempt to discern the blurry shapes around me, barely visible through the deluge. With one hand gripping the hilt of my knife, I slowly stepped away from the tree I was hiding behind and immediately felt vulnerable and exposed. Like someone was watching.

A cold trickle of fear slid down my spine as I froze, certain I was being watched.

Slowly, I lowered to a crouch, goose bumps rippling over my skin. My heart thrummed in my chest, instinct telling me to retreat. *Immediately*.

My gaze locked on the brick building in the distance, the low wall I'd have to scale to safety.

Go!

I lurched forward and took off in a sprint, startled as a *pop, pop, pop* sounded around me. The wind of a bullet split my hair in a puff of air as it whizzed past, hitting a tree just a few feet in front of me. Bark exploded through the rain.

I dove to the soggy ground, expecting to feel the heat and impact of a bullet rip through my body. My knife flew from my hand, and panic seized me.

Have I been hit?

Scrambling over the wet leaves, I felt for my knife. Finding it, I crawled forward, desperately grabbing rocks and roots to help propel myself forward.

More gunshots.

A rock exploded next to my shoulder, tiny shards stinging the side of my face. Boots pounded the ground behind me.

Adrenaline burst through my veins, igniting an otherworldly speed and strength that could only be explained as the untapped impulse of a human's will to survive.

I made it to the edge of the woods and paused with only a short dip in the terrain before the brick wall that would be my salvation. Problem was, the dip was barren of trees and brush. I would be exposed, but what choice did I have?

My pulse roared in my ears as I sucked in a breath and dropped into a crouch, ready to sprint. Just then, ahead of me, a massive figure leaped over the brick wall, rifle in hand.

"James!" I screamed. "Get down!"

Gunshots.

My heart stopped, the world around me blurring to slow motion as I watched his body jerk backward, his steps faltering by the impact.

Two bullets pinged off the tree next to me.

Keeping low, I scrambled along the tree line toward James, now on the ground. Bullets zipped past me, and with a scream, I hurled myself behind a large boulder at the tree line.

Tears ran down my cheeks, and in that moment, I thought of two people. James and my sister. In *that* order.

Pulling my knees to my chest in an attempt to make myself as small as possible, I focused on the cracking of twigs in the distance as the shooter made his way through the brush to my location. Closer, closer, until I could actually feel the footfalls shaking the ground beneath me.

Lightning streaked the sky, the jarring flash of light illuminating the figure stepping out from behind a tree, his eyes as black as coal. I recognized him instantly.

Enrique Salazar.

My grip tightened around the knife as I slowly stood, readying myself to fight to the death.

"Colette Archer."

Dressed in full camo, pistol in hand, Enrique stopped a few feet in front of me, eyeing me like a beetle he was about to crush with his boot. "I believe you know a friend of mine, Avery Bell." His voice was low, gravelly.

I lifted my chin. "She's no friend of yours."

"Tell that to the men watching over her in my bed at this very moment."

As suspected, Avery had gone back to her abusive lover, as so many do. My stomach rolled.

"Let this be a lesson to you, *and* your sister, that anyone who meddles in my life will pay the price."

I took a step forward, raising the knife. "Touch my sister and I'll slice your throat."

His eyes twinkled as he raised the gun, pointing it at my face.

Fear ran like acid over my skin. Not for myself, but for Jade—for Anna and Presley.

I thought of James, his face, the kiss, watching his body fall to the ground. Because of *me.* Anger shot through me.

I lunged forward, slashing the knife through the air when—

Pop!

Enrique Salazar flew backward like a rag doll and crumpled to the ground.

I spun to see James, gun in hand, barreling through the woods. My heart nearly exploded as I surged forward, my eyes locked on his, and his locked on mine.

"Are you okay?" I screamed through the rain, stumbling to a stop in front of him, although he didn't hear me.

With his focus on one thing, and one thing only, James grabbed me and pulled me into his arms. "Are you okay?"

I tried to push away so I could check him over, but he held me in place.

"Are you okay?" His voice was pitched, panicked. Scared. "Are you okay, Cole? *Answer me*!"

Breathless, I said, "Yes, yes . . . I'm fine."

I pulled out of his grasp, my hand coming away red with blood that slowly washed away with the rain pounding onto us.

"Oh my God, James, you're shot." I ran my hand down his arm. "You've been—"

"I'm fine." He swallowed hard, his gaze on mine so intense that my heart skipped a beat. Lifting his uninjured arm, he cupped my face. "You're okay. *Fuck*. You're okay." Relief shone from his puffy, red-rimmed eyes.

"Yes." I pressed his hand against my face. "We need to get you to the hos—"

But James was no longer listening to me. His attention was now fixed on the body behind me, his gaze cold and hard.

Sirens blared in the distance. Someone had obviously heard the gunshots and called the authorities.

"Stay here—*right* here, okay?" he said, all business now. "I've got to make some calls."

I nodded, watching James step through the brush toward Enrique Salazar's body as he pulled his phone from his pocket.

38

Colette

Within hours, the small town of Broken Ridge was crawling with federal agents, local and state police, and journalists from all over the country.

Enrique Salazar was alive, due to a perfectly placed bullet wound to his thigh. Thanks to James, the DEA now had their man in custody, as well as a wealth of information about the ruthless Salazar drug cartel. The war on fentanyl took a massive turn.

Never leaving my side, James fielded the questions and calls like a pro. Cool, calm, and collected, despite his injured arm. Though he had much to do, I remained his top priority.

After I gave my statement to the authorities, James escorted me to my room where Jade was anxiously waiting, containing herself as best she could.

James pulled her into the hallway and updated her, relieving a bit of her stress. When he was done, Jade disappeared downstairs to make tea, a thinly veiled attempt to give James and me some privacy.

He dropped to his knees at my feet where I had curled onto a chair by the window, his armor completely gone. "Cole . . . I'm—"

"No." I held up a hand. "James, don't—"

"I'm so sorry, Cole." With a guttural groan, he pushed upright, shoving his fingers through his hair. "I should have never asked you to be a part of something—anything—that involved that motherfucker." The words spat out like fire, James barely able to contain his anger, at Enrique *and* himself.

I stood, closing the inches between us to grab his hands and tug him to his feet, then pull him close. "You've saved my life *twice*, James. I owe you . . . everything." I placed my palms on his chest to keep him in place. "Please . . ."

Uncontrollable tears welled in my eyes. Without thinking, I pushed up on tiptoe and pressed my lips against his.

Thick, strong, warm arms enveloped me as this amazing, frustrating man devoured me with a dizzying kiss that left me breathless. Lust fanned over my skin like a wildfire, igniting a carnal desire in me so intense, it blocked all rational thought and common sense.

I had never, ever felt such a craving for another human being in my life.

Kissing, kissing, kissing, I raked my hands down his back, around his waist, settling on his thick leather belt. His breath hitched as I unbuckled it, then slid the leather through the loops. And then he stopped. Pulled back.

His chest heaving, James looked down at me, his eyes ablaze with the same craving and desire that I was feeling. But instead of allowing me to cross that line, he pulled my hands from his belt, pressed them against my chest, and took a step back.

"No."

My stomach dropped to my feet. "No?"

He shook his head. "No."

Speechless, I gaped at him.

"I don't want that from you. Not right now, but soon. I want . . ." He pointed his finger, lightly tapping my heart. "That. That first, then," he glanced at the bed, "that."

Breathless, I closed my palm over his hand resting on my heart. That was the moment I fell in love with James Black.

And that was the first time I considered fighting the cancer. The first time in fourteen years that I really wanted to live.

James tucked me into bed, and with his phone ringing incessantly from his pocket, he kissed me on the forehead, on the heart, and promised he'd be back.

"I'll see you soon," he said, repeating the words he'd said after cooking me breakfast earlier that morning.

A promise.

Only I wasn't so sure I was going to be that lucky—again.

39

Colette

I glanced in the rearview mirror, looking to see if James's truck was following me for the tenth time since entering the mountains.

It was a cold, black night, the headlights of the truck I'd borrowed from Jade cutting through the tunnel of trees that lined the narrow, pitted dirt road. The storm had moved on, leaving a light mist swirling around the thick firs, catching the light from my high beams and reflecting an eerie glow around the truck.

The last time I'd seen James, he and his team were scouring the mountainside where Enrique had set up to monitor the B and B.

The town was in an uproar with the most excitement it had seen in years. The bed and breakfast had been roped off, as had half the mountainside. Crowds gathered in the streets, hoping to glimpse a peek at the drama in the woods. It was chaos—and therefore the perfect time to complete my plan.

I'd texted Leo, taking him up on his offer for a "real Montana experience." He responded within seconds, informing me that he had to work late due to one of his bartenders calling in sick, but wanted to see me.

At nine o'clock—not long after the shooting—he'd texted again, informing me he was on the way to his cabin. I'd waited an hour to ensure there was no way James was going to drop in. Luckily, under the cover of the circus that had become the town, I was able to slip out undetected.

I checked the GPS again, veering onto a narrower dirt path that resembled more a driveway than a road. The fog grew thicker the deeper into the mountains I drove. I couldn't see more than a few feet from the beam of my headlights.

Finally, the headlights illuminated a rusty old mailbox with a broken flag. I turned left and descended the long dirt road deeper into the trees until I spotted the vintage Mustang I'd seen parked outside of Creed's Tavern.

My headlights reflected off the windows of the small log cabin, sweeping across the interior, no doubt alerting Leo to my arrival.

I rolled to a stop under a pine and took a second to scan the surroundings. The cabin was small, a simple square structure. No more than two rooms, I guessed, or maybe one big one, nestled among the trees. Two windows flanked the front door. No porch, no chairs, no fluff. Just a cabin in the middle of nowhere.

Only Leo's vehicle sat parked under a tree to the side, no sign of his brother, Dylan, or any other visitors.

A gust of chilly wind blew past me as I stepped out of the truck and glanced over my shoulder at the cliff peeking out of the treetops in the distance. There wasn't a single star in the sky that night.

I crossed the small yard, dead leaves crunching under the boots I'd chosen for the occasion.

The door opened to Leo's blinding white smile.

"Hey, there. Right on time. How's the shitshow in town?"

"Chaos." I smiled, careful to keep my racing pulse in check as I stepped up to the door.

The gossip in Broken Ridge was running rampant, but thankfully, the whispers didn't include the name of the "tourist" who was involved in the shooting. The only information that had leaked was that a dangerous drug lord had been taken down. I was lucky, but it wouldn't be long until my name slipped out.

"Rough night at work?" I said quickly, changing the subject.

Leo rolled his eyes and shook his head, beckoning me inside. A fire crackled in the stone fireplace, the smell of smoke thick in the air.

"That's the thing about bartenders, most don't take the job seriously. Hung over, headache, stubbed toe, whatever, they call in. It's not uncommon." He took my jacket and hung it on a nail on the wall. "I'm pretty sure one just called in so that she could watch the commotion from the streets. Anyway, I'm gone now until four o'clock tomorrow. What do you think of the place?"

I stepped deeper into the two-room cabin, noticing the silence. No television, no music. Not much in the way of furniture. A sofa sat in front of a large flatscreen mounted to the log wall. A small kitchen to the right, a door to the left that led to a bedroom where the flicker of a candle danced along the wall.

Sex.

"Sex correlates to the loss of your sister. You're playing with fire, Colette."

Sex.

"You're going to get yourself killed."

Sex.

One more time. One final time.

My heart tripped in my chest, and I began to feel that inexcusable loss of self-control again.

That desperation.

40

Leo

"How was the drive?" I asked as Colette slowly scanned my cabin with the scrutiny of a CBP officer. It wasn't much, I knew that, but what did the girl expect?

A second passed before she turned, her eyes locking on mine with such an intensity that my heart skipped a beat. It was the same crazy, laser-focused expression she gave me before mounting me like a dog in heat at my apartment the night before.

Colette Archer was crazy. And I was into it.

"Not bad," she said, her blue eyes sparkling like a cat, almost as if she were neither human nor animal. Like she was something else entirely.

A strange feeling came over me. Doubt, or was it fear?

"Would you like some wine?" I asked, studying her.

She dipped her chin. *Yes.*

Keeping my head on a swivel, I walked to the kitchen and uncorked the bottle I'd taken from the bar earlier. She stayed silent, not speaking a single word as I poured the wine.

Glancing out the window, although not sure why, I crossed the room and handed her a glass, keeping one for myself. "Cheers."

"Cheers," she said, a small devious smile curling her lips. Watching me over the rim, she downed the entire glass.

"Holy shit." I laughed, then took a deep sip of my own. "That was impressive."

Colette set the empty wineglass on the end table. "So is this," she whispered as she grabbed my dick and squeezed until a yelp escaped my throat.

I coughed, tears stinging my eyes, then downed the rest of my wine. I was going to need it.

After setting my glass next to hers, I led her into the bedroom I'd spent the last hour scrubbing clean. The candle I'd lit to remove the musty odor of the old cabin was working well, although something told me now that my guest didn't give a shit about the scent of the house. She wanted one thing, and one thing only.

When I clicked off the lights, darkness enveloped us, only the candle lighting our way to the bed. I leaned down to kiss her, but she turned her cheek.

As I reached for her shirt, she slapped my hands away, dropped to her knees, and unzipped my jeans with such vigor that it threw me off balance. Two hands with long, thin fingers gripped my thighs, keeping me in place, as if she was annoyed I couldn't handle her strength.

She pulled my dick from my boxers, and a long trail of spit dripped from her mouth onto the already throbbing head of my penis. With her eyes on mine, she tugged me in long hard strokes.

Colette Archer was officially the hottest woman I'd ever met.

"You like that," I said.

She released a throaty groan that left me unsure of her answer. After stroking me almost to explosion, she pulled off my shirt, pants and underwear—I hadn't bothered with shoes—then stood and pushed me onto the bed.

I grinned, my body bouncing against the mattress. "You're kind of wild, aren't you?"

This time she didn't smile. Instead, she kicked off her boots, slid out of her jeans, and kept her eyes on me as she removed her panties.

"Lay all the way down," she demanded.

I did as I was told. Colette crawled on top of me and hovered above the head of my dick, which was pointing up to the ceiling like a damn pole.

"Take off your shirt," I said.

To my surprise, she obeyed, her voluptuous breasts overflowing around a blood-red lace bra. After sheathing me with a condom, she slowly lowered herself, pressing my tip against a pair of wet, soft lips.

"Are you ready, Leo?"

I swallowed the knot in my throat and nodded, more ready than I'd ever been for anything in my life.

Her knees widened, spreading across the comforter as my dick slid into a warm, wet pussy.

Closing my eyes, I thought about how lucky I was.

41

James

My phone rang as I clicked on my high beams, glancing at the line of trucks behind me.

A few members of the local state police crew and I were headed to the far side of the mountain, where someone had spotted Salazar's car on the side of the road where he'd parked before hiking down in his pursuit of Colette. FBI remained on the scene, awaiting a team from the DEA, including my boss, to arrive at Broken Ridge.

I clicked on my cell. "What?"

"Congrats, man." Blaze's voice was as alert as ever, fueled with the chaos he'd been fielding at headquarters as information came in from Broken Ridge.

I didn't respond because it didn't feel like a celebratory moment. Yes, a ruthless drug lord was now in custody, but only because I'd used Colette as bait—and almost gotten her killed in the process, putting extra stress on a body that was already working overtime just to live. The guilt was absolutely crushing.

"I hear it's a circus down there," he said. "Just got off the phone with—"

"What do you need from me, Blaze? I'm kinda busy here."

"I hear ya. Well, before all hell broke loose in Broken Ridge, I was working on the Archer project you gave me . . ."

"Yeah?"

"I've got more information for you, and something tells me I shouldn't wait."

I straightened in my seat.

"To recap, you requested, one, that I confirm that the girl known as Sarah Kay is, indeed, missing; two, to determine Brock Adams's whereabouts, the man who confessed to witnessing Bryan Carter and Joey Flores rape and murder Anna and Presley Archer. And three, you requested a deeper dive into Leo Creed to see if there is any connection to Enrique Salazar, the drug lord you just miraculously captured."

My jaw clenched.

"I'll start with the missing woman," he said. "Sarah Kay, nineteen, originally born in New York before moving to Butte, Montana, does not exist."

My pulse quickened. "You're sure?"

"Yes. One hundred percent sure. There is currently no missing woman by that name in the tri-state area or the entire United States."

I knew it. Sarah Kay was a ruse to get to Leo Creed, exactly as I'd suspected. But that still didn't answer what Colette and her sister were after with Leo Creed—or Dylan, for that matter.

"What about Brock Adams, the sick fuck who watched the girls being raped? Where is he now?"

The pause on the other end had me slowing, looking for a spot to pull over.

"Dead. Brock Adams is dead."

"Dead?"

"Died exactly two weeks ago today."

"How?"

"House fire. Gas explosion blamed on faulty pipes."

"What did his autopsy find?"

"That's the thing. Not all of his bones were recovered, only a femur and tibia, both burned to a crisp."

"Where's the rest of the guy?"

"Undetermined."

"So, let me get this straight. His house was burned up, caused by faulty pipes, but the remains of his body were removed sometime after? That doesn't add up. Are they considering his death foul play?"

"The local cops called in the state crime lab, but the fire destroyed any evidence that might have been left behind. The guy was a hermit and lived in the middle of nowhere, and it was days before someone found him. Notes say scavengers could have gotten ahold of the bones and dragged them into the woods. So, no, although it is suspicious, I think the cops have simply written it off as an unfortunate accident. They have other things to focus on."

My mind began to race.

"Here's where things get interesting," Blaze said. "While searching for Brock Adams's whereabouts, I discovered some interesting facts in a few confidential folders included in his file."

"Confidential?"

"Correct. While his buds, Bryan Carter and Joey Flores, were tried as adults for the Archer sisters' murders, Brock was not. He was only sixteen at the time, considered a minor, and therefore his information was kept under tight lock and key."

"A lock and key I'm hoping you destroyed."

"Of course. According to interview transcripts, Brock wasn't the only person at the party when the Archer sisters were raped and killed. There were two others, also minors."

"What the *fuck*?"

"Yep. In his interview, Brock mentions two other people were also there, watched the gang rape, and did nothing to stop it. But their names aren't in this specific report."

"Hang on." I needed to digest this news. "The two kids who raped and murdered Anna and Presley Archer are currently rotting in prison, and will be for a long time. Right?"

"Right."

"But there are also now *three* other people supposedly involved on that day? One, a bystander named Brock Adams, who was just killed in a suspicious house fire exactly two weeks ago."

"Correct."

"And now, two other partygoers that watched and did nothing, but their names aren't included in the Archer file or Brock Adams's file."

"Correct. Brock ratted out Bryan and Joey, but claimed he didn't know the other people at the party. Claimed he'd never met them before and didn't know their names."

"Bullshit."

"Agreed."

"And now he's dead, and no one will ever know," I grumbled into the phone.

"I wouldn't be too sure about that. Guess who traveled to upstate New York exactly two weeks ago."

My stomach dropped before he even said the names.

"That's right. Colette and Jade Archer visited Brock's hometown for exactly one night before returning to New York, only to pack up and head to Broken Ridge a few days later."

"Holy. *Shit.*"

"Yeah. I'm guessing one of those sisters knows how to tweak with gas lines."

Jade. And this also explained the mystery bruising on Colette's body.

"And you have no idea who these other two people are?"

"I didn't say that. Now, let's move on to Leo Creed, who you requested I search for any link to Enrique Salazar. I was digging through a cartel related to the Salazars'—so, a totally separate case—and noticed the names Anna and Presley Archer noted in a report. This shocked me, needless to say. In this report, Leo was being interviewed for his connection in the fentanyl bust in your hometown a few years back. Turns out Leo and his brother were born and raised in the Bronx, fifteen miles north of the Archer sisters. Different school zones. Leo was specifically asked about the Archer double homicide. These notes confirm the information from Brock's file that there were two others at the party the day the Archer sisters were killed . . ."

"Tell me Leo gave their names?"

"He didn't have to. He *was* the other person at the party, along with his brother, Dylan Creed."

I slammed the brakes.

Leo didn't have information on Colette's target. Leo Creed *was* the target.

A viper, indeed—and one that was about to strike.

"Why the hell weren't they arrested, charged like Brock?"

"Leo said he and his brother left before the murder.

Claimed they weren't even in the house when it happened. Cops couldn't prove that they were, and bada-bing, they were cut loose."

"But that differs from Brock's story that Leo and Dylan were there, and they watched the Archer sisters die and did nothing to stop it. Something that I'm sure he told Jade and Colette before they burned his damn house down."

"Correct."

"Fuck."

The last piece of the puzzle slowly clicked into place. Colette's secret—her final dying wish—was to avenge her murdered sisters.

I hit the gas. "Get me Leo's address now."

42

Leo

My breath caught as Colette lowered onto my dick, her tight pussy squeezing me like a vise into a speechless stupor. I was completely lost in the weird, laser-like gaze above me as she began to work me slowly, her hands pressed against my chest, pinning me in place with each rise and fall of her body.

Sweat beaded over my skin as she quickened her pace, deepening each thrust. I could feel her clit rubbing against the base of my cock each time she lowered. The woman was so fucking hot, I was struggling not to come, so I closed my eyes and tightened my grip around her waist.

I noticed the quietness of that moment, and how off it was that she wasn't making any sound whatsoever. No groaning, or panting, no calling me *Big Daddy* as she had in my dreams the night before.

I opened my eyes, trying to rein in the need to come. My gaze landed on a piece of paper lying next to us on the bed.

It wasn't there when Colette straddled me minutes earlier. The wrinkled paper was unfolded next to her, where her ass was pounding me like a plunger.

I recognized it instantly.

My gaze lifted to hers as she continued to ride me with an expression so intense, it contorted her face like a sheen of evil.

An instinct, a red flag, began to awaken deep inside me.

"What's that?" I asked, my voice weak, my breath labored.

She didn't respond, just kept riding me, pinning me in place so I couldn't move.

"I told you," I said, a bit stronger now. "I don't recognize the chick in that picture. I don't know who Sarah Kay is."

"Maybe you should take another look." Colette's voice was deep, gritty, sending a shiver up my spine.

Releasing one hand from my chest while increasing the pressure of the other, Colette lifted the paper and held it against her chest, just below her chin.

That's the moment I recognized the girl whose photo I'd only barely glanced at a few days before. How could I not? She was the spitting image of the woman on top of me.

My blood turned to ice.

The woman in the picture was Anna Archer, the ghost who had haunted my dreams for the last fourteen years.

A rush of heat preceded a spike in pulse that felt like my heart was about to explode out of my chest. Panic—sheer panic.

"There is no missing girl, is there? There is no Sarah Kay."

Colette's gaze sharpened like the tip of a spear pointed directly at my soul.

I knew then that I was in trouble. I immediately scanned the room for a weapon, but it was too late.

With my dick buried inside her, Colette pulled a small knife from between her breasts, hidden in the strap of her lacy red bra.

I froze as the cool, steel blade pressed against my jugular.

Her eyes narrowed and lips pressed into a thin line, Anna and Presley Archer's sister bent forward, her face inches from mine.

The tip of the blade pierced my skin as she shifted her body and leaned next to my ear, her entire weight pressing against my rib cage.

"Anna Archer is the woman in the picture," she whispered in a chilling voice next to my ear. "Anna Archer is the young woman you watched being raped, sodomized, and suffocated exactly fourteen years ago today. This, Leo Creed . . . is for my sister."

With her final words, the blade entered my throat, the pain like a branding iron sizzling through flesh and veins. I opened my mouth to scream, but there was no air. Instead, a thick, cloying substance filled my airway. I could feel the blood, hot and thick, running down my neck as well as down my throat.

I'm drowning.

The world began to spin as I looked into those wild, feral eyes staring into my soul, yet she was somewhere else at that moment. A different time. A different person.

As I writhed in pain, gasping for air, she studied me with intent and focus as if she was mentally recording what she saw. As if she never wanted to forget the moment.

The blade slowly dragged across my throat, and I could actually hear the blood squirting out.

I'm not drowning.

I'm dying.

In my last moments, I saw the faces of Anna and Presley Archer.

And they were smiling.

43

Jade

I'd never experienced a night as black as that one in my life. An all-consuming inky darkness that blanketed everything around me, so thick it was as if you could reach out and touch it, parting the night like a curtain in a play.

Heavy cloud cover from a slow-moving storm system blocked the full moon, the thick canopy of trees over my head ensuring not even a temporary streak of moonlight reached my path. The woods were still, eerily quiet as I slipped from tree to tree, one hand gripping the hilt of my gun, the other, a pair of night-vision binoculars. Under the cover of my balaclava, my focus remained locked on the cabin below the cliff, where the silhouettes had just moved away from the window and out of view.

That wasn't part of the plan. Colette was supposed to remain in the living room, directly in my line of sight until the job was finished.

I didn't like that I could no longer see my sister.

Switching to Plan B, I hurried down the mountain, running blind, twigs and branches slicing at my arms and legs. I didn't care. I had to see my sister. It wasn't like her to deviate from a plan.

With my head down and gun up, I breached the tree line and sprinted across the small yard, leaping into the shadows and pressing my back against the cold cabin wall.

Holding my breath, I listened. Everything was still. All I heard was the usual noises of the forest at night.

Ducking under the front window, I crept to the front door, crouched, and listened again.

Silence.

My pulse spiked.

There should be noise from inside, voices, the shuffle of movements, *something.*

After a quick glance over my shoulder, I slid the binoculars into my sling pack, quietly pushed open the front door, unlatched as we'd planned, and crept over the threshold. The living area was vacant, as was the kitchen. Both rooms were so dark and silent, I could hear the drum of my heart in my chest.

My eyes focused on the bedroom where candlelight danced on the walls. Keeping my head low, I tiptoed over the hardwood floors, pausing in the shadows at the doorway.

Still not a damn sound.

I closed my eyes, inhaled once, released it, then raised the gun and stepped into the bedroom.

I froze as the scene came into view. The back of my sister's head, her unmoving body, the sweet, metallic scent of blood ripe in the air, making my stomach roil.

Colette was frozen like a statue as she straddled Leo Creed, his limp naked body ghostly pale over a growing pool of blood beneath him. The gray comforter on the bed was saturated with a staggering amount of it. A dark red, like paint, splattered the comforter and the walls around them. It didn't look real, like the final scene in the movie *Carrie*.

For a second, I wondered if Colette was hurt, if she'd somehow died in that position, death freezing her in place.

"Cole," I whispered.

My sister didn't react, didn't so much as flinch as I pulled up my ski mask and cautiously stepped deeper into the room. If she wasn't dead, she was in shock, and would probably attack anyone who touched her.

I'll never forget that smell. Ripe and pungent.

I whispered her name again. When she didn't respond, I continued to advance, unsure if she knew I was there, although my gut told me she did.

She always did.

"Cole," I whispered, then raised my voice as panic overcame the need for secrecy. "Cole!"

Keeping my gun low but my finger on the trigger, I approached the bed, skirting the wall, making sure she heard my steps.

When I was parallel with their bodies, I stopped. As if in slow motion, Colette's head turned toward me, her eyes as flat and cold as ice.

I will never forget that moment for the rest of my life.

My sister's skin was covered in blood, as if someone had brushed her face red with war paint. Her lips, her hair, her chest, her arms . . . all were sprayed with Leo Creed's blood.

Our eyes met with an intensity that made the earth shudder beneath my feet.

We didn't speak for a long moment, just stared at each

other with the weight of a thousand words—until the sound of an approaching vehicle shattered the silence.

A spark of fear shot like lightning up my spine as I turned toward the window, squinting at the pair of headlights coming up the driveway.

"Shit."

I looked back at my sister, who remained frozen on top of Leo's dead body. She wasn't all right. Her eyes had glazed over, and it was if she was no longer in the room. She was in shock.

And that's when I realized he was still *inside* her. Colette had done exactly what they had done to Anna. Kill him while she fucked him.

Karma. What goes around comes around, in its purest, coldest form.

Headlights bounced across the walls.

"Cole," I hissed, lunging toward the bed. "We've got to go. Someone's coming."

When she didn't move, I screamed again, hoping to jolt her senses. "Get up! Let's go."

I grabbed her arm and yanked at her, but her resistance was like dead weight.

"Fucking *shit*, Cole. Snap out of it."

My pulse skyrocketing, I shoved my gun into the waistband of my pants, hooked my hands under her arms, and heaved her off of Leo's body, his flaccid penis making a suction-like pop as it pulled out of her.

Colette crumpled to the floor as the vehicle pulled next to the house. I didn't know if she'd somehow been drugged, or was hurt somewhere that I couldn't see. But I didn't care. What mattered was getting her out of the house so that she wouldn't spend the rest of her life behind bars.

"Get up!" I hissed, gathering her clothes and anything

else that might link her to the scene, which I then realized was crazy because her DNA would be all over the dead guy's dick. We'd planned to burn the place like we'd done to Brock Adams's house, but now we didn't have the time with this unexpected visitor.

And we weren't done.

"Cole." I fell to my knees, grabbed her shoulders, pulled her up, and shook her. "There's one more. There's *one more.* We can't die tonight, and we can't go to jail tonight. The job isn't done, Colette."

Awareness flashed behind her eyes.

The engine of the truck was silenced. I considered the window on the far wall of the bedroom. With no back door to the cabin, it was our only option.

"Come on." I pulled up my sister, relieved when she finally responded to my touch. Holding hands, we ducked down and scrambled across the floor as heavy footfalls crunched on the rocks outside.

Suddenly, her hand left mine.

I spun around—and the stubborn look in my sister's eyes told me everything.

Colette was staying. She knew her DNA was everywhere. Hell, our rental truck was parked out front for the world to see. Whoever was here could run the tags, call the rental place, and have our names in an instant. There was no way we were getting out of this. Our plan had gone to shit . . . until she realized *her* DNA was everywhere—but *mine wasn't.*

"Go." The deep, commanding voice that came out of Colette wasn't her own.

"No." Tears filled my eyes. "*No*. I'm not leaving you."

"We're not done," she snapped, tears filling her own eyes

—hers of frustration, not fear. "You said it yourself. *Finish this*, Jade."

The front door flung open.

"Go!" She shoved me away. "Finish this! For *them.* Finish it!"

My heart pounding, I spun around and flung open the window, then launched myself through it, rolling twice down a sloping hill before finally slamming against a tree. Scrambling to a crouched position, I crawled back up the hill and turned around, watching the window just as James Black, federal agent, stormed into the room.

"Oh no," I whispered over heaving breaths. "*Fuck.*"

Emotions churned inside me, the question of if I should stay or leave warring in my head in a dizzying haze of confusion and panic.

We're not done . . . do it for them.

With a guttural scream, I spun around and took off like a rocket through the trees, until I hit the rocky terrain that led to the cliff where Colette had dropped me off at midday to keep an eye on the place while she prepared for her evening visit.

My chest heaving, I grabbed the night-vision binoculars from my bag, lowered onto my stomach, and zoomed in on the cabin.

Five minutes passed. Ten. Fifteen. My heart was about to burst out of my chest.

Finally, the front door opened and out stepped James with Colette cradled in his arms like a baby. I watched him carry my sister to his truck and open the door, the brightness of the interior light momentarily blinding me. Carefully, he lowered her into the back seat. Pulling her legs to her knees, she curled into the fetal position. He covered her with a blanket, and I knew she was okay.

James whispered something in her ear, quietly closed the door, then strode to the truck—our rental truck—that Colette had driven to the cabin. The headlights clicked on, the engine roared to life, and I watched the truck descend the driveway and come to a stop on the side of the road, past Leo's mailbox.

I lifted the binoculars toward the highway in the distance, expecting to see the red and blue lights of police cars barreling down the road.

There were none.

Completely baffled at this point, I watched James as he jogged back up the driveway and disappeared again inside the house. Minutes ticked by, and I wondered what the hell he was doing. What was going on?

Then the front door burst open, and I watched James sprint across the yard, hurl himself into the truck, and peel out of the driveway.

Confused, I watched the truck brake at the bottom of the hill, next to my rental truck.

One minute passed. Two—

The ground shook like thunder as the cabin exploded, a huge ball of fire illuminating the woods as if it were the middle of the day. I pulled the binoculars from my eyes and threw myself backward, staring at the massive cloud of black smoke barreling into the sky above bright orange and red flames.

44

Colette

I turned my head against the backrest as the explosion shook the windows.

James didn't look at me. He simply reached over, covered my hand with his, and squeezed.

It was done.

My gaze raked over the strong lines of his face, the intensity in his gaze, the focus, conviction sparking with the commitment he'd just made to me.

Me and him, he'd said.

Together.

Bonnie and Clyde.

"What time is the flight?" I asked, my voice weak.

He glanced at the clock. "Seven-thirty a.m.. Dr. Tisevich has arranged everything—the ride from the airport, the hotel. She's very excited to meet you."

A smile caught me.

I was ready, dare I say excited, for the future.

With James by my side, I was ready for the next fight.

45

Jade

My ears rang as I looked to the truck as it slowly pulled away from the scene—leaving the rental truck for my escape. A relieved exhale whooshed from me.

My sister was safe, and although I didn't know exactly how James was going to play out this whole mess, my heart told me he was going to take care of Colette. One way or another, that man was going to save her.

I waited until the taillights faded into the mountains, then refocused on the flames licking into the sky.

Colette had delivered on her end of the pact. It was now my turn to deliver, although the plan had greatly shifted. My sister only had one target, but I now had two.

Before Colette left on her journey to fulfill her end of the pact that night, she'd confided in me that Enrique Salazar was *not* the person who had attacked her in the bathroom two nights earlier. He was too big, too tall. This meant that there was still an additional player who had entered this game of cat and mouse.

And hell on earth wasn't going to stop me from finding who hurt my sister.

I inhaled deeply, my pulse beginning to race. *One at a time.* Dylan Creed's face flashed in my mind, a tattooed spitting image of his brother. Adrenaline lit inside me as hot as the flames roaring below.

My turn.

Now, it was my turn to end it.

ABOUT THE AUTHOR

Amanda McKinney is the Amazon Charts bestselling and multi-award-winning author of more than thirty romance and thriller novels. Her books have received over fifteen literary awards and nominations, including the prestigious *Daphne du Maurier Award for Excellence*, and have been included in lists such as *POPSUGAR's 12 Best Romance Books*, and featured on the *Today Show*.

Sign up for Amanda's newsletter for new releases, promos, personal stories, and plenty of fun extras!

www.amandamckinneyauthor.com

www.ingramcontent.com/pod-product-compliance
Lightning Source LLC
LaVergne TN
LVHW010605100826
845148LV00014B/2851

* 9 7 8 1 7 3 5 8 6 8 1 6 5 *